The COLOR

of

HOPE

By
Julianne MacLean

Cover Photo Credit: Charles Doucet/BookCoverArt.ca
Cover design: The Killion Group
Editor: Pat Thomas

ISBN: 1927675081
ISBN 13: 9781927675083

Lost and Found

One

Nadia Carmichael

Have you ever done something you wish you could undo? What am I saying? Of course you have. Everyone has regrets. Some are just more life changing than others, and some go beyond a single moment of carelessness. Some regrets are born out over a period of months, or even years of misbehavior, because you didn't have enough self-awareness or life experience to recognize the error you were making at the time.

For me, the greatest mistake of my life resulted in a shock one autumn morning when I was twenty-seven years old and couldn't hold down my breakfast.

"Are you all right in there?" Rick asked, pounding hard on the bathroom door. "I need to get in. I'm going to be late for work."

I moved to the sink to splash water on my face and swig some Scope, which I swished around in my mouth from cheek to cheek. "I'm almost done," I replied, wiping my mouth with a tissue I'd pulled from the gleaming – and no doubt expensive – silver-plated dispenser. "I'll be right out."

I paused to take a breath and calm the sickening sensation of panic that rose from my belly to my chest.

Or was it really panic? Maybe it was nervous excitement. If this wasn't a flu bug or food poisoning, and I was actually pregnant – *pregnant* – what would it mean for my future?

By the time I collected myself and emerged from the bathroom, Rick had moved on. He was no longer pounding on the door.

I padded softly across the polished hardwood floor to the kitchen, where I found him with his back to me at the cappuccino maker.

"The bathroom's free," I mentioned as I slid onto one of the high stools at the kitchen bar.

"Thanks." He picked up his coffee cup and disappeared down the hall.

I heard the sound of the bathroom door closing and the water running.

By the time he finished showering, I was dressed and heading out the door to work. "See you tonight," I called out, and went straight to the pharmacy to buy a pregnancy test.

That night, I picked up some groceries to cook dinner for Rick. Not that I had much of an appetite. I'd felt queasy all day, which wasn't easy to cope with because I worked as a receptionist in a law firm in downtown LA, and my face was the first thing clients saw when they walked through the door. The pay wasn't great, but at least I wasn't cleaning toilets.

It was half past seven before Rick finally walked through the door. I turned on the stove and slid the wok – fully prepped with freshly chopped vegetables – onto the burner.

He entered the kitchen but didn't look up from his iPhone. "I'm here," he said. "What did you want to talk about?"

I faced him and wished he wasn't so impossibly handsome. With that athletic build and thick, dark hair, he always looked like a dream come true in his tailored black business suits. He wore suits to work every day, which always turned me into an idiotic puddle of infatuation, despite my sincere efforts to keep my head.

How could one man be so difficult to resist? There was no point questioning now. It was too late, because I'd already lost every shred of integrity I possessed when I dove head first into this terrible disaster of a relationship five months ago.

Now here we were, facing each other in his kitchen, dealing with the fallout while I feared karma was about to bite me in the ass.

"Go take off your tie and pour yourself a drink." I turned back to the stove and stirred the vegetables. "Then I'll tell you all about it."

⁓

I deserved what was about to come my way, I told myself as I spooned the stir fry onto two plates and carried them to the table. I knew, before I sat down, exactly how this was going to play out. Rick might be every woman's romantic fantasy – because he was a drop-dead-gorgeous professional who earned millions, and when he looked at you, he made you feel like the most beautiful woman alive – but that's where the dream ended. He had made it clear on countless occasions that he wasn't the marrying kind. He wasn't looking for a lifetime commitment. It's part of the reason why we ended up together. He enjoyed the fact that I had plucked him out of a suffocating relationship, even though I had destroyed my own happiness in the process.

'Thank God for you,' he whispered in my ear one night on an elevator. 'You're the escape hatch I need.'

I am ashamed by how those words seduced me, and how happy I was to be anything at all to him.

After setting both plates down on the candlelit table, I poured myself a glass of sparkling water.

"You're not having wine?" Rick asked as he stood up from the computer chair to join me.

"Not in the mood," I replied, formulating how I was going to explain why.

I decided to eat first. I'd let him finish that glass of wine.

Then I would drop the bomb.

❝❝I beg your pardon?" Rick's eyebrows lifted. He set his glass
down, wiped his mouth with a napkin, and leaned back
in his chair.

An ambulance siren wailed in the street below his luxury
high rise condo, but I was not disconcerted by it, or by the fact
that he was clearly shocked and displeased. There was a time I
might have crumbled and wept over the loss of a man's attentions
and begged for a second chance – but after what I had done to
reach this juncture in my life, I was astoundingly calm and firmly
braced for the oncoming rejection. I expected it. Perhaps I even
wanted it – because I needed to believe there was some justice in
the world.

"I'm pregnant," I said. I gave him a few seconds to digest my
words before I continued. "I threw up this morning, in case you
didn't notice. So I took a test on my lunch hour."

He stared at me with those spellbinding blue eyes. "I thought
you were on the pill."

"I was," I explained. "I don't know what happened. I didn't
forget to take any."

He frowned at me. "You must have. You were careless and
forgot. Or you're lying. Maybe you wanted this."

"No," I argued, dropping my fork with a noisy clank onto my plate. "I didn't do this on purpose. Our relationship has enough bad blood in it to begin with. I wouldn't dare add any more poison."

His eyes narrowed. "How am I supposed to trust you? *You*?"

Rage, hot and brisk, flooded my bloodstream. How dare he suggest that I was the one who caused all the hurt, as if I were a wicked siren who seduced and lured him into this wreckage. I wiped my mouth with the linen napkin and threw it onto the table. "That's the pot calling the kettle black, don't you think?"

"Is it?" He shoved his chair back and rose to his feet. "I feel like a damned trout that was flipped around in a frying pan and tossed into the fire. And you know what I'm talking about."

I picked up my plate and carried it to the sink. My chest was heaving, as if I'd just climbed ten flights of stairs.

I hate you. I wanted to say that and more as I ran the water and rinsed my plate, because I blamed him for everything – for the inconceivable magnitude of my disgrace. For the destruction and collapse of this new world that could have been so good for me. Five months ago, I'd been blessed with a miracle, but I threw it all away for the dream of being with a sophisticated man with money.

Why?

Was I that shallow? That much in need of security? That weak to temptation? That self-destructive? And if so, was it really my fault that I had turned out this way? How much bad luck could one woman take before losing touch with her soul?

Or maybe I was just shifting the blame. Maybe I had to accept the fact that I'd screwed up a lot of things recently, and this was my comeuppance.

"It doesn't matter if I forgot to take the pill," I said. "But I didn't. All we can do is move on. We have to decide how we're going to handle this." I shut off the faucet, set my plate in the dishwasher, and made my way back to the table.

Rick sank back into his chair. "You're sure?" he said. "Maybe you should go to the doctor to get it confirmed."

I shook my head. "A positive test result is over ninety-five percent accurate. I'm pregnant, Rick. It's a fact. I know it wasn't something either of us planned, but this is where we are. So what are we going to do?"

It's rather unfortunate, don't you think, that some people are dealt a bad hand in life?

At the same time, I don't want to suggest that we have no control over the road we choose to take, or that we shouldn't accept full responsibility for our attitudes and actions. I will be the first person to stand up and say that our past does not have to dictate our future. It's what we do *now*, in this moment, moving forward that counts.

So if I'm going to take you forward – or backward as the case may be – and seek your understanding, I should at least share with you the events that wrestled me into this situation in the first place. That way, when you hear the *other* side of this story, maybe you'll be able to forgive me for what I did, and the choices I made.

The first card of misfortune dealt to me was the untimely death of my birth mother, who suffered a stroke during delivery. My biological father was married to another woman at the time, so I was promptly shuffled off to an adoption agency.

My second bad luck card came a week later when I was diagnosed with a septal defect, more commonly referred to as a hole in the heart. It usually resolves itself naturally, but in 1983, the state of New York required adoption agencies to reveal an adoptee's medical records to prospective parents. My chances of finding a family with open arms were therefore diminished, because no one wanted a kid with the possibility of a giant medical bill attached to her future.

I spent months in the hospital, and was then placed in foster care while the agency waited for my heart to heal.

I have no memory of my first few years, but I shudder to think about how distressing it must have been for me to be pulled from the loving warmth of my mother's womb and not understand, intellectually, the concept of her death. Did I grieve for the loss of her on that day and in the coming months? Did anyone pick me up, hold me, talk to me, or make me feel loved? Or did I lay alone, untouched, in a sterile white crib?

I don't know the answers to those questions and probably never will. But based on my behavior as an adult woman and how I dealt with relationships, I suspect that I missed out on the sort of bonding experience that shapes most children whose mothers don't die in childbirth.

I was four years old when someone finally adopted me, and for better or worse, I became part of a new family.

My mother worked as a maid in a Washington DC hotel that catered to visiting civil servants and politicians. My father was a bricklayer with a drinking problem.

Their divorce was finalized when I was nine, which was probably for the best, because I spent far too much time hiding under my bed when they argued. The sound of my mother's shrieking voice filled me with dread because she never backed down from a fight and always called my father out when he blew the entire week's grocery budget at the tavern on payday.

My father wasn't talkative. He responded to her complaints with the back of his hand. To this day, I still jump at the sound of breaking glass or a lamp being knocked over in another room.

After my father left, Mom and I lived in our tiny apartment for a few years, until Dad stopped paying child support. That's when everything began to spin out of control.

I'm sure there are periods of your own life that shine brightly in your memory because they were especially happy times, and there are other times you might equate with an earthly version of hell.

For me, a memorable set of events occurred in 1998 when I was twelve and Mom was late with the rent for the third month in a row.

"Please, Mr. Osborne," she said at the door while waving at me to go back to my room. "Just give me until next payday. I'll have the whole cheque for you then. I promise."

"That's what you said last month," he replied, "and the month before that. I got a waiting list for this place, and I ain't putting up with this crap when I don't have to. It's time you found a cheaper place to live."

Mr. Osborne shoved an envelope into my mom's hand and walked away.

"What is it?" I asked from the hallway beyond the living room.

Mom shut the apartment door, broke the seal on the envelope, and read the letter inside. "It's an eviction notice." She carefully refolded it and slipped it back inside the envelope. "It means we can't live here anymore. We have to pack up our stuff."

"And go where?"

More than a little concerned, I followed her into the kitchen to where her purse was sitting on the table. She rifled through it and withdrew a pack of cigarettes.

"I'm not sure yet," she said, placing one in her mouth and lighting it. "But if worse comes to worst, we can always head out west and stay with my parents."

I'd met my adoptive grandparents only twice in my lifetime, and the idea of driving across the country to live with complete strangers who had never even sent me a birthday card was not particularly appealing to me. I had friends here in Washington and I liked my school. Most days, at least.

Mom opened the refrigerator door. The light from inside illuminated her face. How relaxed she appeared in her tight jeans and red spike heels, as if her only concern was what she would feed me for dinner. Would it be rice and canned corn again? Or Velveeta sandwiches? I was pretty sure there wasn't much else in there.

A few weeks later, I came home from school to discover my key wouldn't work in the lock.

For two hours, I sat outside the building in the frigid November chill, waiting for Mom to come home from work, certain that she'd be able to straighten everything out.

But we were not allowed back into our apartment. Ever. All our belongings had been removed to a storage unit in the basement of the building. Mr. Osborn left a note saying that if we didn't collect everything within thirty days, he would have no choice but to dispose of it himself.

The super let us in to find our suitcases and pack enough things for the next week or so, which we stuffed into the back of Mom's rusted out Ford Tempo.

She had enough cash to pay for a motel room that night, but it was a dumpy establishment with a giant spider in the bathtub.

The next morning, I went to school as usual and Mom went to work. She picked me up at the mall at suppertime after I finished my homework in the food court.

"Are we going to stay in that motel again?" I asked, dropping my backpack onto the floor at my feet.

Mom lit a cigarette before pulling out of the parking spot. "Not tonight. I have sixteen dollars in my purse, and that's gotta last until I get paid on Friday."

"But today's only Tuesday. Where will we sleep? And I'm hungry."

She gestured towards the back seat. "Grab my purse. I took some leftovers from the hotel kitchen."

I reached around to fetch it and found a plastic bag inside with cold French fries, a roll, and a Styrofoam container full of warm chowder.

Normally, I wasn't a fan of soups, but I was so hungry I devoured it in three minutes flat. It was the best thing I'd ever tasted, but until that point, I think I had believed all soup came out of a can.

"What about you?" I asked. "Did you eat?"

"Yeah," she replied. "I get my meals at the hotel."

"That's lucky."

She scoffed and peered at me with a raised eyebrow. "What do you say?"

"Thank you for bringing this."

"Damn straight." She dragged on her cigarette and tapped the ashes out the window.

After scraping the chowder bowl clean, I snapped the lid back on, then ate the roll and French fries.

"So where are we going to sleep?" I asked, assuming Mom had it all figured out.

She flicked the blinker and turned onto the freeway. "I'm not sure. We may have to sleep in the car."

"What?" Little did I know it was only to be the *beginning* of our wretched homeless period. "No way! It's November! What about going to the bathroom? And I'll need to change for school tomorrow!"

She merged into the middle lane and pressed on the accelerator. "Stop whining. We'll find one of those rest stops where we can go inside and hang out. They have bathrooms. You have a book, right? And your Walkman?"

"The batteries are dead," I tersely replied, because I wasn't happy about this. Not at all.

"That sucks. Well, I don't have money to buy you new ones right now."

Resting my elbow on the side door, I cupped my forehead in a hand. "Why can't we just go home? I want to go *home*!"

A muscle twitched at her jaw and she gripped the steering wheel tight in both fists. "You think I don't want that? I'm at the end of my rope, here, Nadia, with sixteen bucks to my name. If you want to yell at someone, yell at your deadbeat father."

"But he's not here!" I sobbed.

"Exactly!" For a long moment she paused, then spoke in a calmer voice. "But I'm here, and I'm doing the best I can, so don't give me any more grief. I have sleeping bags in the trunk, so we'll spend the night in the car, in the rest stop parking lot. Just pretend like we're camping."

She drove faster down the freeway while I put my feet up on the dash and sat back in angry silence.

CHAPTER

Six

❧

I'm not sure what time it was when I was startled awake by an aggressive pounding on the hood of the car. Curled up on my side in the back seat, I sat up and squinted into a blinding light aimed at my face.

"What the hell do you want!" my mother screamed.

Confused and disoriented, I shaded my eyes with the back of my hand. Was it a cop checking on us? I wondered.

Mom sat up in the front seat and shouted at the man at her window. "Get the hell away!"

A burning sensation exploded in my belly as I realized the man was no cop, and my mom was behaving like a rabid dog backed into a corner. All my muscles tensed and I screamed when a second man rapped on the window by my head.

"Mom!" I cried.

"Got any money?" the man asked me. Then he rattled the door handle, trying to force it open. Thank God it was locked.

Mom quickly turned the key in the ignition and burned rubber to get us out of there. The tires squealed, and I'm sure we left twenty feet of skid marks.

I was crying uncontrollably by the time we pulled out of the parking lot onto the freeway. "Who were they?" I asked.

"I don't know," Mom replied. Her knuckles were white on the steering wheel as she checked the rear-view mirror.

Still in the back seat, I tossed the sleeping bag aside and tried to take deep breaths, to stop crying and calm my racing heart.

"That was scary," I said. "I don't want to go back there."

"We won't."

I'm pretty sure she was speeding. She must have been going at least eighty miles an hour.

That's when I heard the wail of a siren, and turned to look out the back window at a set of red and blue flashing lights behind us.

"License and registration please," the police officer said when Mom rolled down the window.

He shone his flashlight into the back seat and aimed it at my face. Like before, I squinted and held my hand up to block the blinding ray of light that stung my eyes.

"Is that your daughter?" the cop asked.

"Yes." Mom fished through her wallet for her licence. I noticed her hands, with those long red painted fingernails, were trembling. The cop took the light off me and used it to examine the licence she passed to him.

I felt nauseous by then, like I was going to throw up. I just wanted to go home.

"Do you still live at this address?" the cop asked.

Mom handed him the vehicle permit, which she'd retrieved from the glove compartment. "Not exactly," she replied. "We got evicted yesterday. We stayed in a motel last night, but I don't get paid until Friday, so that's why we were camping out in the car. We were at the rest top back there, but a couple of suspicious looking characters banged on the window and asked us for money. That's why I was speeding. I was really freaked out. I'm *still* freaked out."

THE COLOR OF HOPE

I felt frozen with fear in the back seat, convinced the cop was going to haul us off to jail and lock us up for life.

"You don't have anywhere to stay tonight?" he asked. "No family or friends to take you in?"

"No. It's just me and my daughter."

He leaned down to look at me. "You okay back there?"

Terror gripped me. I couldn't speak. All I could do was nod my head quickly up and down.

The cop handed my mother's licence and vehicle permit back to her. "You could try the homeless shelter, but you have to get there early."

Mom shook her head. "I wouldn't feel safe there."

He leaned down to look at me again. "Where do you go to school?"

My heart pounded thunderously in my ears, but somehow I managed to make my tongue work, and told him what grade I was in, and the name of my school.

"I'll get her there on time tomorrow," Mom assured him, "and we'll be fine as soon as I get paid. I already have a lead on a new apartment. Someone at work…"

I suspected she was making that up, because she hadn't mentioned that to me.

"This is just a rough patch we're going through right now," she added.

The police officer was quiet for a minute.

"All right," he said at last. "I'm going to let you off the hook with a warning this time. No more speeding. You got that? And we'll check out those suspicious looking characters you mentioned. Drive safely, now." He returned to his paddy wagon while Mom turned the key in the ignition.

"Jesus," she said. "He didn't even call it in or check my license. I guess it's our lucky day, because I really can't afford to pay a speeding ticket right now."

She pulled onto the road and drove slowly for at least a mile, nervously checking her rear view mirror every few seconds, just in case the officer changed his mind about letting us go.

Sure, I thought. What a lucky day.

Eight

ayday on Friday was like waking up Christmas morning. We'd slept in the car in a different parking lot each
night, and thankfully Mom didn't get pulled over again for
speeding.

As soon as she deposited her check, she picked me up after
school and we searched through the classifieds together, looking
for a cheap place to live. Unfortunately, we couldn't view anything until Saturday. Mom wanted to save her entire paycheck for
a down payment and not blow it on a motel room, so we decided
to spend one more night in the car.

Christmas would have to wait until tomorrow.

She went back to work for the evening, and I went to the
mall.

Later, when she finished her shift, I met her at the hotel service entrance. If good luck was waiting to strike, that wasn't to be
the moment, because just as we were walking to her car, it began
to snow.

"Mom," I said. "We're going to freeze. I can't do this again.
I'll die."

"Oh, don't be such a drama queen," she replied as she unlocked
the car door and climbed in. She leaned across to unlock my side,
and I got in beside her.

There were pop cans and food wrappers all over the floor. I had to kick them aside.

"You're not going to die," Mom said. "Think about it. People camp in tents on the way up Mount Everest where it's always snowing and there's hardly any oxygen."

"And people *die*!" I argued. "There are books written about it and climbers end up on *Oprah* telling about how they lost all their fingers!"

Mom turned the key in the ignition, but nothing happened. A few dashboard lights briefly flickered on, but otherwise, there was just a clicking sound. She tried again and again, but there didn't seem to be any power in the battery or electrical systems.

Before I had a chance to ask what was wrong, Mom screamed, "No! Dammit!" She started slapping the steering wheel and kicking the pedals.

"Mom, stop!" I pleaded, because I couldn't take it if she lost her mind and took off. Then what would I do?

After uttering a few choice curse words – the ones she always punished me for saying out loud – she tipped her head forward onto the steering wheel and shut her eyes.

"What else, God?" she asked. "What else do you want to throw at me this week?"

I was shaken and frightened, and had a lump in my throat the size of a boiled egg, but I was determined not to cry.

"We made it this far," I said. "I'm sure we can make it to tomorrow."

She leaned back in the seat and blinked up at the roof. "But it's snowing."

"So?" I replied. "People climb Everest you know. And it's really cold at the top, but they say the summit's great."

I would have done anything, said anything, to make her love me enough not to leave.

She turned her head to look at me, and the defeat I saw in those eyes filled me with dread. It was like a kick in the stomach, but then she smiled, and a wave of relief washed over me.

"I have an idea," she said, "but I'm going to need you to stay here for a bit."

"Where are you going?" My heart pounded as I watched her pull her car keys from the ignition and drop them into her purse. *Please don't go.*

She dug around in her purse for something, then withdrew a tube of lipstick, lowered the mirrored visor, and slid some color onto her lips. It was candy apple red.

"There's a room on the tenth floor of the hotel," she said. "It was trashed the other day. The TV screen was smashed and there were some holes punched in the wall. No one's staying there until they get it fixed up, which won't happen until Monday. I think I can get us in there."

"Are you allowed to do that?" I asked tremulously.

"Not really," she replied, "but who's going to notice or care? The manager takes weekends off, and I'm pretty sure I can sweet-talk the desk clerk."

"Mom…" I was worried about what she might do to get that key.

"Relax," she assured me. "He's a really nice guy with a heart of gold. I'm going to tell him the truth about what we've been through this week. I'm sure he'll help us out. I'll be back in ten minutes."

Ten minutes. I was pretty sure I could survive that.

Ten minutes later, a blanket of icy snow had covered the windshield and I could hardly see out. I felt trapped and scared, and started planning what I would do if Mom didn't come back.

If she *never* came back.

But surely that wouldn't happen, I told myself over and over. She didn't have much money. She wouldn't leave her car behind.

I nearly jumped out of my skin when a knock rapped at my window.

I rolled it down, and there stood my mother with her arms folded across her chest to keep warm in what now appeared to be a raging blizzard. Her bleached blonde hair blew wildly in all directions.

But she looked happy.

"Good news," she said with a smile. "Our luck has changed. I got the key to the room. Grab your stuff. We'll go in the back door and take the service elevator up. Dennis said no one will bother us. He's on for a twelve-hour shift and he'll call up if there are any problems."

"You're sure?" I asked before I reached for my bag. "I don't want to get you in trouble."

"It's fine," she cheerfully replied. "I promise. All the big wigs are off duty tonight. We just won't have a TV, that's all."

I reached for my bag. "I don't care about that. I just want a warm bed."

"You got it. Now hurry up. Let's go. I'm freezing out here."

Half an hour later, I was wallowing in the bliss of a warm bath, followed by the pleasant sensation of a hair dryer blowing my long locks around, while I sat forward on the toilet with my head between my legs.

Ah, sweet luxury. I made a vow never to take hot running water and electricity for granted again. It's a miracle in itself. Who invented and perfected the hair dryer? I wondered that night, when I felt clean and safe for the first time in days.

Thank you Dennis, whoever you were. It was a good night.

I just wish that brief stroke of luck could have lasted a little longer.

Ten

M om woke me at eight the next morning with a gentle shake. "You don't have to get up," she whispered. "I'm going outside to get a boost from Dennis, then I'm going to see an apartment. It's a monthly rental, so we should be able to move in today if we get it. Just stay here and sleep in. I'll be back in a few hours."

I nodded groggily and fell back asleep.

I'm not sure what time it was when I woke again to the sound of a knock at the door. Assuming it was Mom, I rubbed my eyes and took my time tossing the covers aside and shuffling across the patterned carpet.

At least I had the sense to look through the peephole before I opened the door, for there in the hallway – their shapes oddly skewed by the tiny round lense in the door – were two uniformed police officers.

Panic shot into me. *Oh God.* Where was Mom? What was I supposed to do?

I stood in front of the door, breathing hard, hoping and praying they would leave, but another knock sounded and I took an anxious step back.

With eyes wide as saucers, I stared at the security chain and wished I had set it in place after Mom left. Maybe it wasn't the smartest decision I ever made, but I darted forward and quietly inserted the little knob into the track and slid it across.

My hands shook, however, and the chain rattled into place.

Bang, bang, bang!

"This is the police. Open the door."

I peered through the hole again and gulped down a breath when I saw one of the officers draw his weapon, while the other inserted a key into the lock.

This isn't happening, I thought. *Oh, God, are they going to shoot me?*

The lock clicked, the door opened, and I stupidly launched my body forward and pushed the door shut again. "My mom's not here!" I shouted. "But she works here. She'll be back soon."

There was a pause. "What do you mean, 'your mother works here'? Who is she? What does she do?"

"Her name is Rhonda Carmichael and she's a maid!"

"What's *your* name?" the cop asked.

"Nadia." I paused. "I'm sorry. We had nowhere else to go! It was snowing last night, so my mom asked for a key. We didn't think it would matter!"

I heard the sound of their voices quietly discussing something. Rising up on my tiptoes, I peered through the peephole again.

The taller officer holstered his weapon, bowed his head, and put his hands on his hips in a relaxed fashion.

"You're not in any trouble, Nadia. All you need to do is open the door. We're here because there was a report of some noise in the room this morning, and the last people to stay in there did some damage. We're just here to check it out."

I swallowed uncomfortably over the knot of panic that was still boiling in my belly.

"Everything's going to be fine," the cop said. "We just want to make sure the room is safe and you're okay. So please open the door."

I paused to take a deep breath and calm myself. Then I reached out, slid the security chain back across the track, and let the officers in.

It was only in that moment that I realized I was wearing my flannel pyjamas, and I hadn't yet brushed my teeth.

The two cops gave me a once-over, then their expressions relaxed.

"Where did you say your mom was?" one of them asked.

She's out looking for an apartment because we need a place to live." I gestured toward the unmade bed and my small open suitcase on the chair. "Obviously."

The cop nodded. "I see. There's no one else in here with you?"

"No."

"Mind if we check it out?"

I gestured again with my hand. "Go ahead."

One officer kept an eye on me while the other checked the closet, the bathroom, and under the bed.

"Did your mom have permission for you to be in here last night?"

My voice shook. "I don't really know."

The other cop came out of the bathroom. "It's all clear, but we'll have to call the manager."

"I thought he was off duty for the weekend," I replied.

"He came in because someone called to let him know there was some unauthorized activity in here."

"Is it that big of a deal?" I asked.

"Yeah. This was a crime scene up until yesterday."

My head drew back in surprise. "Was there like…yellow tape on the door, and everything?"

"Yup," the cop said.

"Oh." As I thought about it, I wasn't surprised that Mom had neglected to mention that to me last night. She would have known I'd be afraid to sleep here.

Just then, she walked into the room. "What's going on?" she asked with a frown.

"Mom!" I dashed into her arms. "I'm sorry. I didn't know what to do."

She hugged me. "It's okay, Nadia."

No one said anything for a long moment, then the taller cop sauntered forward. "I'm sorry, ma'am, but you and your daughter are going to have to come with us downstairs. The manager will want to see you."

I was still clinging to my mother with a death grip, and couldn't pull myself away from the heavy rise and fall of her chest beneath my cheek as she sighed.

"Fine," she said, "but can you give us a few minutes to pack up? My daughter needs to get dressed."

"You've got five minutes."

I went to rifle through my small open suitcase. "Did you get the apartment?" I asked her as I took some clothes with me to the bathroom.

"No," she replied. "It was rented only minutes before I got there."

My heart sank. If only the car hadn't needed a boost.

Half an hour later, what we'd believed to be a stroke of luck the night before turned out to be the biggest setback of the week.

Mom was fired from her job, and we were rudely escorted from the building.

"A t least we didn't end up in jail," Mom said to her father from a phone booth somewhere in Kansas a few days later.

She had collected her vacation pay and an extra week's salary that was held back when she first started at the hotel, and we sold all the furniture from the storage unit, so we had enough cash to make it across the country and stay in cheap motels along the way.

"Yeah, I know," she said into the phone while she tapped the Plexiglas with the toe of her leopard-skin boot. "I'll look for work as soon as we get there. A couple of weeks tops, Dad. That's all I'm asking. We'll find our own place, I promise." She paused. "We just need a fresh start, that's all."

Her gaze met mine. She shook her head and rolled her eyes heavenward.

"No, I haven't heard from him at all," she said. "I don't even know where he's living. His phone got disconnected months ago. He could be in Mexico for all I know." Another pause. "Yeah, yeah, he's breaking the rules. No kidding. But what am I gonna do? Hire some fancy hot-shot lawyer to take him to court? You know I can't afford that."

She continued to kick lightly at the side of the phone booth, then rested her forehead against the Plexiglas.

"I gotta go," she said. "But wait! Say hi to Nadia." Mom held the phone out to me.

"Hi Grampy," I said.

"Hi Nadia," he replied. "You doing okay?"

"Yeah, I'm good."

He didn't say anything for a few seconds. I wasn't sure what to say myself.

"Hurry up," Mom whispered. "It's long distance."

"Give the phone back to your mother," Grampy said. "We'll see you soon."

I handed the phone back to Mom.

"We'll be there in a couple of days," she told him, and then hung up.

When we stepped out of the phone booth, I looked up at the clear blue sky. The sun was shining, but the temperature had dipped below freezing and there were iced-over puddles on the pavement. I shivered and folded my arms across my chest.

Mom dug into her purse for a cigarette, opened a fresh pack, and lit one. She took a deep drag and blew the smoke out with a great sigh of relief.

"Let's get some lunch," she said. "Maybe we'll meet a rich, handsome lawyer in there, and all our troubles will be over."

I glanced at the red-painted roadside diner, and took note of the pickup trucks and eighteen wheelers in the parking lot. "I don't think rich people eat in places like this."

She nudged me playfully. "A girl can always dream."

⟶

"Don't do what I did," Mom said, wagging her finger at me as we crossed the border into New Mexico. "Don't marry a loser. Find yourself a rich man. Doesn't matter what he looks like. If he's smart and he has money, grab onto him and don't let go. That was my mistake. I let my hormones make my decisions for me. Your dad…" She smiled as she remembered earlier days. "Your dad was the best looking guy in high school. He had these broad shoulders and a swagger that gave all the girls nervous breakdowns when he walked by. I was lucky to be the one he wanted. And I loved him. I really did. But where did that get me?" She pointed at her purse. "Pass me another cigarette, will ya'? Thanks."

I dug through her purse for her cigarettes and a lighter, because the one in the car had stopped working ages ago. A few seconds later, she was inhaling deeply and blowing smoke out the open crack in the window.

"Love just ain't enough," she said. "You listening?"

I nodded at her, even though my twelve-year-old heart didn't want to hear that. It was the *last* thing I wanted to hear.

"You gotta choose a husband with your head, not your hormones," she insisted. "You gotta marry a guy who's going to be able to provide for you and not blow all your money on beer and cigarettes." She darted a quick glance at me. "You understand what I'm telling you? Are you going to remember that?"

"Yes, Mom," I replied, because I knew it was what she wanted me to say.

It did, however, make sense to me. I was only twelve, but I recognized the wisdom in her words. I remembered all too clearly how my father got drunk most nights and lost his temper, and how we never seemed to have any money left over for fun things, like going to the movies or buying new clothes. I didn't want to end up married to a man like my father, but I didn't want to end up alone either.

As I gazed out the window at the frozen landscape passing by in a blur, I pondered the reasons for my pessimistic outlook. I'm sure there were happy girls my age who believed in fairy tales, but I wasn't one of them. I think that because I was adopted, I had a greater fear of ending up alone, and a more passionate need than most to have a baby one day. *A genuine blood relative.*

To know you were really related to someone by blood was something I'd never experienced. It was a mystery to me. Often I felt a piercing envy when I watched my friends interact with their siblings, even when they were fighting and screaming at each other.

It was during those moments I felt the most intense emptiness inside me – a loneliness that nothing could touch.

I longed for a sibling, but I knew I didn't have any because I'd been told my real mother never had any other children previously. I was curious about her. What had she been like, and would she have kept me if she'd lived? Or would she still have given me up? And what about my birth father? Did he not want me? Was it because of my birth defect – the hole in my heart that turned me into a reject?

It wasn't something I ever discussed with my mom, not after the first time when she and Dad accused me of being ungrateful for everything they'd done, when no one else wanted me.

I understand now that they felt hurt and rejected by my desire to know more about my birth parents, so after that I kept those questions to myself. I didn't explore my feelings or try to gain a better insight into my soul, which probably contributed to my separation anxiety and fear of abandonment.

Consequently, when something good finally came my way, I was afraid to trust it.

Discovery

Diana Moore

What is hope, exactly? Is it the longing for something, such as the fulfilment of a dream? Or is it a sense of optimism within you, a sense of trust, an unwavering belief that everything is going to be okay?

My name is Diana Moore, and for the most part, I've lived a charmed life. I was raised in a loving home by parents who adopted me as a newborn. My father is now a senator and my mother is a respected philanthropist. I had the best of everything growing up, and I was fortunate enough to pursue and succeed in a career I am passionate about. Today I am a successful divorce attorney, and I usually do well for my clients.

To an outside observer, I have no reason to ever be unhappy. I am a healthy, attractive, and financially secure, independent woman.

But how important are those things when hope and optimism leave you? What happens when you believe you've been blessed by a miracle, but then it's immediately ripped out of your hands? How can you truly be happy when you've been betrayed in the worst possible way by those you trusted, and all your beliefs – in others and yourself – have been obliterated? What happens when you simply give up on people, and stop letting them in?

I can't answer that question for everyone, but I can share my own story. Perhaps you'll take something away from it. Something that gives you a measure of hope.

⎯᧒⎯

It was the spring of 2011 when my world first began to shift on its axis. I was twenty-five years old and working at a law firm in Los Angeles, with the lofty goal of becoming a partner one day. I knew it would take years, but I felt confident that it would happen eventually, because I was an ambitious, positive thinker, and I was performing exceedingly well. I'd even been dubbed 'Rookie Superstar of the Year' when I brought in more new clients than any other first year lawyer in the firm – ever.

But I'll give credit where credit is due. It probably had something to do with the fact that my father was a popular senator, and there were some who considered him to be a likely candidate for President. I was therefore a high-profile addition to the team at Berkley, Davidson, Simon, and Jones. New, young clients with relationship problems began calling the firm to ask for me specifically.

That's when I met Rick, but not because he was getting a divorce. I saw him for the first time at a charity baseball game for the Children's Wish Foundation in the fall of that year. As luck would have it, I was wearing a bulky sweatshirt and a pair of faded blue jeans with a baseball cap on my head, and I was sitting in the back row of the bleachers at a local little league ball field.

"Holy cow, that is the most beautiful man I've ever seen," my friend Candace said, touching my arm and raising her water bottle to her lips.

"Who?" I looked around the ball field.

"Not on the field," she said. "In the parking lot by the black Audi. Eight o'clock. Yep, right there, moving along the fence. Black suit, blue tie."

"Wow," I replied, and nearly choked on the last bite of granola bar I'd popped into my mouth.

The gentleman in question was tall, dark, muscular, and handsome. As he drew nearer, I saw that he was blessed with one of those extraordinary faces with well-defined, chiseled features and captivating blue eyes. He entered the ball field, stepped onto the bleachers, and his smile sent every woman into a swoon.

"Who is he?" I asked, sipping my water.

My friend Candace was an attorney as well, but she specialized in property law. She started at the firm a year before I did, and to our mutual delight, her office was situated next to mine, near the photocopy machine.

"I don't know," she said, "but I'm going to find out."

Before you assume that Candace and I were a couple of fast women on the prowl, I should set the record straight and mention that she was happily married to a lovely man, and they were expecting a baby. That afternoon, Candace was eating for two and had a belly she could use as a tray to balance a small cheese plate. She was not looking for action. To the contrary, she was on a mission to hook me up with my future husband, so that we could all live happily ever after together, and our children could go to the same preschool.

Later that afternoon, she attempted to set her plan in motion. When the game ended and everyone moved onto the field to thank the ball player, Buddy Gilroy – who had surrendered his afternoon to pitch for a team of little leaguers – Candace pretended to recognize Rick, and asked him if he worked at another law firm in our building.

"No, I'm Buddy's agent," Rick explained with that killer smile as he shook her hand. "Rick Fraser."

Candace charmingly apologized for the confusion and introduced herself – and me – while complimenting him on the great work he was doing, arranging for his client to donate his time to such a worthy cause.

Then Candace jolted with surprise and reached into her pocket. "My phone's vibrating." She whipped it out and said, "Can you excuse me for a sec?"

As she backed away from us to answer it, I knew that was all a sham. Her phone hadn't vibrated, and there was no one on the other end.

Rick and I stood for a moment, watching Buddy sign baseballs for the kids while a news crew recorded everything.

"Do all your clients do charity work?" I asked.

"Most of them," he replied. "Some have regular organizations they support, but others offer their time to anyone who asks. Buddy's like that. When it comes to charity work, he has eclectic tastes."

"That's great to hear."

Rick turned to me. "Which law firm do you work for?"

"Berkley, Davidson, Simon, and Jones," I replied. "I mostly handle divorce cases."

The sunlight caught a glimmer of something exciting in his magnetic blue eyes, and I felt a thrilling spark of attraction. It's a wonder I didn't faint from the rush of it.

"Are *you* married?" he asked.

"No. It's not really on my To Do list at the moment." I don't know why I said that. I suppose I wanted to convey an impression of being light and easygoing. "Work keeps me pretty busy."

"Not too busy, I hope," Rick said with a devastating grin. "I mean, you gotta enjoy yourself."

"Absolutely," I replied. "That's one of the first lessons you learn when you handle divorces." He tilted his head questioningly, so I decided to elaborate. "I see too many couples that stop having fun together, and eventually their daily life just feels like drudgery. I don't ever want to feel like that."

He seemed intrigued by my comment, and his gaze raked boldly over me. "So what do *you* do for fun, Diana?"

There was no mistaking the flirtatious tone of his voice, the spark of interest in his eyes, and I responded in kind, with a provocative smile. "I'm always open to suggestions."

The attraction between us was palpable, and when Candace returned just then, I had to shake myself out of the spell I was under.

Later, as we were walking off the field, Rick said, "We should grab a drink sometime."

"I'd love it," I replied, and we exchanged cell numbers.

When I got into the car with Candace, she grilled me about everything Rick and I talked about while she was pretending to chat on her phone, and I felt like an infatuated schoolgirl. I could barely contain my elation. I couldn't wait for him to call.

To my utter delight, my phone rang ten minutes later, and it was him.

"Hey," he said in a low and sexy voice that sent shivers across my body. "How about tonight?"

"Tonight sounds great," I replied with a smile.

We arranged to meet for dinner.

Over the next few months, Rick and I spent every possible waking moment together. On the weekends, we went hiking and biking, and for long drives up the coast. He introduced me to his friends, and I introduced him to mine. We enjoyed the same music and movies, and could barely keep our hands off each other.

It was an instense physical relationship, and within six months, I had moved into his condo. It wasn't a decision we consciously made; it simply evolved naturally because I stayed over most nights. When the lease expired on my apartment, it didn't make sense to keep it.

I was madly, crazily in love.

And that's when my life got *really* interesting.

Thirteen

"Why haven't I met your sister?" Rick asked one night over dinner at one of our favorite sushi restaurants. "Because we live in LA and she lives in London." My sister Becky was finishing a PhD in Classics at Oxford.

"But she comes home for the summers, doesn't she?" he asked. "Last year you disappeared for two weeks with your family, and you didn't even invite me."

I sipped my wine. "You'd actually want to come?"

Every summer, my family sailed from Bar Harbor, Maine up to Nova Scotia for Chester Race Week. It was a Moore family tradition, and a few years ago, Becky met her birth mother in Chester. It was a mind-boggling coincidence – or maybe it was destiny – that they both ended up in the same small town at the same time. A few puzzle pieces fell into place, and ever since then, our family considered the summer sailboat race in Nova Scotia to be a sacred thing.

"But you don't sail," I said to Rick.

"I could learn," he replied. "I'm a quick study and a strong swimmer."

I laughed. "I certainly hope you wouldn't end up doing the breast stroke in the chilly Atlantic. I'd never forgive myself."

He scooped up some rice with his chopsticks and grinned at me. "So I can come? I think your dad and I would hit it off."

Perhaps in that moment I might have suspected that Rick was into me because he thought my father could be the next president, but of course, that didn't even enter my head. I was simply happy to know that my rich, gorgeous boyfriend wanted to meet and spend time with my family. It meant we were becoming more serious, and I couldn't imagine a more desirable husband than Rick Fraser. Walking down the aisle to stand next to him and say 'I do' would be like hitting a home run, and I was a self-confident high achiever who believed I deserved nothing less.

Most importantly, I trusted him.

Fourteen

On a warm night in June of 2012, the telephone rang. It was my sister Becky calling from Nova Scotia where she had taken a summer job at the Chester Yacht Club.

"How are you?" she asked. "It's so great to hear your voice."

"It's good to hear yours, too," I replied as I moved into the living room and sat down on the black leather sofa.

From Rick's condo on the twenty-seventh floor, the view of the sunset never failed to amaze me. Vivid splashes of red and orange lit up the sky and reflected off the tinted glass windows of neighboring skyscrapers.

"What's up?" I asked. "How's sailing school?"

My sister was teaching kids to sail in summer day camps, and working on her college thesis on the side.

"It's a lot of fun," she replied.

"And how's Kate?"

Kate was the birth mother Becky had met a few years back. Since that life-changing event, she'd spent her summers in the vacant in-law suite in Kate's home overlooking the water.

Naturally we were all overjoyed when Becky found her real mother because her adoption records had been sealed for years, and before that she had no idea if her birth mother was dead or alive.

Unlike me. At least I knew my birth mother was dead. She died in childbirth and I was an orphan. There was no hope I'd ever reconnect with her.

Was I envious of Becky's good fortune?

Yes, most definitely. But above all things, I was happy for my sister because I loved her dearly. We were as close as true blood sisters could be.

"Kate's great," Becky replied. "She and Ryan are really happy together. They're so easy to get along with, and Ryan lets me use his Jeep anytime. But enough about me. How's your gorgeous man?" Becky asked. "You texted me that he wanted to sail up here with you in August. Are you two getting serious?" I recognized a note of teasing in her voice.

"Maybe," I replied. "I don't know. God, I can't believe I found him."

"You sound happy," she said.

I nodded. "Yes. Everything is going really well."

"I'm glad." Becky paused. "But what about LA? The last time we talked you said you weren't crazy about the idea of settling down there forever. Too much Botox."

I chuckled. "It's different from the east coast, that's for sure. I love the weather here, but I really miss the snow. And I never imagined I'd ever raise my kids so far from Mom and Dad."

"I know what you mean," she said. "Sometimes I feel torn between coming here for the summers to be with Kate, and going home to be with them."

"But Dad's busy in Washington," I reminded her, hoping to ease any guilt she might be feeling. "It's not like they have a lot of spare time to be full-time parents like they used to be. Not that we need that anyway. You and I are fully cooked. And I'm sure they want you to get to know Kate better. They're not feeling rejected, if that's what you're worried about."

"No, I'm not worried about that," she said. "Mom's been really supportive, and she and Kate talk on the phone all the time. They're getting to be good friends. How weird is that?"

"I'm sure they have lots to talk about," I replied, imagining what two mothers of the same daughter might want to share with each other.

"So are you going to bring Rick up here for Race Week?" Becky asked, steering the conversation back to its original thread. "I'd like to meet him."

"I'll think about it," I said, then we moved on to other things, like the hot guy Becky had met a few weeks ago at the yacht club. Apparently, he owned a winery in the Annapolis Valley. I was keen to hear more.

Fifteen

It's strange how it didn't even occur to me that the peculiar things that happened to me that summer resembled what had happened to Becky when she was reunited with her birth mother. The fact that they'd found each other at all still seems like a miracle to me, and I suppose I could say the same about my own bizarre experience that year.

"You like to get around, don't you?" a client said to me one morning when I met him for the first time at the office. He wore blue coveralls, he reeked of fuel oil, and he desperately needed to scrub the grease out from under his fingernails.

I half chuckled, because I believed humor was usually the best method of diffusing a potentially awkward situation. "I beg your pardon?"

"I saw you last week when I went to talk to my wife's lawyer. We chatted. Don't you remember? You were sitting at the front desk."

This made no sense to me. "At the front desk… I'm not sure I know what you're talking about. What law firm?"

"Perkins and McPhee. They handle divorces, too. Last week you were there. Now you're here. Wait a second. You're not one of those corporate moles, are you? Are you working for *them*?"

Mr. Casey regarded me with suspicion as he took a seat in one of the leather chairs facing my desk. I moved around the desk to sit down. "I've been working here faithfully for two years," I told him, "and I don't work anywhere else. Are you sure you're remembering correctly?"

I was familiar with the legal firm of Perkins and McPhee. They had a reputation as ambulance chasers, and did those cheesy television commercials, shouting into the camera liked used car salesmen.

He stared at me with a look of confusion. "I'm sure it was you…I think."

I straightened some papers on my desk and decided that my client was muddled from all the stress of his messy divorce. "It was probably someone who looked like me," I suggested. "So tell me, how can I help you, Mr. Casey? How long have you and your wife been separated?"

He frowned at me, then sat forward in his chair and uneasily began to answer my questions.

⁓

Three weeks later, I was on my way out of the courtroom when the security guard at the door said, "Are you a time traveler or something?"

Briefcase in hand, I stopped in my tracks. "I beg your pardon?"

I knew most of the security guards in the building, but this guy was new.

"Either you have a time machine," he said, "or you're freakin' brilliant."

I stared at him briefly, feeling slightly amused and shamelessly cocky after my impressive performance in court just moments before. "I don't have a time machine," I replied, "but I like to think I'm a teensy bit brilliant." I smiled at him. "Honestly, I don't know what you're talking about."

"Yes, you do."

"No, I don't."

"Yes, you *do.*" He seemed rather insistent, which knocked me off kilter a bit.

The last few stragglers began to file out of the courtroom, so I had to step aside to clear the door.

"I don't understand," I said.

He waited for a few more people to pass between us, then explained, "Last week you were here dropping something off to your boss. We talked outside for ten minutes while we had a smoke. You said you were answering phones for your boss, but taking night classes so you could apply to law school. Now here you are, all decked out in a fancy suit, handling somebody's divorce. I hope you're not like that guy in that movie. The one who pretended to be a pilot and a doctor after he faked all his diplomas."

"*Catch Me If You Can,*" I replied, then I shook my head. "First of all, I don't smoke, and I assure you, I'm not a fraud. I graduated from UCLA law school."

He grimaced and scratched his temple. "Then you must have a double."

For a long moment I stared at him as I recalled the bizarre conversation I'd had with my client, Mr. Casey, who thought I was a spy, working for his wife's lawyer.

Something strange was happening here, and I began to wonder if there truly was a mysterious doppelgänger out there – someone who looked just like me and was also working in the legal profession.

Or maybe it was something else…

I went home that night, poured a glass of wine, and immediately called Becky before Rick got home. "I'm so glad you answered," I said. "The weirdest thing happened today."

"What was it?"

I sank onto the sofa and watched storm clouds shift and roll across the sky. "Get this. The security guard in the courtroom thought I was someone he talked to recently, and he said she was my double. It's the second time someone said that to me this month. A few weeks ago, a client said he saw me working at another firm."

"That *is* weird," Becky replied. "Maybe this woman's a psycho who saw you in the tabloids and had plastic surgery to look just like you."

I laughed softly and shook my head. "Thanks, sis. That helps a lot."

"I'm just kidding. Did the guard tell you the woman's name?"

"No, he didn't know it, but my client told me the name of the firm where she worked. I think she's a receptionist. Today the guard told me she wanted to go to law school. I'm kind of creeped out. You know what they say? If you see your double, it's supposed to be a bad omen."

"An omen of death, actually," Becky informed me. "The poet, Percy Shelly, drowned himself after he saw his double."

"Not helpful," I said.

Becky's voice was playful. "Sorry, I couldn't resist. But that's just old folklore. Don't worry about it. What are you going to do?"

We were both quiet for a moment.

"I'm curious about her," I said.

"I don't blame you." Becky paused. "Are you thinking what I'm thinking?"

I lifted my feet and rested them on the tinted glass coffee table. "Yeah…probably. That I might have a twin?"

"Stranger things have happened," she replied. "And it's possible, because all three of us were adopted – you, me, and Adam."

I inhaled deeply. "I wish I knew more about my birth family. All I know is that my mother died in childbirth, but she'd had no other children, so this person who looks like me would have to be a twin, not just a regular sister. But if I had a twin, wouldn't Mom and Dad have adopted both of us? I can't imagine they'd let us be separated."

I couldn't bear to think that my parents would do something like that. It didn't seem possible.

"Maybe they didn't know."

"Maybe she's just someone who *looks* like me," I said, secretly hoping that was the case, because the idea of having a long-lost twin seemed too much to comprehend. How would a person deal with something like that? It would change everything. My life would never be the same. And what if my new sister turned out to be someone I didn't want to invite into my life? What if she was a druggie or a leech?

"I'm probably being ridiculous," I said, "imagining that this person is my missing twin. It's like something out of an old movie."

"How can you find out?" Becky asked. "Can you go to her firm and see her? If she's the receptionist, she'll be right there to greet you when you walk through the door."

I took my feet off the coffee table and shifted my position on the leather sofa, which creaked when I moved. I couldn't seem to get comfortable. I felt restless and uneasy.

"What if she *is* my exact double?" I asked. "How weird would that be, to look at a stranger and see your own mirror image? What would I say to her?"

"That's a tough one," Becky replied. "At least you'd be prepared, but if she's never heard about you, she might have a heart attack when you walk through the door. Can you get someone else to go in and check? What about Rick? If he tells you she definitely is your identical twin, you can find out her name and maybe then you could call her, or send a letter. That would give her a chance to absorb everything and decide if she even wants to meet you."

"That's good advice." I looked up when I heard a key in the door. "Rick's home. I should go. I'll let you know what happens."

"Call me later when you decide what you're going to do," Becky quickly replied.

I hung up and went to greet Rick at the door.

Sixteen

"I think this is the weirdest thing I ever heard," Rick said, leaning back against the kitchen counter and sipping his wine. "But if you need someone to go check her out, I'm your guy. I'm pretty sure my morning's clear tomorrow. I can go then, if you want."

I slid my hand into an oven mitt, opened the stove door and withdrew a sizzling pan of broiled chicken. "Hand me that, will you?" I pointed to the serving dish on the center island.

Rick brought it over. "That smells great. What is that?"

"Ginger and lime," I replied. "Now go grab the cucumber salad out of the fridge and we can eat."

A few minutes later, we were sitting across from each other at the table.

"What if she really is your twin sister?" he said, cutting into his chicken breast. "How will you handle that?"

I shook my head as I leaned over my plate. "I don't know. It could be a really great thing. I've always wondered about my real family, and I have to admit, I was kind of jealous when Becky found her birth mother. I felt left out, like that would never happen to me, because my mother was dead. Part of me was afraid that Becky would drift away from me, because we weren't really blood relatives, and she'd want to be with people who shared her genes. I was terrified of that."

All my life I'd had sporadic nightmares of Becky being kidnapped or taken away. Was that possibly a residual memory of the moment I was separated from my twin at birth? Had I never truly recovered from that trauma?

Get a grip, I said to myself. I still didn't know for sure if this woman was my twin. Maybe all this was just a silly delusion.

"Lots of people share the same genes," Rick said, "but they can't stand each other. You and Becky are close. Nothing's ever going to change that."

I picked up my wine and took a sip. "I'm nervous about this," I said, "but I can't possibly ignore it. I need to know who this woman is. Could you go over there for me tomorrow? I'd really appreciate it."

His mouth curved into an irresistibly devastating grin, and I melted like butter. "How grateful would you be, exactly?" he asked.

I set down my fork and gave him the look he wanted – the look that answered his question with a sensuous smile.

We went to bed early that night without putting away the dishes.

The next morning, we kissed each other good-bye in the front seat of his Audi when he dropped me off at work.

"You'll call me as soon as you see her?" I asked, gathering up my purse before I got out.

"Yeah," he replied. "I'll call you soon."

I stepped onto the curb and felt a rush of nervous butterflies invade my belly as I watched him drive away.

An hour later, I was seated at my desk with a cup of coffee, reviewing a file. I nearly jumped out of my chair when my cell phone rang. I scrambled to pick it up.

"Hi," I said, recognizing Rick's number in the call display. "What happened? I'm going nuts here."

"Well…" he replied, taking his good old time to elaborate. "I did see her, and there's no doubt about it."

He paused, and I waited, breath held, for him to continue.

"There's no doubt about *what*?" I pressed.

"That she looks exactly like you. Seriously, Di, I couldn't believe it. I thought I was in some kind of parallel universe, because she didn't know who the hell I was. She has to be your twin, unless this is a sci-fi flick and she's your robotic clone."

I stood up and moved to the window to look out at the city below. "Did you talk to her?"

"Yeah, though I played it cool. I said I was looking for the restroom and she gave me directions. Her voice was just like yours, too. It was so weird."

"Did you get her name?"

"Yeah, there was a name plate on the desk. It said Nadia Carmichael. I double checked before I left and I even said, 'Thanks, Nadia,' and she said, 'No problem.'"

I felt my eyebrows pull together in dismay. "My God. You're sure she looked exactly like me? She wasn't just...*similar*?"

"She's your mirror image, Di, and that can't be a coincidence. You know that little beauty mark above your lip. She even has that, but on the opposite side. I don't know much about the science of this stuff, but there's no way she could be anything but your identical twin sister."

I felt slightly nauseous all of a sudden, and returned to my chair to sit down. "I can't believe this. What should I do?"

"I don't know," he replied, "but I have to get to work. Let's talk it over when we get home."

"You're not free for lunch?" I asked, feeling desperate to know more about his brief encounter with the twin I never knew I had.

"I have to meet a client," he said, "but I'll come home early tonight. I'll bring Chinese."

"Okay."

I hung up and swiveled in my chair to look out the window at the city skyline.

Was all of this really happening? Did I truly have a flesh and blood twin sister?

Who was she? What was she like? Where had she been all this time?

And did she know about *me*?

That night, Rick told me everything about how he had walked into the reception area of Perkins and McPhee, and was greeted by a woman who looked exactly like me. He told me he'd been stricken speechless – an odd response from a man who was always suave and had a clever reply for everything.

"I thought about telling her the truth," he said, using his chopsticks to scoop his chow mein noodles out of the box, "but I wasn't sure you'd want me to. You need to think about this, Di. If she is your twin, it's going to change everything. If you meet her and tell her who you are, there will be no turning back. It'll be like a marriage. She'll be part of your family forever."

I listened to what he was saying and knew he was right about the permanence of such a connection. There were so many issues to consider. How would this affect the family I already had? I was fortunate to have two amazing parents who loved me more than life itself. I never once felt less valued because I was adopted. They made me believe I was special and rare, and they told me they were blessed to have found me.

Maybe it was selfish, but I didn't want to give up my distinctiveness, my special individuality either. If there was another person exactly like me, wouldn't that make me less of an original?

And what if my twin was a better version of me? What if she was wittier, smarter, or more kindhearted?

I knew my family. If they opened their hearts to her, they would do so with love. Would that make me suddenly half as important to them? Would I stand in my twin sister's shadow because she was new, and because she'd been lost to us – might need extra attention? Or would she always stand in *my* shadow?

And what about *her* family? Would they welcome me as a daughter? Would I even want that? I didn't know anything about them.

"How did she seem?" I asked Rick, as I poured more chicken fried rice onto my plate.

"What do you mean?"

I shrugged. "I don't know. Did she seem confident? Smart?"

I wanted desperately to know more, to know every last detail about the kind of woman she was. Had she been adopted by loving parents like mine? Did she have siblings to replace the twin she'd lost? Or did she grow up as an only child with abusive parents who lived in a ghetto?

The notion of such a life for my twin stabbed me in the gut, and I knew in that moment that I was already deeply involved – whether I wanted to be or not. I couldn't possibly walk away now, no matter what sort of person she turned out to be. I needed to know the truth, and I needed to know that she was okay.

"I only spoke to her for a minute," Rick said, "but she wasn't as…" He stopped.

"Wasn't as what?"

He dug into the bottom of his chow mein box, finished it off and set it on the coffee table. "I'll be honest, Di, because I know you want the truth. She wasn't as classy as you."

"*Classy...*" I struggled to understand what he was trying to say.

"She didn't look like the law school type," he explained.

"What makes you say that?"

He leaned back on the sofa and rested his arm along the back of it. "She was wearing a low cut top, and bright red lipstick. Huge dangly earrings. I'm surprised any law firm would want someone like that in their storefront, if you get my drift."

"You mean she looked trashy?"

He inclined his head flirtatiously and pointed a finger at me. "That's your word, not mine. I'm sure, if she's your sister, she's a lovely and intelligent woman."

I tipped my head back on the sofa and stared up at the ceiling, because I needed to digest the information. If this woman *was* my identical twin, how alike would we be?

More specifically, how much impact did environment have over genetics?

I resolved not to make any decisions about meeting her until I did some research of my own.

Nineteen

T hat night, my desire to know more about the science of identical twins kept me up until three in the morning.

I learned that in this decade, monozygotic twins occur approximately once in every three hundred thirty-three births. They share one hundred percent of the same genes because the mother's fertilized egg splits in two after conception, not before. Nevertheless, identical twins don't share the same fingerprint, because genetic changes continue to occur in the womb after the splitting of the embryo.

I was most interested in researching twins who were separated at birth, and discovered that no matter what sort of environment they were raised in, they usually shared similar IQ's later in life, and had similar body mass indexes.

Based on other studies I read, however, it seemed apparent that environmental factors did play a significant role in the development of each individual, whether they were reared apart, or together.

Twins who spent their lives apart had the greatest number of differences, though they often chose similar professions, which was a notable similarity between Nadia and me, as we both worked in law firms, and Nadia, allegedly, wanted to go to law school.

I wished I knew more about her. So far, I could only document two characteristics: she smoked and she did not share my taste in fashion – though that was likely a result of her financial situation. I didn't smoke and my parents had paid for my post-secondary education, and because of their distinguished profile, I was in demand by high paying firms after law school. I was offered a six figure salary, which was unheard of for someone at my level. On top of that, Rick was generous and did not ask me to contribute to the condo fees, so my closet was full of Armani suits and designer purses.

But who was Nadia Carmichael? I was desperate to know what sort of life she'd led. I Googled her, but found nothing to satisfy my curiosity. She wasn't listed in the phone book, and there were dozens of Nadia Carmichaels on Facebook. Some had flowers or pets as their profile pictures, and none of them matched my face.

I also searched the adoption agency, but they had gone bankrupt years ago because of a series of law suits.

By the time I stumbled into bed with bloodshot eyes, I knew I couldn't possibly live with these questions rolling around in my head for the rest of my life. I had no choice in the matter. I was going to have to meet her.

Changes

Twenty

Nadia

I 'll never forget the day that crazy letter arrived on my desk at work. It was a dismal, gray morning and the sky was pouring buckets of rain outside. I had waited at the bus stop for nearly twenty minutes, struggling with my crappy orange-and-white polka dot umbrella. The metal spokes were bent and broken, and the rain poured off the nylon like water from a gutter. Naturally, the bus was late.

By the time I arrived at work and sat down at my desk, my hair was frizzy, my shoes were soaked and squeaky, and my damp leggings made my thighs itch.

On the upside, a couple of clients canceled their appointments, so I was able to steal a few minutes to play Solitaire on my computer.

"Quite a day out there," the courier said when he entered the reception area at 10:00 and approached my desk. He placed four envelopes on the high granite counter and handed me the gadget for my electronic signature.

"I got soaked, too," I replied as I signed the screen and passed it back.

"You need a car for days like this," he said.

"Tell me about it."

After he left, I finished my card game on the computer before I flipped through the packages. Everything was addressed to the lawyers, except for one that said *Nadia Carmichael. Personal and Confidential.*

This was different. No one ever sent me personal mail at work, and certainly not by courier.

I wasted no time ripping open the envelope. I withdrew a handwritten letter, which was equally odd. I couldn't remember the last time I'd read a letter someone actually wrote with a pen.

Dear Nadia,

I'm sure this is going to seem strange to you, but I'm writing because I think we might be related. My name is Diana Moore and I was adopted out of the Jenkins Adoption Agency in New York in 1986. I was raised in Bar Harbor, Maine, but I moved to Los Angeles a few years ago to attend UCLA.

Recently, I was told there was someone at Perkins and McPhee who looked exactly like me. A good friend of mine visited you there recently and confirmed that we are in fact mirror images of each other. I am wondering if we might be twins.

I'm not sure what year you were born, but if it was 1986, there is a chance we are true sisters.

If you are willing to meet me, I would love to arrange a time and place.

If not, I will understand and respect your wishes. It's a lot to take in. I've written my email address on the back of this letter, and I hope you will reply. If you would prefer to send a letter by regular mail, I work at Berkley, Davidson, Simon and Jones, and that address is also on the back of this letter.

Hoping to hear from you,
Diana Moore

I blinked a few times and cocked my head to the side. *What the hell?*

Quickly, I flipped the page over and read the woman's email address, and the address of the firm where she worked.

She was a lawyer? I felt instantly intimidated and angry at the same time, though I couldn't explain why I should feel angry. She was contacting me because she believed we might be twins.

Twins! No, it couldn't be true. I had no family. I was raised as an only child, my birth mother was long dead, and Mom told me very early on that I had no biological brothers or sisters. She assured me of that.

How the hell did this woman know my name? Had she hired a private investigator or something?

She said she sent a friend here. When had that happened? I glanced around the empty vestibule and felt uncomfortably violated, to think that someone had been in here to scout me out and evaluate me.

I threw the letter down on the desk and stared at it while my heart thundered in my ears.

One of the partners walked in at that moment. He stuck the point of his folded wet umbrella into the giant ceramic vase that stood by the door and said, "Good morning."

I sat up straighter and tried to shake myself out of my shocked state. "Good morning," I replied.

He passed by and opened the glass door that led to the inner offices and boardroom. As soon as the door clicked shut behind him, I slouched back down in my seat, stared at the letter for a few seconds more, then rolled my chair forward to Google Diana Moore.

At first, it made me sick and infuriated that this well-respected, rich and accomplished woman existed on the planet with *my face*, and that she had been adopted as a newborn baby by a freaking future candidate for the President of the United States!

I'd always known I'd been dealt a lousy hand with my congenital heart defect and a dead mother on my birthday – followed by a childhood with an abusive, alcoholic father and a mother who chain smoked and couldn't hold down a job – but how much worse could it get? Now I had to accept the fact that I'd had a sister, but she had been removed from my life at birth because she was perfect, and I was not.

I hated Senator Moore and his wife in that moment, because clearly they had money. They could have taken both of us. How could any decent human being separate two orphaned twins at birth, and never tell them the other existed?

Senator Moore wouldn't be getting *my* vote at the polls any time soon. That was for damn sure.

I rested my elbow on the desk and cupped my forehead in a hand. What the hell was I supposed to do with this information? Friend her on Facebook and say, "Oh Joy! I can't wait to meet you! We're going to be the best sisters ever!"

No. That was *not* happening.

A sudden urge to shove my dream of being a lawyer up some-one's big fat ass overwhelmed me. I wanted to stand up right now, walk into my boss's office, quit my job, and go back east, as far as possible from Ms. Diana Moore. Maybe I could be a stockbroker instead.

But that would never happen. I was terrible at math.

I lifted my head and looked at my computer screen. Diana's face stared back at me, mockingly. I was staring at a family photo-graph, where they all stood together on a dock next to their yacht – which evidently, they sailed up the coast every summer to race around in circles and win trophies. The picture must have been taken a number of years ago because the article said Diana had just been accepted to UCLA.

I noticed that she had a pretty sister with blonde hair, and a brother, Adam, who was African American. According to the article, all three children were adopted.

I wondered what my life might have been like if they'd taken me home with them, too. Would I be a lawyer today? Would I be living in the Hamptons and going to cocktail parties at the White House?

What a crock! And what an unbelievable confirmation of the fact that I was the unluckiest person alive.

I reached for Ms. Moore's letter, crumpled it up in a ball, and pitched it into the trash can under my desk. "Screw all of you," I said. Then I called the office manager to tell her I was taking my break. I picked up my purse and went downstairs for a smoke.

Ten minutes later, I practically leaped off the elevator and ran the full length of the carpeted hall in my leggings and high heels, in a mad rush to return to my desk. When I pushed through the door, Ida, the office manager, looked up at me with surprise.

"Good Lord, is there a gunman behind you or something?"

I stood for a moment, fighting to catch my breath. "No."

While she rose from the reception chair and logged out of the computer, I moved around the desk and waited for her to vacate my post.

"Twelve o'clock lunch today?" she said.

"Yeah, that's fine," I replied.

As soon as she was gone, I picked up the trash can and rifled through the contents to retrieve the crumpled-up letter from my twin.

Twenty-two

Diana

On the day my letter was delivered to Perkins and McPhee, I checked my email every five minutes, waiting and hoping for a reply. Nothing happened all morning, then shortly after lunch, it appeared in my inbox, like a flash of light in a dark space.

Her name, Nadia Carmichael, sent my heart into a fast-beating frenzy. *Was I obsessed?* Maybe a little. Thank God I wasn't in court that day, because I could barely focus on anything beyond my email.

I clicked on the message to open it. It was long, and I felt a rush of nervous excitement. What did my twin have to say? I prayed it wouldn't turn out to be an explanation about why she didn't want to meet me, because by now, I had crossed the point of no return. I simply could not exist without seeing this woman and speaking to her.

Leaning forward, with my hand still on the mouse, I began to read her message…

> Hi Diana.
> Needless to say, I was shocked when I opened your letter this morning, and it's taken me a few hours to digest what you told me. I am sitting here at work, still

feeling very distracted. I haven't known what to do, or how to respond.

I should tell you that when I first read your letter, I was upset. It's one thing to learn you have a twin who was stolen from your life, and all this time you never knew. It's another thing to actually SEE your own face on another person. (I looked you up on the Internet. Sorry, I couldn't resist.)

The thing that bothers me most in all is this (and I need to know the answer): Did your parents know about me? Did they separate us intentionally? If they did, I don't think I could ever forgive them. Please tell me the truth.

If they chose not to take me, I do have some idea why. You probably don't know this (I have no idea what you know about me), but I was born with a heart defect, so no one wanted to adopt me until later, when that problem was resolved. I was four years old when I was adopted, but I'm fine now, in case you're wondering.

And yes, I was born in 1986. March 15. You?

I wish I could write more, but I'm at work and I have a ton of stuff to do. I think we should definitely meet, though. Do you realize that we work only a few blocks away from each other? It's kind of freaky to think that we have been sharing the same sidewalks and didn't even know it.

When would you like to meet? I am free most nights except Tuesdays and Thursdays when I go to night classes.

Nadia

I sat back in my chair and exhaled. None of this seemed real. It was like something out of a movie. My head was spinning. I could barely move.

At least her email wasn't a rejection. I was worried when I read the first few paragraphs.

March 15, 1986. That was my birthday, too.

After a few deep breaths, I sat forward to read the email a second time, and felt badly that she had been upset by my letter, but it couldn't be helped. There was no way to tell someone she could be a twin without causing her some shock and distress.

Eager to respond right away before she changed her mind about meeting me, I hit reply, but paused with my fingertips on the keyboard.

How should I address the question she asked me? *Did my parents know about her?*

I had no answer to give, at least not yet. I'd told my sister Becky about the possibility that I might have a twin, but I'd asked her not to tell Mom and Dad until I made contact with Nadia myself and figured out if this was real.

Now that I knew there was a strong liklihood Nadia was a twin sister, I would have to talk to my parents and find out what they knew. But first, I would reply to Nadia's email and set up a place to meet.

My hands trembled as I began to type.

Nadia emailed me back within five minutes and agreed to meet me for dinner that night, at a restaurant within easy walking distance for both of us.

There was still some vital information I had to unearth before I met her, however, so I picked up my cell phone and dialed my mother's number in Washington.

"Hello?" she said, after the first ring.

Though I dreaded what I was about to ask her, the sound of her voice nevertheless eased the tension in my neck and shoulders. "Hi, Mom."

I swiveled around to look out the window.

"Hey," she said, "I don't usually hear from you in the afternoons. Is everything all right?"

Leave it to my mom to sense a tremor in my world. She knew me better than anyone. "Funny you should ask," I replied. "Some weird stuff's been happening, and I don't know how to explain it."

"Why don't you start at the beginning," she suggested, and I could just picture her sitting down on the upholstered chair by the fireplace, ready to listen to every detail.

"What'll you have?" the bartender asked me as soon as I sat down. I'd arrived at the restaurant early and did a quick walk-through, searching for an exact replica of myself seated at one of the tables, but there was no such person, so I decided to wait at the bar.

"Pinot Grigio, please," I replied.

While he poured my wine, I dug into my purse for a compact and checked my lipstick and teeth, just to make sure I didn't have a poppy seed stuck somewhere, then clicked the mirror shut and took a deep breath to calm my nerves.

Part of me still felt like this was a strange dream, and my mysterious double was going to stand me up because she didn't actually exist.

As I sat there waiting, I couldn't keep my thoughts still. Questions came at me, like ping pong balls, from all angles. *What would it feel like to look at her? Would I pass out from the shock of it? Did she have the same sense of humor as I did? What movies did she like? Did she hate raw onions, and was she unable to sleep at night if her feet were cold?*

The bartender slid the glass of white wine toward me. I immediately picked it up and took a sip.

The door opened and three men in dark suits walked in. I tried not to stare at everyone who entered. Feeling impatient, I drummed my fingers on the bar.

After a few minutes, I checked the time on my cell phone. It was still early. Not yet six o'clock. Nadia wasn't late – at least not yet. I really needed to try and relax.

The door opened again, and this time a woman walked in. Her long, dark, wavy hair was pulled back in a high ponytail, and she wore pointy-toed black pumps and leggings with a fitted gray blazer, and a bright red scarf to match her lipstick. She paused just inside to remove her sunglasses. As she dropped them into her oversized purse, and glanced around the bar, I knew in an instant that it was her.

I couldn't believe what I was seeing.

In the space of a single heartbeat, our eyes met, and my stomach did a somersault.

I'm sure, in this moment, you are imagining how you would react upon seeing your exact likeness, but I assure you, it's nothing like you could ever predict. I was in shock. It was frightening and disturbing.

Yet I was smiling.

As I slid off the stool, and my twin slowly made her way toward me, our gazes remained locked on each other's. I wanted to shout, "Holy crap!" but I held my tongue.

Nadia was not smiling, however. Her eyes were focused on my face with a curious intensity. Then her brows drew together in bewilderment, as if she couldn't believe what she was seeing.

When she reached me, I half expected her to poke my cheeks to make sure I was real.

At last we came to stand before each other, and her expression softened.

"We're definitely twins," she said, and I nearly fainted at the tone of her voice, because she sounded just like me.

"Yes." I held out my hand. "I'm Diana."

"I'm Nadia."

Our hands were an exact fit.

In unison, we dropped them to our sides, then continued to stare at each other, examining all the details.

I noticed she had a T-zone complexion, like me. Her hips were about the same width, and even the veins on the tops of her feet were identical to mine.

My eyes lifted and I studied the color and texture of her hair. It was thick and wavy, like mine was on the days I didn't use a flat iron.

How strange, to see myself in another person and know that we shared the same genes. Because I was adopted, this was a first for me.

"Wow," the bartender said, and his voice pulled me out of my reverie. "You guys must be twins."

We both shot a glance at him, as if his comment was a terrible intrusion, then our eyebrows lifted and we smiled at each other.

"Yes," I replied, and felt my eyes fill with tears. "We're sisters."

Nadia's eyes sparkled with wetness as well. Then she stepped forward into my arms. We embraced each other while we wept, and I felt as if I had just found the sister I had been missing – and grieving for – all my life, though I never consciously knew it.

Twenty-four

As soon as we sat down at our table in the back of the restaurant, I reached for the wine list, which was standing up on the white tablecloth, next to the charming accent lamp in the center. "We should get a bottle," I said. "I think we may be here for a while."

"Definitely," Nadia replied.

"Do you like red or white?" I asked, trying not to sound like I was interrogating her, but I was curious about her tastes and preferences. How identical were we?

"I'm okay with either," she replied. I continued to peruse the list, until I felt her lean forward over the table, as if she wanted to share a secret with me. "Actually, I'm a beer drinker," she whispered, "but this is a classy place, so I'll opt for wine."

My eyes lifted and I regarded her over the top of the menu. Demurely, I closed it and set it aside. "Actually, a cold beer would go down really well right now," I said.

We grinned at each other, as if we were sharing a private joke, and I felt as if I was on an exciting first date.

We were definitely clicking. The chemistry was palpable.

Oh my God. She was my twin sister.

The waiter arrived at our table. "Good evening, ladies," he said. "Can I get you started with something to drink?"

I took the liberty of placing the order. "Could you bring us a couple of beers?"

He didn't even flinch. "Certainly." Then he began to list off all the brands they carried. I deferred the selection to Nadia.

"Bud Light," she said.

He complimented her on her choice and left us alone again.

"This is so weird," I said, resting my forearms on the table. "I feel like I should apologize, because I can't stop staring at you."

"I'm doing the same thing," she told me. She waved a finger, gesturing at my eyebrows. "You must go to a really good aesthetician. I love the arch of your brows."

I touched my forehead. "I go every four weeks to get them shaped. But if I didn't, they'd look exactly like yours."

"You'll have to tell me the name of place. I'll give the lady a heart attack if I show up the day after she does you. She'll think your hair follicles are on steroids."

I laughed. "This is nuts." We continued to stare at each other, and I was tempted to pull out my cell phone and refer to the list of questions I'd compiled to ask Nadia, but I left it in my purse.

"I want to know all about your life," I said. "Tell me about your family and where you grew up. Do you have any brothers or sisters?"

She glanced uneasily to the left, and I knew immediately that she was uncomfortable.

"I grew up in Washington," she told me, but I interrupted her before she could go any further.

"Really? My parents live in Washington now. They have an apartment there."

She nodded, as if she already knew.

But of course she would know. My dad wasn't exactly a nobody.

"I didn't have any brothers or sisters," she told me. "My parents couldn't have kids, which is why they adopted me. I think it was my dad's fault, but who knows."

"What do your parents do?" I asked her.

The waiter arrived just then with two glasses of beer. "Are you ready to order, or would you like a few more minutes?"

"A few more minutes, please," I replied, and he left us alone again.

"Continue," I said to Nadia. "You were telling me about your parents."

She picked up her beer, guzzled a few sips, and set it back down. "My dad was a mason, and my mom worked as a maid in a hotel."

"Which hotel?"

"The Wellington."

My emotions swirled about, and I leaned back in my chair. "You're joking."

"No, why?" she asked.

"Because I must have stayed at that hotel a hundred times. We lived in Bar Harbor, but Dad had to travel to Washington a lot for work, and that's where we always stayed. When did your mom work there?"

Nadia stared at me with fascination. "I'm not sure when she started, but she worked there until I was twelve. Then we moved to LA."

"That's crazy!" I laughed. "I stayed there when I was a kid. Your mom might have cleaned our room."

As the words spilled from my lips, I knew I'd said the wrong thing. I didn't normally suffer from foot-in-mouth disease, but for some reason tonight, sitting across from my identical twin made me feel as if it was okay to say anything.

We were both quiet for a moment.

"Did *your* mom work?" Nadia asked.

"On and off," I replied, thankful to change the subject. "She did PR and communications for some non-profit organizations." We each sipped our beer. "But I should answer your question from the email," I said. "You wanted to know if my parents knew about you. I called my mother this afternoon to ask, and she was just as shocked as we were to discover what happened. They didn't know, and if they had, they definitely would have adopted you, too. No matter what. She was very upset they weren't given that chance."

Nadia's eyebrows flicked up, as if to say, "That's typical." Then her eyes turned cold.

"Where are your parents now?" I asked.

Again, Nadia glanced to the left, and I could see that she was uncomfortable. She didn't want to talk about her family, and it made my insides churn with dread. Had her childhood been unhappy? I couldn't bear to think of that. It made me feel guilty for being adopted by perfect parents who loved me more than breathing.

"My dad had a drinking problem," Nadia said. "He left when I was nine. I have no idea where he is now. They got a divorce, which was probably a good thing because he had a mean streak. And my mom…" She paused. "She died a few years ago."

"I'm so sorry." I didn't know what else to say. I wished I could make it better somehow, but I felt as if I was standing on the outskirts, in the dark. If this was a play, I didn't know my lines.

Nadia shrugged, but I could see there was nothing cavalier about the gesture. She simply didn't enjoy talking about her parents, or want to become emotional.

"Lung cancer," she flatly said. "Smoked like a chimney. On that note, if you don't mind, I need to pop outside for a minute. Like mother like daughter," she cheerfully said, though there was a note of apology in her voice.

"No problem." I sat back and picked up my beer.

As soon as Nadia left the restaurant, the waiter returned. "Everything okay here? Can I get you anything?"

I picked up the menu. "I'm sorry, we haven't even had a chance to look at this yet. My friend – I mean my *sister* – just went outside for a minute. She'll be right back."

"No problem. Take your time." He left again.

As I read over the menu, however, I was compelled to check the door repeatedly, because I wasn't entirely certain my sister intended to return at all.

When the door opened and Nadia walked back into the restaurant, I laid the menu down and flopped back in my chair, realizing that if she hadn't returned, I would have been devastated. All my life, I'd been unaware – *unconscious* – of the fact that I'd shared my birth mother's womb with a sister, and that she had been torn from my side. Now that I knew it, I found myself wrestling with both heartache and happiness.

The knowledge of her existence was like a fluorescent light over my head, buzzing noisily for a few seconds as it flickered on in a dark room. Suddenly, I was enlightened.

At the same time, I was grief-stricken that we'd been denied the opportunity to grow up together. Those were years we could never get back. They'd been stolen from us. It resembled a successful bank heist, carried out in the middle of the night. We hadn't even known it occurred.

I couldn't bear to imagine losing her again. Now that I'd found her, I needed to hold on. Get to know her. Heal this newly discovered anguish that had always been there, secret and subtle in its presence.

I suspected she must be feeling the same way. She had to be.

As she sat down, I said, "Are you okay?"

"I'm fine," she replied. "Sorry about that. This is a lot to take in."

"Hey, you don't have to apologize to me. I get it. I was just thinking about how I never knew you existed until today, but maybe in a way, I did." I looked around the restaurant at all the other people sitting at tables, smiling, talking, and laughing.

"I wonder if that's why I was always so focused on filling my life with challenges to keep me busy," I said. "For as long as I can remember, I've been a high achiever, desperate to succeed, as if success would fill a hole somehow and distract me from thinking too deeply about who I really am. I never knew anything about my birth mother. I never even tried to learn who she was. I suppose I didn't want to think about it. Maybe I was avoiding something I knew was missing. Something painful."

Nadia placed her elbows on the table and rested her chin on the heels of her hands. "Funny," she said, "there was never any doubt in my mind that something was missing from my life. I always knew it, and I always felt deprived, as if I was floating out to sea with nothing to hang on to but a banged up life ring. I thought it was because we didn't have any money, and my mom was always working, so I was alone a lot. But now that I think about it, I probably knew that I had lost my real family, and I wasn't where I was supposed to be." She, too, glanced around at the other patrons in the restaurant. "I've always had a hard time connecting with people, because I expect them to leave me eventually. I never had a best friend I could trust to stick around forever." She leaned back in her chair. "That word...*Forever*. I roll my eyes whenever I see it engraved on bracelets, or written in greeting cards."

"I'm sorry, Nadia," I said. "I'm sorry that we were separated, and I'm especially sorry about your mom." After a long pause,

I was brave enough to ask the question: "Are you involved with anyone? A boyfriend? Are you married?"

"No," she said, "I've had a few relationships, but nothing has ever lasted more than a few months. Boyfriends always tell me I'm too clingy. What about you?"

"I'm living with someone," I replied. "Actually, he's the friend I mentioned in my letter – the one who came to your office to check and see if you were my double. He asked for directions to the restroom."

Nadia's head drew back in surprise. "Oh, my God, yes. The other day…I remember him. Really good looking. Colgate smile."

I was amused by her description. "That's him. His name is Rick, and he encouraged me to contact you."

Nadia's chest rose and fell with a heavy sigh. "Well." She picked up her beer and took a sip. "You're a lucky girl. Are you going to marry him?"

For a long moment I sat there, uncertain, unable to answer. I just stared across the table at her.

Then I confessed something I hadn't confessed to anyone. Not my mother, not my sister Becky, or any of my closest friends.

"We don't really talk about the future," I said. "To tell you the truth, I'm not even sure he ever wants to get married, or have children. He seems to be allergic to anything permanent."

"What do *you* want?" Nadia asked, and I was strangely comforted by the sight of my reflection in her eyes.

How odd, that I felt I could trust this woman with my deepest insecurities – a woman I'd only just met – and that she would understand. It was as if I had met my alter ego. Another version of myself. Was that overly romantic and naïve of me? Was I too trusting?

Perhaps.

"I want to get married and have kids," I told her. "Not right away, of course. I'm just getting started with my career, but by the time I'm thirty, I'd like to have certain things secured."

"*Secured.*" Nadia dropped her gaze to her lap. "That's an interesting word. I've always believed that nothing can ever be truly secure. You never know when the rug is going to get pulled out from under you. One of us could walk out that door tonight and get hit by a bus."

"True," I replied, "but you can't live your life like that, expecting the worst to happen. You have to hold on to the hope that everything is going to turn out right. Eventually."

"Mm...*eventually.* I'm still waiting for that day. Haven't seen much sign of it."

The waiter returned, and this time we didn't send him away. We picked up our menus and ordered the first thing that looked appetizing. I ordered the trout and Nadia ordered chicken.

The conversation took a lighter turn after that, and we spent the next portion of the evening comparing notes about our favorite foods, movies, and music.

Lingering over dessert and coffee, we shared stories from our childhoods and talked about our first crushes. Nadia told me about how she and her mother were homeless for a while. Then she described her mother's illness, and how the final weeks had been painful and difficult.

Before we knew it, the restaurant was closing down, and it was time to leave. But I didn't want to.

It wasn't easy saying good-bye to Nadia after dinner. I stood on the sidewalk and watched her walk away from me, toward the subway. I wondered if that's what *I* looked like from behind when I walked at a brisk pace in heels. It was an unusual vantage point, to see yourself from such an angle.

But she wasn't actually me, I reminded myself. She just *looked* like me. We were not the same person. We were two unique individuals with very different life experiences.

When I arrived home, Rick was lying on the sofa, his tie loose about his neck, his legs crossed at the ankles. There was a baseball game on the large flat screen television, but Rick was texting on his phone. He glanced up and set it on the coffee table when I locked the door behind me.

"How did it go?" he asked, sitting up. "I've been thinking about you all night."

I shrugged out of my blazer and draped it over the back of one of the kitchen stools, then poured myself a glass of ice water from the spout on the fridge.

"It was unbelievable," I told him. "I still can't believe this is happening. I just had dinner with a twin sister I never knew I had, yet I feel like I've known her all my life."

"So it wasn't awkward or anything?"

"Not at all," I replied. "Well, maybe there were a few awkward moments, because she's had a hard life, and I feel kind of guilty about that."

I moved into the living room and sat down beside him.

"Why?" he asked, massaging my shoulder. "It's not your fault."

I sipped my water. "I don't know. I guess I feel like I was the lucky one – lucky to be adopted into such an amazing family. When I was growing up, I never felt deprived. If I sensed something was missing, it had to be on a subconscious level, because I had such abundance in my life. But Nadia was born with a heart defect, so she wasn't adopted until she was four. She has no memory of the first four years of her life, which she spent in foster homes. Later, her dad was an alcoholic, and abusive. He left when she was nine."

"Geez, that is rough," Rick said.

"Yeah. But it gets worse. He stopped paying child support, so she and her mother got evicted from their apartment and had to live in their car for a while. They drove out here to live with Nadia's grandparents, but that didn't work out too well either. They ended up on the street again, living out of their car until her mother met some guy who let them live at his place. Nadia said he was really nice but not very handsome, and that her mother was just using him for a place to live."

Rick continued to knead my shoulders. "She should write a novel."

"Tell me about it. So you can see why I would feel guilty." I closed my eyes and tried to relax while he used the pads of his thumbs to rub in circular motions down the length of my back.

"But it's more than that," I continued. "When I imagine her in any of those situations, alone and frightened, I feel a pain in my gut, and it makes me want to double over in agony. How could this have been happening to her while I was living a perfect life, not far away? I wish I had a time machine, so I could go back and tell my parents that she was out there in the world, and in trouble. They would have rescued her, without a doubt. I hate that we didn't know. It makes me want to sue the crap out of someone."

"Too bad the agency went bankrupt," he said.

"Yeah."

His hands moved up to my shoulders. "So where do you go from here?"

"I'll ask my parents to come for a visit," I replied, "and start making up for lost time."

I believed, in that moment, with every fibre of my being, that it was right thing to do. It may surprise you to learn that I still believe it today, despite what happened later.

CHAPTER

Twenty-seven

⁕

Nadia

Have you ever wondered how many degrees of loneliness there are? I'm sure you must understand what I'm talking about. Surely everyone has experienced *some* form of loneliness in their life, whether it's temporary and fleeting, or painful and on-going.

Maybe your husband went on a business trip, and you felt lonely in your empty bed. Or maybe your best friend moved away and you were devastated; you missed her terribly, and you were certain your loneliness would never go away.

I've experienced varying degrees and intensities of loneliness in my life. Much of it takes me back to my childhood, when my parents argued and my father left, and I never saw him again. I spent a lot of time alone when my mother worked long hours, and I was never sure that she wouldn't leave some day, too. I felt very much alone in those situations, and I became accustomed to it, because it was ever-present.

It goes without saying that no child should ever be without a loving family, but sometimes it simply can't be helped. We can't all grow up in a perfect world. Sometimes a child has to learn how to be independent, self-sufficient, and tough – on the inside and out. I believe I learned that early on, but in the process, I learned other things, too, like how to keep people at a distance. How to keep from caring too much and to rely only on myself.

These were things I would eventually have to *un*learn. But first, I had to hit rock bottom, and experience loneliness from a whole new perspective.

—⟨

As I rode the subway to meet Diana's family and potential future husband for the first time, I marveled at the fact that I was not nervous. To the contrary, I felt hopeful and excited, which is a far cry from my initial reaction when I opened and read Diana's letter at my desk on that fateful rainy day.

My first reaction had been anger. I was jealous of the life that had been handed to her and not to me. But our dinner together had somehow wiped that away. By the end of that night, my animosity vanished, for I experienced something profound – something I'd never experienced before. I'm not even sure how to explain it.

My mother, on her deathbed, told me she loved me, and I believe with all my heart that she did. In spite of all her failings, I knew she tried her best, and I loved her for sticking around all those years.

My first meeting with Diana, however, introduced me to something new. What I felt for my twin – in the first instant when we embraced – was a connection few people in the world can ever truly comprehend. It was a different kind of love. Though we had spent our lives apart and were virtual strangers, by the end of the evening, my eyes were wide open, and I realized that she was the missing link to *everything*. She was the answer to all my questions about my purpose in the world. Suddenly I had a true sense of self. I knew exactly who I was.

Diana was everything I ever wanted to be, but never believed I *could* be – because I wasn't smart enough, lucky enough, or pretty enough. When I met her and saw myself in her, I began to feel inspired.

This is what I am capable of. That's what I told myself. I admired her confidence and all the outer details that were so damn impressive.

I went home that night, amazed by the fact that we were so much the same. The only difference was our financial circumstances and our life experiences, but weren't those things external? That had nothing to do with my genetics. Or my soul. The past was finished now. The future was mine to make of it whatever I wanted.

Diana may have benefited from a higher education and social connections, but *my* experience had taught me how to be tough, and how to survive. Mine was not a cushy life, so at least in that department, I was ahead of her. I knew a certain breed of hardship that she knew nothing about.

Please don't think I was riding high or feeling arrogant because Diana's family was rich and powerful, and I considered them to be my free ticket to the easy life. That was the last thing on my mind when I rode the elevator up to her condo on the twenty-seventh floor.

What mattered to me most was that I would meet her family, people who would become my family as well. Diana had made it clear that her parents wanted to get to know me. They loved *her*, and I would share in that love.

This meant I would no longer be alone. I had lost both my parents and I had no siblings, but now I would be part of a family. A real one.

As the elevator doors opened and I stepped off, I paused briefly in the corridor, because my heart was overflowing with gratitude. My eyes filled with moisture.

What an incredible turn of luck this was. It was like a second chance at life. I prayed that it would hold, and nothing would happen to screw it up.

When I raised my fist to knock on Diana's door – that's when the nerves kicked in.

What if they didn't like me? What if Diana had glossed over the truth – that her family was, in actuality, a tight band of hoity-toity snobs, and as soon as they discovered my parents were blue-collar workers, they would be horrified and concerned for their high-class daughter's welfare.

I paused and took a deep breath. Then I knocked.

A few seconds later, the door opened, and I found myself standing in front of a mirror. A mirror that smiled back at me.

Most of my anxiety drained away, and I felt a burst of euphoria. I hate to use the word infatuated, but that is the only one that comes to mind. It's a fairly accurate description of my emotions in that moment.

My twin. The other half of me. And she was so beautiful.

Was this real?

Perhaps the best part was that she stared back at me with matched joy and fascination, as if she had been counting the minutes until we could see each other again. Her eyes glistened, and I could have wept.

"Hi," she said almost breathlessly, and it seemed private, meant only for me. "I'm so glad you're here." She gave me a quick hug in the entrance hall.

Thank goodness I'd texted her earlier about what I should wear. She told me she was wearing jeans, so I wore jeans as well. I made an effort to class up my appearance with a pale blue blouse that looked like silk, but was actually a very nice synthetic.

As I entered the apartment, I was overwhelmed by the spectacular view of the cityscape beyond the floor-to-ceiling windows, and the sleek contemporary décor, but then Diana's parents stepped into view from the kitchen.

Her mother, Sandra, was slim and blonde with blue eyes and high cheekbones, and her father, Gerald, was even more attractive in person than he was in pictures and on television. He, too, was slim and fit. His hair was thick and dark with a distinguished hint of gray. They were an attractive couple, and when they greeted me, it was with genuine warmth and openness.

"We're so happy to meet you," Mrs. Moore said, holding out her hand to shake mine.

I was relieved she didn't move to hug me, because that would have been too much too soon. A handshake was a good choice.

The senator held out his hand also. "Hi Nadia," he said, "I'm Gerry."

His casual hello eased my mind about the hoity-toity snob issue, and I felt my shoulders relax.

"Nice to meet you," I said.

"Come on in." Diana led me into the living room, and again, I was distracted by the view. "What can I get you to drink? How about a Bud Light?"

I glanced at Mrs. Moore, who was holding a glass of white wine.

"I'll have what your mom's having," I replied.

"Sure." Without missing a beat, Diana went into the kitchen.

"Let's all have a seat," Mrs. Moore suggested, gesturing to the black leather sofa and facing chairs.

We all sat down, and the conversation flowed naturally, which taught me a thing or two about high-level social skills. I was proud of myself for catching on as quickly as I did.

"This is quite something, isn't it?" Mrs. Moore said. "We couldn't believe it when Diana told us about you. I'm still in shock. I can't imagine what it must have been like for the two of you to learn about each other, and then make contact."

"It was definitely a shocker," I replied. "It took me a while to absorb everything."

Diana arrived with my glass of wine. I took it out of her hands, and gulped a mouthful.

"Nadia was at work when she read my letter," Diana explained. She sat down and touched my arm, looked me in the eye. "I should probably send an apology to your boss, because I doubt you were at the top of your game for the rest of the day."

"You definitely should." We all laughed, and I took another sip of wine.

"Diana also tells us you grew up in Washington," Mrs. Moore added. "It's odd, how we were so close to each other, but didn't know it."

"It has to make you wonder about fate," Senator Moore said. "Maybe you were always meant to cross paths. I only wish it could have happened sooner."

"So do I." Diana's gaze locked with her father's.

In that moment, I saw, in his eyes, a look of apology and regret. It was impossible not to recognize the depth of their attachment.

He was an ambitious man who wanted to give his daughter everything, but in this instance, he had failed. He had not known his little girl lost a sister on the day she was born – a sister who could have been restored to her if they'd been informed.

The door opened just then, interrupting my brief moment of reflection.

Diana's mood lifted. "Rick!" She stood and moved to greet her future fiancé at the door. "I'm so glad you're back, and you brought dinner. Come on in. You have to meet someone."

He set a large plastic bag full of live lobsters on the kitchen counter, then followed Diana into the living room.

As he stood before me, I found it a challenge not to stare, because he was the most attractive man I'd ever seen in my life. I had the same reaction when he walked into my office the other day and asked for directions to the restroom.

Broad-shouldered and charismatic, with wavy dark hair and a pair of expressive blue eyes, he had the overwhelming presence of a movie star. I felt as if I'd been shot out of a cannon into some kind of fantasy world on prime time television. Were these people even human? They seemed too perfect to be real.

My sister had definitely scored a home run with this guy. I could barely catch my breath.

"Wow." Rick leaned forward and shook my hand. "Amazing. You two look exactly alike. It's a pleasure to meet you."

"Nice to meet you, too," I replied, lowering my hand to my lap.

"Though it's not really the first time we've met," he reminded me. "Diana must have told you about my reconnaissance mission into your office."

"Yes," I replied with a chuckle. "I remember you."

"Rick, what would you like to drink?" Diana asked him.

"Whatever's open," he replied.

He turned to greet the senator and Mrs. Moore, while I sat quietly, feeling shy all of a sudden, like an outsider. They chatted about the flight from Washington.

When Diana returned from the kitchen with Rick's wine, handed it to him, and sat down next to me, I was relieved.

"How are you doing?" she quietly asked me.

"I'm fine," I assured her.

"I hope you're not allergic to shellfish," she said. "I'm not, so I assumed you weren't either."

"No," I replied in a light tone, "but I've never had lobster before. Except in chowders and casseroles."

"Really? Well, you're in for a treat then."

We smiled at each other, and I realized I was entering into a new phase of my life – a phase full of novel experiences that would change the person I was.

The lobster turned out to be delicious, but it wasn't easy to crack the shell. I didn't know where to start. Thankfully, Diana sat beside me, and she was very discreet as she showed me what to do.

Thirty

Over the next three months, the speed and depth of my relationship with my twin grew at an exponential pace. Diana and I spoke on the phone at least once a day and exchanged emails and texts constantly, to share even our most trivial thoughts. We met for lunch whenever our schedules allowed it, and she invited me for dinner every weekend.

She and Rick took me to movies and ball games, introduced me to their friends, and invited me to parties and clubs. It wasn't easy at first, because I didn't feel I fit into their world – and I certainly couldn't afford a twelve-dollar drink at the places they frequented – but they were quick to make me feel at ease. They had a way of effortlessly inviting me into conversations, and one of them was always quick to whip out a gold credit card and take care of the bill.

Diana and I soon became a novelty among her friends and co-workers. People were fascinated by my existence, and wanted to know every last detail about how we found each other and what it was like to see our exact likeness in another person.

On one particular night, over dinner at a restaurant with a few other couples, Diana said, "I just hope Oprah doesn't come calling."

"It's bound to happen," one of her friends said. "Especially considering your dad's popularity right now. I'm amazed you've kept Nadia a secret this long."

Diana sat back and turned to me. "What would we do? What if someone approached us to write a book or something?"

"A book," Rick said with a nod, holding up his wine glass and pointing at her. "You guys should consider that. You could make a fortune."

Diana and I gazed at each other for a moment. It felt as if we were reading each other's thoughts.

"I think it would be interesting from a scientific point of view," I said.

"Yes," Diana agreed, "it could attempt to answer questions about how much of a role genetics plays in the development of a person...versus their environment and how they were raised." She paused and our eyes remained fixed on each other's. "But I'm not sure we'd want to open ourselves up like that," she added.

"I'm not sure either," I agreed, because the circumstances of my life up until that point weren't exactly things I wanted to share. I imagined that people would compare me to Diana, and judge me accordingly.

"Yes," they would say, "this definitely proves environment plays a large role, because look how Nadia turned out, versus how Diana turned out."

The waiter brought our desserts just then, which was a welcome interruption, because I didn't feel like explaining my insecurities to the others.

I picked up my dessert fork and was about to dig into my caramel topped cheesecake.

Rick, who sat beside me, leaned a little closer. "I'm sorry about that," he quietly said. "I didn't mean to put you on the spot."

I glanced up at him. "It's fine," I replied. "You didn't."

He gave my shoulder a friendly squeeze before he tapped and cracked the sugary shell of his Crème Brûlée.

Thirty-one

"So tell me everything you know about him," Diana said to me one evening as we sat on the sofa in her living room.

"He's a financial consultant," I replied, "and Bob said he's a fun guy. That's all I know."

Rick poked his head out from the computer alcove around the corner. "Who's Bob?"

"A guy I work with," I told him. "He's new."

Diana piped in to explain further. "Bob set Nadia up on a blind date, and they're going out for dinner tomorrow night."

Rick stood and moved into the kitchen to refill his water bottle. He'd just come from the gym and was still wearing his shorts and T-shirt. "A financial consultant, eh? I don't know about that…"

Diana chuckled. "What do you mean? What do you have against financial consultants?"

"Nothing at all," he replied, tipping his water bottle up to take a swig. "Where's he taking you?"

"I'm not sure yet. Somewhere nice I hope. He's picking me up at 7:00."

"On a school night," Rick said. "Don't stay out too late."

Diana waved a dismissive hand at him, and he went back to his chair at the computer.

"So what are you going to wear?" she asked me.

"I don't know yet."

"Want to check out my closet? You can borrow anything you like."

I smiled at her. "That would be so great."

We both rose from the sofa to go into her bedroom, and she gave Rick a kiss on the cheek as we passed by.

Strangely enough, my blind date's name was Richard, which made me wonder if I was living in some sort of parallel universe. When he buzzed my apartment, I told him I'd be right down, and as I descended the steps, I tried to imagine what I would do if he turned out to be Rick's doppelganger as well, and Diana and I were about to become twin couples.

When I reached the ground floor, however, and spotted him waiting in the entrance hall by the mail boxes, I was relieved to discover that although he had dark hair and was good looking, he bore no other resemblance to Diana's other half.

"You must be Nadia." He held out his hand to shake mine.

"And you're Richard."

"Nice to meet you," he said, "but my friends call me Rick."

I almost chuckled. "Do you mind if I call you Richard?"

"Whatever," he replied after a brief hesitation. "My car's parked just outside. You ready to go?"

I nodded and followed him out of the building to a shiny silver Mercedes at the curb.

I didn't live in the greatest neighborhood, so this swanky car of his stood out like white on black.

I paused a moment to get my bearings. Whose life was this, anyway? I wondered. Surely it wasn't mine, because I couldn't possibly be wearing a six-hundred-dollar dress, a four-hundred-dollar pair of shoes, and a purse that was probably double the price of everything combined.

Richard unlocked the passenger side door with the press of a button on his key ring, and the loud beep startled me out of my dithering. He opened the door and waved me closer, then held it open while I got inside. A few seconds later he was circling around to the driver's side.

Don't get clingy, I said to myself. *We're just having dinner.*

He started the engine and pulled onto the street, then gave me a curious look. "You're not quite what I was expecting."

"No?" I replied. "Is that a good thing or a bad thing?"

"Not sure yet." He stopped at the corner and turned left. "We're only just getting started."

I wasn't thrilled with his non-committal answer, but I was determined to remain aloof.

Richard took me to an expensive restaurant, where we engaged in the sort of casual conversation most couples endure on a first date.

I did my best to learn all I could about him. Though he clearly made truckloads of money, I didn't take him for one of those Old World, Old Money snobs. He told me that his parents owned a hardware store in Iowa, but he hated all things rural, and preferred a more cosmopolitan lifestyle, which was why he'd moved to LA. He talked about his work, and had no qualms about describing his wild college days when he was a member of a fraternity, partied every night of the week, and barely made it to graduation.

I laughed at some of the stories he told about bizarre drinking games and freshman girls puking out windows. Part of me felt as if I should feel more at home with someone like him, but that wasn't the case. To the contrary, I was disappointed in myself for laughing and trying so hard to act as if we shared a connection.

It reminded me of who I was on the inside – a woman desperate to be accepted, and to be invited into someone else's world. Someone else's life.

I tried to tell myself I had my own world now – a twin sister who cared about me – and I didn't need this man to validate my self-worth. Nor did I have to fawn over every word he said, and sound so bloody impressed, as if he and I were the same.

We weren't. First of all, I never went to college, so I didn't get the whole fraternity thing.

Second, I had horrendous memories of a man in my life who drank too much, and for that reason, I was intensely aware of how many gin and tonics Richard tossed back during dinner.

Later, when we walked out, Richard reached into the breast pocket of his jacket for a pack of cigarettes. "Want one?" he asked, holding it out to me.

"No thanks."

"Bob said you smoked."

How did Bob even know that about me? I wondered. I'd quit cold turkey not long after I met Diana, and that was before he started at the firm.

"Not anymore," I said.

"Ah, come on." He pushed the pack at me. "Just one. You know you want to."

My heart began to race, because yes, I *did* want to. I could smell the fresh fragrance of the tobacco, still in the package, right there in front of my nose.

"No thanks," I said, though I was teetering on a cliff edge.

"Suit yourself."

Richard lit up as we walked back to his car. Thankfully it wasn't long before my urge to do the same retreated, and I was proud of myself for resisting the temptation.

"Where do you want to go now?" Richard asked. "I know a great club not far from here."

"I should probably get home," I replied. "I have to work in the morning."

"But it's Thursday," he argued. "Practically Friday. Come on, just one drink. I talked too much about myself at dinner, and I want to know more about *you*. You're intriguing."

Intriguing. No one had ever called me *that* before.

"All right," I said, wanting to give him one more chance before I threw in the towel. "Just one drink. But then I really need to get home."

He held up a hand. "Scout's honor. I promise I'll have you home by midnight."

S trobe lights in the club flashed through a white haze from a smoke machine. The music was so loud, the floor vibrated under my feet. I could feel the heavy rumble of the beat in my chest.

Richard slid closer to me on the leather upholstery. He had passed a fifty-dollar bill to a bouncer when we first entered the club, and the bouncer showed us to a private circular booth on the second level with a view of the dance floor below.

Despite my protestations, Richard ordered me a second Cosmo as soon as I finished the first. That was when I decided it was time to text Diana.

I'm at that club called Revolution. He's a bit of an ass, holding me captive. I don't feel like dancing, but he just ordered me another Cosmo.

I pressed send, and felt my phone vibrate a few seconds later while Richard paid the waiter for our second round. I read her reply:

Can you tell him you have to work in the morning?

I quickly texted her back:

I already did, but he's pushy.

Keep me posted, she wrote.

I slipped my phone into my purse and took a sip of my drink. Because the music was booming, it was impossible to carry on a conversation without shouting.

Not that it mattered. Richard hadn't asked me a single personal question since we arrived. For him, it was bottoms up, over and over, while he watched the crowd on the dance floor and bobbed his head like a rooster in time with the music.

Suddenly, I remembered my mother's advice about marrying a man with money, but I couldn't imagine spending my life with this turkey head. He could be as rich as the Pope, but he reminded me too much of my father.

"Let's dance," he said in my ear, brushing the tip of his nose through my hair.

"I'm not really up for it," I replied.

"Come on. Bob said you were a party girl."

I swung my irritated gaze to meet Richard's. *"Did* he?"

Why would Bob think that? He barely knew me.

Was it because of the way I dressed? Was that what Richard meant when he said I wasn't what he'd expected?

"I'm sorry," I said, "but I have to go." There was no way I was getting into a car with this guy. I'd seen how much he had to drink. So I grabbed my purse and slid out of the booth. "You don't have to get up. I'll just grab a cab. Thanks for dinner. It was fun."

Rising too quickly to my feet, I wobbled as I tugged the hem of my dress down to cover my knees. It had been awhile since I'd had any hard liquor, and I didn't enjoy the tipsy feeling.

I pushed through the tight crowd, searching for a path to the door. When at last I stumbled outside onto the sidewalk, I gulped in a breath of fresh air. *Thank God.* I was so happy to be out of there.

The heavy rumble of the bass beat from inside the club pounded in my head, so I started walking toward the nearest intersection to flag down a cab.

One drove by, but he didn't stop for me, so I continued, spurred on by the sound of my heels clicking rapidly over the concrete.

Then someone called my name. "Nadia!"

I turned around, and wasn't sure what to think when I recognized Richard jogging to catch up with me.

"I'm sorry," he said, out of breath as he came to a halt. "I shouldn't have let you leave like that. Let me drive you home."

It was the first gentlemanly thing he'd said to me all evening. But still…

"No, really," I replied. "It's no problem. Look, there's a cab now." I raised my arm to flag it down, but it sped by.

"I can drive you," he insisted.

"No, I'm fine."

"What's the problem?" he asked. "I paid for dinner, and it was a damn good meal."

"It was delicious," I agreed, and felt my shoulders tense.

"You should be grateful," he said.

"I am."

But I wasn't. I wanted to kick him in the nuts and run.

I should have done it when my instincts told me to, because the next thing I knew, I was being dragged by the wrist into an alleyway. Richard shoved me up against the side of the building. The back of my head cracked against the brick.

"Let go of me!" I grunted, struggling fiercely, punching him in the face, thrashing about.

He pinned me tightly to the wall. Then he began to tug my skirt up.

I struck him in the face and bit him on the mouth when he tried to kiss me, but it only roused him further. Though I had witnessed my father beating my mother on countless occasions, I had never been beaten myself, so it came as a terrible shock when he slapped me across the face.

Then suddenly he was pulled away from me, as if by a giant vacuum into the air. He flew across the alley and hit the opposite wall.

I watched in stunned silence as another man punched him in the jaw, which caused him to fold like paper and crumple to the ground.

My rescuer – dressed in faded jeans, a black T-shirt, and a baseball cap – straddled Richard, who was flat on his back, wiping blood from under his nose. Grabbing hold of Richard's lapels in two fists, the man lifted him up and spoke in a vicious growl.

"Didn't you hear her say no?" He thrust Richard roughly to the ground. "If you ever talk to her again, I'll smash you to pieces. You got that?"

I was stunned and nearly hyperventilating when I realized it was Rick – *Diana's* Rick – who had come to my rescue. He was holding me steady by my shoulders.

"Are you all right?"

Still in a daze, I managed to nod.

"Let's get you out of here." He led me to his car, which was double parked in the street.

"Just a minute." I pulled free of his grasp and turned back kick Richard in the ribs. "You're an ass!" I shouted. "I hope the rats eat you."

Then I ran to follow Rick, who was holding the car door open for me.

"You sure you're okay?" Rick asked as he shifted into first gear and took us away from the dark alley. His eyes raked over me with concern. "Did he hurt you?"

"I'm fine," I replied, but my whole body was trembling. "How did you find me?"

"Diana sent me out to pick you up. She was worried."

"How did you know where I was?"

"You texted the name of the club. It's lucky I came along when I did. I saw him pull you into the alley."

I buried my face in my hands. "Oh, God, I can't believe that just happened. What would have happened if you hadn't come along?"

He touched my shoulder. "I'm sure you would have kicked his ass."

I glanced up, and let out a sob that was half laughter.

He checked the rear view mirror and shifted into a higher gear. I noticed his knuckles were bloodied.

"Thank you," I softly said, and tipped my head back on the seat.

We drove for a few minutes in silence.

"You should call Diana," he suggested. "Tell her you're okay, and I'm driving you home."

I wasn't up to having a conversation about what just happened, because I was embarrassed by it. I was sure nothing like this would ever happen to Diana. She would know better. Or maybe guys just sensed that she was a woman who deserved to be treated with respect.

"I'll text her," I replied, and reached into my purse for my phone.

> Hi Sis. Thanks for sending Rick. He picked me up and he's driving me home now.

She immediately texted me back.

> Oh good. Call me later.

> Okay.

When we reached my apartment, Rick found a parking spot out front. My hands were still trembling, however, and I was slow to get a grip on the door handle.

"Let me help you." Rick got out and circled around to my side, opened my door, and supported me by the elbow as I set my feet on the ground.

My knees felt like quivering blobs of jelly when I tried to stand.

"I'll come inside with you," he said. "Where are your keys?"

I handed him my purse and he found them for me.

We walked up the stairs in silence. He unlocked my apartment door and flicked on the lights. I went straight to the sofa and collapsed onto it.

While I toed off my heels, he glanced around at the faded paint and scuff marks on the walls, the stained carpet, and the small, dated kitchen that hadn't had an upgrade since the eighties. "So this is where you live," he said.

I leaned back. "Yeah. My decorator's on vacation. So is my cleaning lady."

He nodded with amusement. "Can I get you a glass of water? A cup of tea?"

"Tea would be great." I pointed. "There's a kettle on the counter, and the cookie jar has teabags in it."

While he stood at the sink and filled the kettle, I tried to relax, but it wasn't easy. I laid my hand on my cheek where I'd been slapped. It still burned.

"I should have seen that coming," I said, shaking my head at the stupidity of heading down the street alone. "My date was a jerk from the first minute. All he talked about were all the wild parties he used to go to in college."

After plugging in the kettle, Rick turned to face me. He leaned back and curled his hands around the edge of the kitchen counter. "I'm sorry that happened, Nadia. You didn't deserve it. *No* woman deserves that."

"No, I suppose not. But I still don't understand why Bob thought he could just pimp me out for a night." I gazed at Rick imploringly. "Do I give off slut signals or something?"

His eyebrows lifted, and he pushed away from the counter to move closer, into the living room. He sat down on the ottoman across from me and rested his elbows on his knees. "No, you don't."

I looked down at the borrowed dress I wore. "Maybe not tonight, because Diana dressed me up, but I think the lawyers at work see me differently. They assume, because I just answer phones and wear cheap outfits, that I'm a bimbo."

"I'm sure they don't think that."

"Yes, they do," I argued. "It's why Bob set me up like that. His friend was looking for a good time, and I was the first chick who came to mind. The one who wears spandex pants and low cut tops to work."

The kettle began to boil. Rick stood up to make the tea. "You should kick Bob's ass tomorrow," he said, "or at least tell someone what happened. Is there an office manager you can complain to, or a senior partner? You said Bob was new there. There's usually a probationary period. Maybe they'll get a clue and fire him."

"I don't know," I said, sitting forward. "He's a college grad, and what am I? They'd be more likely to fire *me* and sweep it all under the carpet."

"Don't let yourself be intimidated," he said to me as he poured boiling water into two mismatched mugs. "Remember, your sister is a lawyer, too, and she works at one of the top firms in the country, and your father…Let's just call him your father, okay? He's a senator. He could destroy them if they tried anything like that."

I smiled. "I'm starting to feel better already."

Rising from the sofa, I went to join Rick in the kitchen. He was dipping the teabags, and again, I noticed the blood on his knuckles.

"You must have swung a pretty hard punch," I said. "Can I get you anything for that?"

"It's fine." He handed me my cup. "I'm tough."

"Well, that's obvious," I replied. "*I* certainly wouldn't want to cross you in a dark alley."

We both leaned against opposite counters, facing each other.

"Nadia…" Rick said, looking me in the eye. "You're not a bimbo. You're smart. You could be anything you want to be."

I took a deep breath and let it out. No one had ever said anything like that to me before. At least, no one like Rick Fraser.

"Thanks. I think it's a confidence issue. I wasn't exactly raised to believe I could conquer the world."

"Diana told me you had a rough childhood."

Before long, I was confessing numerous intimate details about the fights my parents used to have, and how we had no money left when we arrived in LA, and how my mother couldn't get along with her parents, so we ended up living in her car again.

"But you survived," he said, "because that's what you are. A survivor."

I finished off the last of my tea. "Yes," I replied, "and somehow I'll survive at work tomorrow when I tell Bob to go stick his head in the toilet and flush it."

Rick laughed. "I wish I could be there for that." He paused. "You're not going to quit are you?"

"Hell, no," I quickly replied. "I wouldn't give him the satisfaction."

Rick finished his tea as well and set the mug on the counter. His phone beeped. He picked it up and checked it.

"It's Diana," he explained as he texted her back. "She's wondering where I am. He pressed send and dropped the phone into his back pocket. "I should go. You're sure you're okay?"

"Yeah, yeah. I'm fine. Go home."

We walked out of the kitchen together, and I stood at the open door while he dug into the front pocket of his jeans for his car keys.

"Listen, thanks again," I said. "I owe you one."

He made a face. "Don't be silly. That was the highlight of my day."

I smiled. "Drive safely."

"Always do."

I shut the door behind him and locked it.

I thought about calling Diana, but I was physically and emotionally exhausted. All I wanted to do was go to bed and start fresh tomorrow.

Diana

I t shouldn't have been a big deal for me to tell Nadia that Rick
and I planned to drive up the coast, just the two of us, for
a romantic weekend getaway. Yet I felt guilty all the same,
for leaving her behind when she and I had spent every weekend
together since the first day we met.

We were not joined at the hip, I reminded myself constantly,
and I was not responsible for her happiness. She was a grown
woman, and so was I, with my own life to lead.

It had been awhile since Rick and I spent a night together in
a hotel, so I booked us into a quaint little five star Victorian B&B
overlooking the water.

We drove up Friday after work, enjoyed a steak dinner at the
inn with a delicious Cabernet, then went for a walk down on the
beach.

Rick never looked more handsome to me. He wore linen
pants and a loose, white shirt, while I wore a flowing Indian cotton skirt and black tank top. As soon as we stepped onto the
sand, I kicked off my flip flops to feel the soft, cool grains of sand
between my toes. A half moon hung low over the water, lumines-
cent as it reflected off the foamy, crashing waves.

"How perfect is this?" I said, reveling in the warmth of his
hand around mine.

We walked for quite a distance and discussed some of his frustrations at work, and his desire to open his own agency. I was supportive, because I wanted him to be happy, and I wanted to be a part of his future.

Soon we entered a private cove beyond some large boulders, and sat down to look out at the dark, sparkling sea.

I closed my eyes and breathed deeply. "Why doesn't it smell like this everywhere?" I asked. "That clean salty fragrance... It's like a drug."

"*You're* like a drug," he replied, and when I opened my eyes, he was gazing at me with heated desire.

His lips touched mine and I slid my fingers through his hair, pulling him close, enjoying the rough bristle on his chin as it rubbed against mine. His tongue probed softly with skillful, caressing strokes, and I let out a soft sigh. I wanted him desperately, and felt my body tremble as his hand slid over my hip and he eased me onto my back.

The sound of the ocean pulsing up onto the shore lulled me into a dreamlike state, and when he rolled on top of me, I wrapped my legs around his hips and clung to him with a yearning that made me forget everything outside of that moment.

His hand roved down over the top of my thigh, and I shivered when he gathered the fabric of my skirt and began to tug it upward.

"Not here," I whispered. "Let's go back to the room."

"Why not here?" he asked.

"Because someone might see us."

He lifted his head and scanned the perimeter of the secluded cove. "There's no one else here. It's completely private."

His mouth brushed lazily across my cheek, over my jawline, down the length of my neck.

I wanted him, truly I did, but I also wanted this to be special.

"Let's go back to the room," I whispered breathlessly. "I have champagne and chocolates waiting for us."

His head drew back, and he smiled at me. "Were you *planning* to seduce me?"

I playfully puckered my lips. "I can't tell a lie. I lured you here for one purpose, and one purpose alone."

Rick sat back on his heels and raked his fingers through his hair. "If this is part of your grand plan to make me all hot and bothered, then play hard to get, you're doing a great job."

I sat up as well and grinned at him mischievously. "It's better when you have to wait for it."

"I can't argue." He stood up and offered his hand. "Those chocolates better be damn good."

"They'll be fabulous," I promised, and with teasing laughter, I let him chase me back to the inn, where I fully intended to make him glad he waited – and hopefully then, we'd put a seal on our future together.

We devoured the chocolate truffles, then made love on the bed. When we woke the next morning to the sun streaming in through the pale cream curtains, and the soothing sound of the waves crashing up onto the beach, we made love again.

Afterward, Rick tossed the covers aside and moved across the room to open the window. Then he returned and slipped back into bed beside me. I entwined my body around his and kissed his neck.

"This is nice," I said. "We needed some time alone together. It's been awhile."

"Yeah, it has."

Resting my cheek on his shoulder, I stroked a finger across his chest.

"Can I talk to you about something?" I asked.

"Sure."

I leaned up on an elbow. "You know I'll be turning twenty-eight next year…" I hesitated.

He had been rubbing the pad of his thumb lightly over my shoulder. He stilled but made no comment. Suddenly I wished I could backpeddle and say simply, "Let's get some breakfast," but I was already into it, so I soldiered on.

"I'd like to talk about the future," I said.

I felt the steady stroke of his thumb slow to a halt. "What about it?"

"Well...We've been together for a while, and there are certain things I want out of life."

"Such as?"

Again, I hesitated. This wasn't as easy as I thought it would be. "I want to get married eventually, and have a family. Don't you want that, too?"

His eyes clouded over. "You know I love you, Di," he said, "but I don't want that right now."

I swallowed uncomfortably. "I'm not talking about right now, this minute. But someday...I'd like to know how you feel about that."

In all honesty, I would have welcomed a pregnancy that night if he was keen. But I knew this was a big step, and I was willing to give him time to ease into it, because I believed he was worth the wait.

Of course, an engagement ring would be nice before we took that leap.

Rick sat up and swung his legs off the bed. My heart began to pound as I stared at his smooth, muscular back. *What was he thinking?* I had no idea. *Had I pushed too hard? Was my timing all wrong?*

He rose to his feet, padded to the washroom, and closed the door behind him.

I flopped back down onto the bed and wanted to sink through the mattress while I waited for him to come out. Then I heard the shower come on.

Feeling frustrated, and a bit insulted, I rose from the bed, went to the closet, and slipped into the cozy white bathrobe with the name of the inn embroidered on the breast pocket.

I buried my hands into the deep pockets and went out onto our private balcony that overlooked the sea. Everything was blue.

At last the door to the bathroom opened, and Rick emerged in a towel. He joined me on the veranda, slid his arm around my waist, and kissed me on the temple.

"I'm sorry," he said. "This is supposed to be a romantic weekend. I hope you're not disappointed."

"Of course not," I replied, wrapping my arms around his neck. "I just wanted to be alone with you. I didn't mean to spoil it, or put pressure on you. We have time to figure things out."

I spoke casually, then I kissed him on the mouth, but it was all pretence. I *did* want to put pressure on Rick.

I wanted children. I could feel my biological clock ticking like a hammer. I wanted a ring on my finger as soon as possible so we could get started with the rest of our lives.

I'd always been ambitious. I was always climbing, eager to reach another summit.

In this case, that drive turned out to be my undoing.

ᴄᴄ᠍ᴗᴖᴖ

"Whose turn is it to deal?" I asked as I gathered up the cards in the center of the table. It was a Saturday night. Rick and I had invited two of his colleagues and their wives over for dinner so they could discuss the possibility of leaving the firm to strike out, as partners, on their own.

By the time we polished off the last of the chocolate cheesecake, the ladies decided it was time for the guys to stop talking business and have some fun. We settled into a friendly game of Scat, gambling for quarters.

"It's my turn," Jennie said, and I passed her the deck.

She started shuffling when a call came in from the security entrance. My eyes lifted to meet Rick's. "Are you expecting anyone?"

He shook his head and rose from the table. "I'll see who it is."

"Hello." He paused. "Yeah, sure, come on up." He pressed the button to buzz someone into the building and returned to his chair. "It's Nadia. She's on her way up."

"I thought she had a baby shower to go to," I replied, which was why I specifically chose that night to host our dinner party, so that we could have some time alone with our friends.

It wasn't that I didn't enjoy being with Nadia, but sometimes it came as a relief not to worry about whether she was feeling comfortable with my friends, or having a good time.

"It must have ended early," he said.

I picked up the three cards that were dealt to me and rearranged them by suit in my hand. Everyone took their turn picking up and laying down a card, and we made it once around the table when a knock sounded at the door.

"I'll let her in." Rick stood.

We continued playing that hand, and when Nadia entered, she said, "I hope I'm not interrupting."

I called out to her over my shoulder. "We're playing Scat. Do you have any quarters?"

She approached the table and shrugged out of her jean jacket. "I might have a few. Who's winning?"

"No one yet," Rick replied. "We just started this round, so feel free to jump in." He went to get an extra chair and placed it beside his.

Greg knocked on the table to indicate he was ready to lay down his cards, Rick whistled, and Jennie ended up losing that hand. She tossed a quarter into the bowl, and I scooped up the cards to shuffle them again.

"How was the shower?" I asked Nadia.

"Fun," she replied. "The food was great, and I loved seeing all those cute little baby outfits."

"Aw…Did it make you want one?" Jennie asked.

I glanced discreetly across at Rick, and wondered how he would react to a conversation about babies.

He was difficult to read. Slouched back in his chair, he tapped a finger on the table while he waited for the cards to be dealt.

"Not in the least," Nadia replied with a surprising hint of disgust. "I don't think I'm the mothering type."

Rick – suddenly interested in the conversation – sat forward and turned toward her. "What are you talking about? You'd make a great mom."

Nadia shook her head and rolled her eyes. I could see she was embarrassed by the compliment.

"Of course you would," I added.

She pointed at Rick and me. "No thank you. Making babies will be *your* job. I'll just be the fun single auntie who's a terrible influence in the teen years."

Everyone laughed. Everyone except for me, because I was busy dealing the cards and keeping an eye on my boyfriend, whose gorgeous, magnetic smile was directed at my twin.

"What do you think about Rick?" I asked Nadia, after we placed our lunch orders at our usual weekday meeting place.

"What do you mean?" she asked.

I leaned back in my chair and wondered if I should even bring this up. Maybe it was a mistake. I wasn't sure where it would lead.

"Do you ever feel like he's *too* charming?"

"I don't know," she said. "He's good looking; no one can deny that."

"I'm not talking about his looks. I'm talking about whether or not I can trust him. You know how I want to have a family someday…"

"Of course."

Nadia and I had talked about it more than once.

"The problem is…" I said, "I'm not sure he wants the same thing, and it worries me."

She picked up her glass of water and took a sip. "What does that have to do with him being charming?"

I shrugged, and looked the other way toward the lunch counter. After a long pause, I met her eyes and said, "Do you ever feel like he's flirting with you?"

Her eyebrows lifted. "Oh, my God, no. Why would you ask that?"

I felt suddenly guilty for suggesting something that sounded like an accusation.

Why did I always feel guilty around Nadia?

I leaned forward and touched her arm. "That came out wrong. I didn't mean it like that. I just think…" I paused. "I'm not sure if he's a true family man, you know? I worry that he might have a wandering eye."

She shook her head at me. "That's crazy. He's totally in love with you, and you're the luckiest woman in the universe. He's nice to me because he feels sorry for me. He tries to make me feel welcome. Just like you do. I don't feel like he's flirting. Do you think he flirts with other women?"

"I don't know. I'm sure they must try to flirt with *him*. That's the problem with having a gorgeous boyfriend. Lots of temptations."

"Do you have any reason to suspect him of anything?" she asked. "Any proof?"

Now I was sounding like one of my distraught clients. "No, and I'm probably being ridiculous. I just thought maybe, by now, we might be talking about marriage, but he doesn't seem to be anywhere close to that."

"Give him time," she suggested. "Guys usually need to be eased gradually into these things. Not that I'm any great expert, but I do watch *Dr. Phil.*"

Our salads arrived, and I promised myself I would try to lighten up about the whole marriage and baby thing. Nadia was right. I was only twenty-seven. There was still plenty of time.

Despite my resolve to be optimistic and easygoing, I couldn't seem to let go of my doubts about Rick's commitment to our relationship.

One night, while driving home from a Lakers game, I turned in the passenger seat to face him. "What's the longest relationship you've ever had?"

He glanced at me with concern. "Why are you asking me this?"

"I'm just curious," I replied. "I dated a guy in high school for three and a half years. Back then, it seemed like an eternity, but it's not really."

"It is for high school," he said, shifting into fourth gear.

He must have realized I was still waiting for him to answer the question, because he sighed with resignation. "About a year and a half, I think. It was right after college."

I nodded to acknowledge his response, then I decided to change the subject.

—6

Two days later, I interrogated him again when we got into bed. "Do you think Nadia's pretty?"

"Of course," he replied. "She's your identical twin, and I think you're the most beautiful woman alive."

"But if you're attracted to me," I said, "you must find her attractive, too."

I hated myself in that moment, for I was clearly trying to bait him. No matter how hard I tried, I couldn't seem to escape my feelings of doubt.

He frowned at me. "What are you getting at?" he asked. "You don't think there's something going on between us, do you?"

"Of course not," I replied.

There was no logical reason for me to think such a thing. Nothing had ever occurred to make me suspect him, and I was beginning to wonder, for the first time in my life, if I should see a therapist.

Was I losing my inner confidence? My firm and stable sense of myself? Was I now half the person I used to be, because I'd discovered I had a twin?

Rick stared at me with concern, then he threw the covers aside and got out of bed.

"Where are you going?" I asked, as he headed for the door.

"I'm not tired."

I'd hoped we might make love, but that suddenly seemed like an unrealistic expectation.

I, too, slid out of bed and followed him to the kitchen, where I found him standing in the glow of the open refrigerator, staring at its contents.

"You're mad at me," I said.

"No shit." He shut the fridge door and moved into the living room, where he sat on the sofa, picked up the remote, and turned on the television.

I sat down beside him. "I'm sorry."

He said nothing for a long while, then at last he met my gaze. "What's up with you lately? You're not yourself, and I feel like you're not happy with the way things are between us."

"Of course I'm happy," I said. "That's why I want to make sure we're okay. Because I don't want to lose you."

He pointed the remote control at the television and quickly flicked through the sports channels.

"Will you talk to me, please?" I implored.

He settled on a football game and tossed the remote onto the coffee table with a clatter. "You've been different since you found Nadia," he said. "Nothing's been the same."

My stomach turned over. I wasn't sure what was about to happen.

"I know," I replied. "I've been spending a lot of time with her, so there hasn't been much left over for you. Or for us. I feel like we've been growing apart."

But Rick was my future. I loved him and I wanted a life with him.

"I can't believe what you said," he replied. A vein pulsed at his temple, and I realized how angry I'd made him. "Nadia is your sister, and she's like a sister to me, too. I've done nothing but try and make her feel at home here, because she's *family*. For you to suggest that I'm…" He stopped and shook his head. "You need to stop thinking that, Diana. It's crazy."

As I sat there, staring at the football game, I felt a little sick to my stomach over what I'd said to him in the bedroom, over what I had insinuated, and what I had suggested to Nadia at lunch. I really needed to get a grip. If anyone had a problem, it was me.

I wanted desperately to fix everything, but somehow, when I tried, I only managed to make things worse.

CHAPTER

Thirty-nine

M y brother Adam, who had been living and working in Australia since the fall of 2011, called me one Sunday afternoon to let me know he was flying to Vegas for a conference the following weekend. It was a last-minute decision, and since I hadn't seen him in a year – and he was keen to meet my twin – we made arrangements to meet up.

I then called Becky, and she decided to fly out to meet us as well, since she hadn't met Nadia yet either, and it was the perfect excuse for a family get together.

The following Friday, Rick, Nadia and I finished work early, threw our suitcases into the trunk of Rick's car, and headed out of the city.

"This is wonderful," Becky said as she shook the ice-filled martini mixer at the bar in our sprawling penthouse suite at the Palms Casino Resort. The suite had a gourmet kitchen, a spacious living room with contemporary leather furniture, a stunning view of the Vegas skyline, three and a half baths, and a pool table.

"You can say that again," Nadia replied. "I never imagined I'd ever set foot in a place like this. I keep wanting to pinch myself."

Becky poured the pink cocktails into our long-stemmed glasses, and we raised them for a toast.

"Here's to finding lost family members," Becky said.

"Cheers to that," I agreed with Becky. Adam was now the only one of us who didn't know anything about his biological parents, but it wasn't likely he ever would, because he'd been orphaned in Africa.

"Your brother's a great guy," Nadia said, swiveling on her leather bar stool to watch Adam sink a few balls at the pool table. "I always wanted a brother, when I was little."

"Now you have one," I said to her.

She swiveled back around and gave me an appreciative look. "I should knock on wood when I say this, but thanks to you, for the first time in my life, I actually feel lucky."

Becky smiled. "Then we came to the right place. Hurry up and finish that game boys!" she shouted into the other room. "Nadia's feeling lucky. It's time head down to the casino."

While Nadia, Rick, and Adam went to check out the blackjack table, Becky and I found two seats at the bar to talk privately for a while. She wanted to know how things were going with Rick.

"I'm trying my best to give him space," I explained, "but it's not easy when I don't want space between us. I want to be closer. I was watching one of those trashy reality talk shows last week, and there was a woman who'd been living with a guy for eleven years, and her family was trying to convince her that he was never going to marry her or have children with her, but she wouldn't leave him because that would mean she'd wasted all those years. I don't want to wake up when I'm forty and wonder where my life went."

Becky reached for some bar nuts in a bowl. "I think every woman feels that way at some point in her life."

"Do *you* feel that way?" I asked. "Are you worried that nothing's going to work out, and you'll never find that special person who wants the same things you do?"

Becky considered it for a moment. "I'm still hopeful," she said, "but it's easier for me at this point, because I'm just finishing my degree, and I'll be moving to Nova Scotia soon, starting a new job. Everything still feels undiscovered."

"The world is your oyster," I said with a smile.

I was happy for Becky. I wanted her to have everything.

"How about we go try our luck at the roulette table?" she suggested.

"Sounds great." We slid off the bar stools and went searching for a spinning wheel that looked lucky.

⁓⧂

More than an hour passed. I scanned the noisy casino floor, searching for Nadia and the guys. "I wonder if their luck was any better than ours," I said.

"I'll text Adam and find out." She dug into her purse for her phone, while I went to check out a poster about a stage show that was playing in the hotel.

"We should go see this," I said. "Looks like fun."

"It's a magic show," Becky replied, after she pressed 'send.'

"Yeah. They're usually pretty amazing."

Her phone vibrated and she swiped the touch screen. "Oh," she said, her brow furrowing.

"What's wrong?"

"Adam left. He ran into his boss and they went to another hotel for a late dinner."

"His boss is a woman," I said. "Isn't that right?"

Becky raised an inquisitive eyebrow. "I wonder what's going on there."

I turned to scan the casino floor, while trying to ignore the monotonous carnival sounds: the discordant music and chiming beeps and bells. "Where are Nadia and Rick?"

"I don't know. Let's go look for them."

We wandered around the gaming tables and through rows of slot machines, but didn't see them. I texted each of them but neither replied.

"Maybe they went to one of the bars," Becky said.

"Can you text Adam and ask him where he saw them last?"

She pulled her phone out again and typed the message.

A moment later, his reply came in.

"He says they were at the slot machines when he left."

We were standing in the middle of the slot machine aisle, and had gone through it twice.

"Maybe they went back to the room." I checked my phone again in case one of them had texted me. Still nothing.

"Want to go upstairs?" Becky asked, and I knew she recognized my concern, my need to check up on Rick and put my concerns to rest.

"Let's find a house phone and call up to the suite."

We found one in an alcove near the washrooms, but there was no answer.

"It's a big hotel," she said. "They could be anywhere."

Then my phone vibrated, and I quickly swiped the screen. "It's Rick," I said with relief. "He says they're in Rain. It's the dance bar."

"It's just over there." Becky turned and pointed.

I was relieved to have finally heard from him, but I wished he or Nadia had texted us earlier to invite us to go with them.

When we finally found them in the club – which was flashing with pyrotechnics – they were waving to us from the dance floor. We pushed our way through the crowd to join them.

By the time the four of us made it back to the penthouse, I
knew I'd had too much to drink, because all I wanted to do
was pass out on the bed.

"Want some chips?" Nadia asked, heading straight for the
kitchen.

"Definitely," Rick replied. "And I need to drink some water."

"Me, too," she said.

I tossed my purse on a table and met Becky's gaze.

"I'm exhausted," Becky said. "I need to go to bed."

"But it's still early," Nadia called out from the kitchen.

I heard the sound of the chip bag ripping open, and went see
what else was there to eat.

"It's three o'clock in the morning," Rick reminded her with a
playful shove. She shoved him back.

I reached for a bottle of water, opened it, and tipped it up for
a drink while I watched the two of them. "I need to go to bed,
too," I said.

I waited for Rick to follow my lead, but he took his water and
the bowl of chips into the living room, sat down on the sofa, and
turned on the television.

"What's on?" Nadia cheerfully asked. She kicked off her heels
and sat beside him.

My muscles tensed with agitation, and heat rushed through my body.

"Good night," I said, moving past them to go to bed.

"I'll be in soon, babe," Rick replied, but it was five in the morning before he slipped into bed beside me.

"You're beginning to sound crazy," Rick said when I stepped out of the shower to get ready for breakfast. "Nothing's going on. What...? I'm not allowed to stay up and watch TV now?"

"There's a TV in here," I argued, gesturing toward it.

"I wasn't tired," he explained. "I wanted to stay up."

Surely my blood pressure was burning a hole in the roof. I wanted to biff a pillow at him.

"She's your twin sister," he said in disbelief. "How can you even *think* what you're thinking?"

"Just get up," I said, brushing my wet hair. "We're supposed to meet Adam in twenty minutes."

Rick groaned in complaint, and tossed the covers aside.

I managed to keep a smile on my face most of the day, but on the inside I was quietly fuming over how Rick seemed to be ignoring me. He talked and laughed with the others, but the wedge between was as obvious to me as the flashing neon lights on the strip.

We went to *Cirque Du Soleil* that night, then returned to the Palms to gamble in the casino again. Nadia stuck close to me, which took some of the edge off, and I made an effort to give each of them the benefit of the doubt and consider the possibility that the problem was with me, not them. Maybe I just needed to lighten up and have a good time.

While Adam and Rick played poker, Nadia, Becky and I did well at the craps table. People began to cheer for us, but before long, our luck took a turn for the worse, so we decided to quit while we were still ahead.

I gathered up our chips. "You guys go find a seat in the bar," I said. "I'll take these to the cashier's cage. And text the guys. Tell them where we are."

A short while later, I found Becky in the Scarlet Lounge with a glass of white wine on the table in front of her. She was reading emails on her phone.

I sat down in the facing chair. "Where's Nadia?"

"She went to the washroom."

I ordered a glass of wine and checked my emails as well.

When Nadia didn't come back after about fifteen minutes, I said, "Do you think she went to find the guys?"

"Maybe."

I texted her: Are you coming back?

Adam walked in and sat down. "I heard you guys won big at the craps table," he said.

"We won two hundred dollars!" Becky proudly told him.

"Does that mean you're buying?"

"Sure. Let's get the waiter over here." She waved a hand to flag him down.

"Where's Rick?" I asked Adam.

"I think he went to the washroom."

"When was that?"

"About fifteen minutes ago," Adam said.

Alarm bells were going off in my head, but I tried to keep cool. "I'll be right back." Grabbing my purse, I rose from my chair.

I walked out of the bar and checked the ladies washroom on the casino floor. There was no sign of Nadia inside so I took a quick stroll through the slot machine aisles and searched around the gaming tables. By this time, I had tight knots in my stomach. I hated feeling suspicious, but I couldn't help myself.

I walked across the sky tube to the tower where our penthouse was located, reached the lobby and pressed the button on the elevator. It was quieter there, away from the sounds of the casino. Impatiently, I tapped my foot on the floor.

Then the elevator chimed, the doors slid open, and I stood motionless, staring. Rick was inside the elevator, stepping away from Nadia after kissing her up against the side wall. With a smile on his face, he turned to get off, but stopped dead when he met my shocked gaze.

"Oh, my God," Nadia said with horror as she covered her mouth with both hands.

Rick looked down at the floor. "Shit."

The elevator door started to close, but he held it back and quickly got off. Nadia followed him.

"Diana, I'm so sorry," she said.

I shook my head at her. "Don't." Then I turned and started walking away, back across the sky tube to the casino.

"Diana wait!" Rick shouted.

My stomach churned with sickening rage as I entered the noisy casino. I wanted to hit something.

I knew Rick had followed me, and when he grabbed hold of my arm, I whirled around and shook myself out of his grasp. "Don't touch me!"

Nadia caught up with us.

"You know as well as I do," he said, "that we've been having problems for a while."

"Is that supposed to make me feel better?" I asked. "Is that supposed to excuse what I just saw?"

"You're too uptight," he argued. "All you want is a ring on your finger and a white dress and a wedding cake. I don't want any of that!"

"That's not true."

He lowered his voice and spoke close in my ear. "Remember the beach? You didn't want to make love because it didn't fit into your grand master plan for the night. Nadia's not like that. She would have made love on the beach."

Nadia grabbed his arm. "Rick, *stop!*" Her eyes shot to mine. Her cheeks were flame red, her eyes full of angst. "I'm so sorry, Diana. I didn't mean for this to happen."

"Well, it did," I replied. "And you can't take it back."

I started back to the bar to find Becky and Adam, but Nadia followed.

"Please, Diana, let me explain."

"I don't want to hear it," I said. "I don't even want to look at you. Don't follow me."

I returned to the Scarlet Lounge where Becky and Adam were talking. Becky glanced up at me. "Oh my God, what happened?"

She knew me well. "I need to get out of here," I said. "Can we go?"

"Of course." She and Adam stood up. We left our drinks behind.

Nadia

It was the understatement of the decade to say that I had never been so down on myself.

Diana wouldn't answer my calls or texts, and we had no idea what happened to her after our blowout in the casino.

Rick and I spent the night in the penthouse alone. He slept in his room and I slept in mine, while we waited for Diana to return. She never did. It wasn't until the next day, when we were checking out, that her brother Adam finally took pity on us and responded to a text. He told us that she and Becky had gone to a different hotel, but they'd hopped on a flight out of Vegas early that morning. They were already on their way home to Bar Harbor.

"Ask him when she's coming back," I said to Rick, while we stood at the hotel reservation desk with our luggage.

Rick texted the question to Adam.

He got back to us almost immediately.

She hasn't decided.

He sent us no more information.

During the three-hour drive back to LA, Rick and I spent the first hour arguing over what had happened. Mostly we blamed each other.

"We had too much to drink, that's all," he said.

"That's all?" I replied. "Seriously? Is that what you really think?" When he didn't accept responsibility, I laid into him, hard. "You've been flirting with me for weeks. Even Diana could see it."

"Hey, it's not like you weren't doing your part!" he argued. "You always look at me like I'm your knight in shining armor. Ever since that night I punched out your loser boyfriend."

"He wasn't my boyfriend," I said with disgust. "And yes, I was grateful for what you did, but I never wanted this to happen. Jesus, she's my twin sister." I touched my hands to my cheeks. "Oh God, how could we have done that?"

He said nothing for a long moment, then to my surprise, he reached over and touched my knee, rubbed it reassuringly. I looked down at his hand, stared at it, befuddled, then frowned at him.

"I'm sorry," he gently said. "You're right. This is really messed up. It shouldn't have happened."

I was still angry with him. Nothing was going to change that, because even if the fault was ours to share equally, I blamed him for being so incredibly attractive.

"You said terrible, hurtful things to her last night," I reminded him.

"Yeah," he admitted, returning both hands to the wheel, "but every bit of it was true." He glanced at me. "Don't pretend she didn't talk to you about our relationship. I know she told you everything. She talked to you more than she talked to me." He shook his head. "All she wanted to do was get married. She was really smothering. I could barely breathe, so last night I finally just snapped. I couldn't keep my mouth shut about it anymore."

I rested my elbow on the door and cupped my forehead in a hand. The world outside the window sped by in a blur and I was reminded of that day long ago when my mother told me to find myself a rich man. "Love just ain't enough," she had said.

Those words seemed so empty now.

"And don't deny your part in this," Rick said. "It wasn't all me. You were giving off plenty of signals."

My self-loathing escalated to a new level, because he was right. I was attracted to him, and wildly so. I'd been in awe of him from the first moment he walked into the reception area at work. I nearly fell out of my chair that morning, and had to fan myself after he left.

I never told Diana that, of course, but whenever Rick looked at me, I melted. Each time he spoke to me, the pull grew stronger. I just didn't dare admit it to myself.

Last night, in the elevator, the willpower I'd been clinging to finally gave way. All he had to do was look at me with those mesmerizing blue eyes, and all the sparks that had been flashing between us for weeks suddenly burst into flame. I wanted him so badly – physically – that I just couldn't say no.

And the kiss had been electric. My whole body surrendered. When the elevator doors opened, I was in a dazed stupor. I could barely comprehend what was happening.

Turning my head to look at Rick, I took a deep breath to try and settle my nerves and think rationally. "So what are you going to do about Diana?"

"I'll apologize for what happened," he said, "because I owe her that. But otherwise, we're done. I don't want what she wants. It's best if she moves on."

His decision seemed so final. He sounded callous.

And where did that leave *me?* I wondered. What was I going to do?

I had betrayed my twin. Was it even possible to fix what I had broken?

Rick and I said very little to each other the rest of the way home, but when we finally entered the city, I had made up my mind about one thing, at least.

"When you drop me off at my apartment," I said, "I don't want to ever see you again. We did a terrible thing, and I wrecked the best thing that ever happened to me."

Keeping his eyes on the road, he touched my leg and spoke imploringly. "Nadia…"

"No." I pushed his hand away. "Don't do that. This is tainted. All I want is for Diana to forgive me. Just please take me home."

When he pulled over in front of my apartment, got out and opened the trunk, he said, "This isn't over."

"Oh, yes it is," I replied, as I took my suitcase from him.

He slammed the trunk shut and got back into his car.

As I stood on the curb, watching the taillights grow distant, I realized with a pang of sadness that I was alone again, and somehow, this time felt worse than all the others.

Maybe it would have been better if I'd never known Diana existed.

O ver the next few days, I tried everything. I called Diana's cell phone repeatedly and left voice mail messages to apologize for what happened and express my regret. I sent her long emails where I struggled over how to explain why I had made such a foolish mistake: I was a lonely person. I just wanted to be loved. I was flattered by the attentions of a man like Rick. I was under some kind of spell.

I was weak. Stupid. Insecure. Desperate.

I told her I would never see Rick again, and I begged for her forgiveness.

All the while, I wondered if Rick was doing the same thing – begging for her to take him back. Maybe he had come to his senses and was on his way out east with an engagement ring, and I would be pushed out of the circle.

Eventually, after about three days, Diana finally responded to one of my emails. It arrived in my inbox while I was at work.

Dear Nadia,

Please stop calling and sending emails. I understand that you're sorry and you regret what happened, but I can't tell you it's okay, because it's not.

Please, just leave me alone.

Diana

The words devastated me. I buried my face in my hands. I wanted to let out a gut-wrenching sob, but there were clients in the waiting area. Somehow I managed to keep it together by tugging a tissue out of the Kleenex box and blowing my nose.

I placed my hand on the mouse at my computer and clicked through to Diana's Facebook page, just to see a picture of her smiling face, but she had unfriended and blocked me.

There was a part of me that hated her in that moment. Beautiful Diana, who had everything. She had no qualms about punishing me. Shutting me out of her perfect world.

I felt a little queasy, but willed myself not to hate her, and not to lose hope. Maybe someday, she would be able to forgive me. Maybe I just needed to be patient, and give her time to heal, and she would invite me back in. But how long would it take? How many more lost years would there be?

A month went by, and the holiday season loomed. It was not my favorite time of year, as I had no family to visit, or any nieces or nephews to spoil. I had a few cousins who lived in Arizona – from my adoptive father's side – but I'd only met them a few times when I was very young. We lost touch after he left us.

Though I did my best to honor Diana's wishes to be left alone, I secretly hoped she might contact me at Christmas time. Maybe she would send a card. It would have been the most cherished gift I could receive, but we hadn't spoken since Vegas, and I knew that was unlikely.

I did send a text to Rick after Thanksgiving, to ask if he'd heard from Diana, or if he knew when she planned to return to her job in LA. He texted me back and told me that she'd arranged to have all her things from the apartment shipped home to Bar Harbor, and as far as he knew, she had taken an extended leave of absence from work.

I prayed she was okay. It killed me to think that I had ruined her life, and that she despised me. Sometimes my regret was so agonising, I would curl up in a ball, as if someone had plunged a knife into my stomach.

In those dark moments, I struggled to remember what Rick said to me one night – that I was a survivor – and I clung to that belief. I also clung to the hope that something good would happen – *anything* – and my future would eventually take on a brighter hue.

I wasn't certain what my future held, but it seemed impossible that I could be dealt any more luckless, crappy hands. There had to be some balance in the universe. Surely.

A week before Christmas, while I was at work, waiting to go on lunch break, a well-dressed gentleman in a black wool overcoat entered the reception area and approached the desk. It took me a few seconds to recognize him, but as soon as I did, my hands clenched into fists.

"Hi Nadia," he said with a smile.

"What do you want?" I quietly asked, because I wasn't proud of the nature of our acquaintance.

Richard – the blind date who had taken me out to dinner and attacked me in a dark alley – set a glittery Christmas gift bag on the high granite counter that stood between us. "I brought you something."

"Whatever it is," I replied, "I don't want it."

He nodded, as if he'd been expecting me to say that. "I can't blame you. But that's why I'm here – to apologize for how I behaved when I took you out."

"Apology accepted," I said flatly. "Now you can leave, and take the gift with you."

"Please…" He tilted his head to the side. "It's just a Christmas cookie from the bakery down the street. I'm not trying to cause trouble. I just want to tell you how sorry I am. I was a jerk that night, and you didn't deserve to be treated that way."

I felt my brow furrow suspiciously as I stared at him across the countertop.

When I still made no move to accept his gift, he buried his hands in his pockets. "I've been going to AA," he explained. "After what happened with you that night, I knew I had to make some changes. I didn't want to end up like my dad."

"Oh." My shoulders relaxed slightly, and I felt obligated to at least give him *some* encouragement, because I couldn't forget how many times my mother begged my father to get help – but he always refused. She told me that if he had gone to AA, we probably would have stayed together as a family. But it was too much for my father. He didn't want anything to get in the way of his drinking, not even his wife and daughter.

"That was a wise decision," I said to Richard. "How is it going?"

He cocked his head from side to side. "Some days are easier than others, but I'm determined. I haven't had a drink since that night I took you out, so I'm also here to thank you – and your friend – for knocking some sense into me."

I couldn't help but smile. "He did do quite a number on you."

"So did *you*," Richard said. "What was it you said to me? Oh yes…'I hope the rats eat you.'"

I grinned sheepishly, then took the gift bag from the counter, pulled out the red and green tissue paper, and withdrew a giant frosted sugar cookie wrapped in clear cellophane. It was a Victorian styled Santa Clause.

"This is a work of art," I said, in awe of the detail in the frosting. "I couldn't possibly bite into it."

"Sure you could," Richard replied. "The baker would want you to enjoy it."

I gave him a doubtful look and carefully placed the cookie back in the bag. "Thank you."

Ida, the office manager, came through the door just then. "Sorry I'm late. I got stuck at the photocopier, but please take your full hour."

"Are you going to lunch?" Richard asked me, as I bent to grab my purse from under the desk.

"Yes."

"Can I treat you? I was just going to grab a sandwich myself."

I wasn't sure about this. Just because he was going to AA didn't mean he could be trusted.

"I'm just going to the deli downstairs," I told him. "Then I have some errands to run."

"Oh, no problem," he replied with disappointment. "Could we at least ride the elevator together?"

As we walked out of the office lobby, I made an effort to sound cheerful. "Sure."

Starting Over

Diana
Boston

"Thanks for coming in, Jackie," I said as I escorted my client out of my office. "Since this is uncontested, everything should move through the system fairly quickly."

I wished all divorces were as cordial as Jackie's. She and her husband had agreed to split everything straight down the middle, including the proceeds from the house, which they had recently sold. There were no children involved, therefore no custody issues to fight about.

But still…It was the breakdown of a five-year marriage, and not without its share of pain.

As I returned to my desk and sat down, I tried to remember why I'd specialized in this area of the law. In the beginning – when I was fresh out of law school – I'd wanted to help people through a difficult time as quickly and smoothly as possible, be their advocate, and share with them my hope and optimism about the future.

Unfortunately, the longer I practiced, the more jaded I became. Conflict and bitterness surrounded me on a daily basis, and after what happened to me in LA, I suddenly understood that a messy divorce could happen to anyone, even me. My parents might enjoy a happy, successful marriage, but that didn't make me immune to disappointment, or safe from disaster. Anything could fall apart, unexpectedly, at any time.

Nevertheless, since returning to the east coast and leaving my high-paying job in LA, I made a sincere effort not to fixate on the ugly events of my recent past.

Not that I didn't suffer, moan, and complain when I landed there. Oh, I did plenty of *that* in the first four weeks. I had retreated to my childhood home in Bar Harbor – which belonged to my parents, who spent most of their time in Washington, DC. I did nothing but go to yoga class, eat ice cream, and laze around in sweat pants. Then, I woke up one morning, looked at my pathetic reflection in the mirror, and said, "Diana, get a grip."

A few days later, I contacted a college friend who had recently opened her own law practice in Boston, and she invited me to join her as an associate until I figured out what to do with the rest of my life. So off I went. I packed my things and found a red brick, colonial revival townhouse to rent in Beacon Hill. I also hired an experienced executive assistant to work with me at the practice. Her name was Marion and she was a lovely, compassionate woman, happily married for forty years.

Marion entered my office and placed a file on my desk. "Do you need anything else before I go?" she asked.

I checked my watch. "Is it 5:00 already?"

"Sure is," she replied. "Time flies when you're having fun."

I smiled. "See you tomorrow, Marion."

A few minutes later, I heard the outer door close, and it grew quiet in the office. Kicking off my heels under the desk, I lounged back and swiveled around in my big leather chair to look out the window at the boats in Boston Harbor.

"No regrets," I said to myself, pleased to be home.

Then my cell phone vibrated on my desk, and I swiveled back around to answer it.

"Hi Becky," I said. "What's up?"

Becky called often to chat, even when I was at work, but on that particular day, the hesitation in her voice alerted me to the fact that something was wrong.

"Have you been talking to Adam?" she asked.

My stomach turned over with dread. "No, why? Is he okay?"

"He's fine," she said.

There was a long pause, and I couldn't take the suspense. "What is it? Tell me."

She took a deep breath. "We weren't sure if we should tell you this, but in the end, we thought it best if you knew."

"Knew what?" By this time, my heart was pounding like a drum.

"Nadia's pregnant."

All the air sailed out of my lungs, and I leaned back in my chair. "Oh God. Is it Rick's?"

"Yes."

The walls felt like they were closing in around me. "How did you find out?"

She cleared her throat, and I knew it wasn't easy for her to deliver this news to me. Nevertheless, she forged ahead.

"Believe it or not, Nadia and I are still Facebook friends," Becky explained. "She doesn't post on my wall or anything, and I certainly don't send her messages, but I assume she creeps my page just like I creep hers. Every once in a while, I check to see what she's up to."

"I didn't think they were even together," I said, still reeling with shock. "The last time I looked at Rick's page – and that was about a month after Vegas – he was dating a bunch of different women. It looked to me like he was enjoying the single life."

"I'm sure he was," Becky replied, "but apparently, he and Nadia hooked up again last spring."

I shut my eyes and covered my forehead with my palm.

Becky continued to explain what she knew. "I only saw it a few days ago – the status update where she announced she was pregnant. A bunch of friends congratulated her."

"I didn't think she had any friends." It was a nasty remark, definitely below the belt, but I was still so angry with her.

"Well," Becky replied, "keep in mind these are Facebook friends. She has thirty-two of them. Anyway, when I saw that, I nearly had a coronary. Her relationship status said single, so I didn't know who the heck the father was. I knew she had been dating some other guy for a while, but then she ended up back with Rick."

"How can you be sure it's Rick's baby?" I asked. "Maybe it's the other guy's."

Becky paused. "I was curious about that too, so I called Adam. As soon as we hung up, he picked up the phone and called Rick, and got the full scoop, every last detail, from start to finish."

I pinched the bridge of my nose. "I suppose you're going to give me all the dirt now."

"Do you want me to?"

I considered it a moment, and decided that yes, I needed to know everything. Otherwise, curiosity would eat away at me forever, like poison in my blood, and I wanted to deal with this directly so that I could move past it. "Yes, I want to know."

"All right, then." She took a moment to gather her thoughts. "Rick told Adam that after Vegas, Nadia said she never wanted to see him again, so he drove off and let it go. You officially dumped him, so he dated a lot. Then around Christmas time, Nadia started seeing some guy she had dated once before. According to Rick, he was a real nut job, but Nadia gave him a second chance because he had joined AA."

"Isn't it a recommendation that addicts aren't supposed to date when they're in treatment?" I asked.

"Yeah," she replied. "That should have been her first clue."

I exhaled heavily. "Poor Nadia. She's not the sharpest tool in the shed when it comes to men." I thought about how she'd kissed Rick – *my* Rick – in an elevator, when she knew I loved him and wanted to marry him.

On that note, maybe I wasn't terribly sharp about men either.

"Anyway," Becky continued, "Rick said the guy stayed sober for about sixty days, then he got loaded one night and smacked her around. She didn't know who to call, so she called Rick, and he came to her rescue."

"Just like the last time," I said. "I think that's what started everything. It was after that when I began to notice an attraction between them."

"To make a long story short," Becky continued, "Nadia got pregnant right away, but Rick told Adam he suspected she did it intentionally, just to trap him."

"I wouldn't put it past her," I said. "So where does it stand now? Please don't tell me they're getting married."

Becky scoffed. "God, no. It sounds like they hate each other. Believe me, when Adam told me the rest of this, I was glad you caught Rick cheating on you. Trust me, Diana. You're better off without him. He wasn't worthy of you."

Becky's words were both satisfying and comforting. Ordinarily, I was not a cruel person, but there was a wounded part of me that took pleasure in the news that Rick and Nadia's relationship had imploded. That they were not blissfully happy and in love and thankful that I got out of their way.

"They've already signed a legal agreement about their separation," Becky continued. "He doesn't want custody of the child, and he didn't even ask for visitation rights. He wants no part of it."

"He doesn't want to know his own child?" I said.

"Nope."

This was inconceivable to me. "Did Adam get the details of the settlement?" I asked. It was my area of expertise, after all, and I couldn't stem my curiosity.

"Rick gave her his car," Becky said, "plus a fifty-thousand-dollar lump sum."

My mouth fell open. "You're kidding me. That's all she got?" I sat forward. "My God, what kind of idiot legal counsel did she have? I would have gotten her way more than that — not to mention some sort of regular support payment until the child reached majority. She'll blow through fifty thousand dollars in a heartbeat. Eventually she'll be living out of her car with her kid in the back seat, just like her mother. It's mind boggling."

"I guess it must have seemed like a lot of money to her," Becky said, "and Rick's car is nicer than anything she could ever afford."

I let out a breath. "Yeah, but Rick was probably thrilled to get rid of it. He was always talking about getting a new one. Something sportier. He sure got off easy."

Becky sighed. "Didn't you once tell me that Nadia's father stopped paying child support when she was young? Maybe she figured she'd be better off to get it all up front."

"Maybe," I agreed, and swiveled around in my chair to look out the window again.

"Was I right to tell you?" Becky asked. "I wasn't sure."

"Yes," I assured her, "you did the right thing."

We were both quiet for a moment.

"So, what are you going to do?" Becky asked.

"What do you mean?"

She paused. "I mean…That baby is going to be your niece or your nephew. Are you going to talk to Nadia?"

Becky and I were both adopted, so we shared an understanding of what it meant to meet a blood relative. We had so few of them.

But this was different. Nadia, my identical twin, with whom I had shared a womb, had re-entered my life and betrayed me in the worst possible way. I couldn't imagine inviting her back into my world.

"No, I'm not going to contact her," I said.

"What about when she has the baby?" Becky asked. "You'll be an aunt."

I watched a sailboat motor out of the marina outside my window. As soon as it reached open water, the crew began to hoist its mainsail.

"I think it's best if Nadia and I live separate lives," I said.

When I hung up, however, I experienced a strange, achy feeling in my heart. I laid my hand over my chest, and massaged my sternum with the heel of my hand.

CHAPTER

Forty-eight

Nadia

Despite all the mistakes I had made in my life, for the first time I felt I was doing something right – something wonderful and amazing, for there was a tiny person growing inside me. Everything else in my past – all the hardships, failures, and foolish errors in judgement – paled in comparison to the bright future I saw before me. I was going to be a mother, and this beautiful child would love me and depend on me forever.

No one had ever depended on me before.

I would no longer be alone, without family.

This time, I was determined not to make a mess of things. What was happening to me was too beautiful. Surely, everything in my past had led me to this moment, this place, this calling. This was my chance. I was finally experiencing a hope and optimism I'd never known before. Whenever I touched my belly or felt my baby kick, joy spread through me like a warm breeze through an open window.

My world was about to change profoundly, and I was determined to be the best mother in the world.

At five months, I was progressing well. The baby was gaining a healthy amount of weight, as was I. Each time the doctor checked my blood pressure, it was normal, and everything looked good on the ultrasounds. I was even able to learn the baby's gender.

She was a girl.

Then, one Monday morning, my boss called me into her office for the annual performance review. I always hated these things and braced myself to hear all about my shortcomings, in meticulous detail, and then be told I was on thin ice.

"Come in and have a seat," Ida said, gesturing to the chair on the opposite side of her desk. "How have you been feeling?"

It was a question I was asked often, whenever someone noticed my belly. "Great, thanks."

"You were lucky not to have any morning sickness," she said. "I was sick for months with both my children."

"That's rough," I politely responded.

She sat back and looked at me for a moment, warmly. "Have you given any thought to how long of a maternity leave you want to take?"

I cleared my throat. "I'd like to take the maximum amount of time I'm allowed, if that's okay."

"Of course it is," she kindly replied. "Those first few months of your baby's life are so important. You're smart to take as much time as you can."

Pleasantly surprised by the sincerity in her voice, I began to relax a bit.

"And when you come back," Ida continued, "there's an excellent daycare right here in the building. Have you gone to visit it yet?"

"I went a couple of weeks ago."

"Did you put your name in?" she asked. "You should do that right away, because they have a waiting list."

"I will. Thank you."

She opened my file, and my body tensed up again as she read over her notes in silence.

"So tell me, Nadia," she said, sounding more businesslike. "How do you think things have been going lately?"

I swallowed uneasily. "Good. I'm very happy here."

She folded her hands together on top of my file. "I'm glad to hear that, because we've all been pleased with your performance. You're dependable, courteous, responsible, always on time, and the clients find you friendly and helpful on the phone. We all feel we're in very good hands with you on the front lines."

For a moment I thought I was dreaming, because this never happened to me. I had never been a star student in school, nor was I singled out for my winning smile and personality at any previous job. Rarely in my life had I been given such praise.

"Thank you," I shakily replied.

"I know you only have a few more months before you go on leave, but before then, I'd like to start training you to take on some extra responsibilities with office management. I'd like to feel that I have a back-up, someone I can trust and rely on to take over my duties when I'm on vacation, and with that, I'd like to promote you to assistant office manager. Would you be interested? It would come with a raise, of course. I've already discussed it with the partners, and they suggested ten percent."

I felt like I'd just had the wind knocked out of me. Slightly giddy, I slapped a hand against my cheek. "Are you serious?"

"Yes," Ida replied with a laugh. "I'd like to start training you next week if you're willing, and of course, the position will be waiting for you when you come back from maternity leave." She paused and leaned over the desk. "We really want to make sure you come back, Nadia. We don't want to lose you."

I smiled at her. "I'm thrilled. And yes, I'm very interested in the promotion." It all sounded like a dream.

She sat back and sighed with relief. "Excellent." Then she closed my file. "I'll start training you next week, and I'll put the raise through right away. You should see it reflected on the next paycheck."

We both stood up. She came around her desk and shook my hand. "Congratulations."

"Thank you."

I felt a tickle in my nose and sneezed.

"Bless you," Ida said, picking up the box of Kleenex on her desk and offering it to me before she escorted me out of her office.

⸜⸝

By the time I arrived home, my sinuses were completely plugged, and my throat felt like it had been scrubbed raw with sandpaper. Every time I swallowed, it burned.

I dropped my oversized purse on the floor, slipped out of my heels, and went straight to my bedroom to change into my pyjamas.

A short while later I was wrapped in a soft fleece blanket on the sofa with a roll of toilet paper in front of me – I needed to blow my nose every five minutes. I could do nothing but click sleepily through TV channels, searching for something good to watch.

I had no appetite, but I knew it was important to keep eating for the baby, so I managed to get some strawberry yogurt down. Later, I warmed some canned soup in the microwave, but the heat stung my throat, so I decided to stick to yogurt and popsicles.

⸜⸝

That night, the uncomfortable pain in my throat and sinuses prevented me from sleeping, but I didn't dare take anything to relieve my symptoms because I didn't want to risk hurting the baby.

When I rolled out of bed the next morning, I took my temperature and discovered I was running a low fever. I called in sick at work, and Ida told me to take care of myself.

Normally, I would have stayed home, drank plenty of fluids, and lay on the couch until I felt better, but this was different. I was an expectant mother, so I decided to call my doctor.

He fit me in for an appointment before noon. I took a cab to his clinic and sat in the corner of the waiting room to avoid coughing or sneezing on the other patients.

At last a nurse called my name, and I shuffled miserably into an exam room. After keeping me waiting a little longer, Dr. Weldon finally walked in, closed the door, and told me to hop up on the table.

"I'm twenty-two weeks pregnant," I told him. "Hopping just isn't in the cards."

He laughed and held the step stool for me while I positioned myself on the crinkly white paper.

"Open wide and say ah." He inserted a tongue depressor into my mouth. "Yes, there's definitely some redness there." Then he listened to my heart and took my blood pressure. He told me everything looked good, so he stuck a thermometer in my mouth and sat down at his desk to jot down some notes.

The thermometer beeped. He stood up and pulled it out of my mouth.

"Do I have a fever?" I asked.

"Yes, but only a slight one. Nothing to worry about."

"It won't affect the baby?"

"No, but if you're uncomfortable, you can take Tylenol. I suspect you'll feel better in a few days, but come back in if you don't, or if your symptoms get worse."

"So I should just stay home and rest?" I confirmed as I set one foot on the stool and slid off the table to the floor.

"Yes. Drink plenty of fluids, and you can rinse your throat with warm salt water. That might help."

Relieved to hear this was nothing serious, but still feeling like a bag of wet sand, I went home.

Unfortunately, my symptoms didn't improve after a few days. The cold moved into my chest, and I was forced to call the doctor again when I coughed so hard I was sure I'd cracked a rib.

"Nope," Dr. Weldon said as he examined me. "Ribs are fine. You might have pulled a muscle though." He asked me to turn to the side and lift my shirt so he could listen to my lungs. "Deep breaths please. Very good." He moved his stethoscope from one spot to another on my back. "Another deep breath please."

It wasn't easy to inhale without coughing.

"I definitely hear some wheezing in there. Now let's have a listen to your baby." He bent forward slightly and placed the scope over my belly. "Very good. Everything sounds fine." After removing the ear buds, he hooked the scope around his neck. "You can lower your shirt now."

I tugged it down and faced forward. Dr. Weldon returned to his desk and consulted my file. "Are you a smoker Miss Carmichael?"

"Not anymore," I replied. "I quit about a year ago."

"Good for you."

He wrote that in the file, then swiveled in his chair to face me. "I know it's unpleasant," he said, "but these things usually take care of themselves after a week or two. I could prescribe Salbutamol – a Ventolin puffer – that might give you some relief.

It's safe to use during pregnancy, but only helps fifty percent of people with symptoms like yours. We can give it a try though."

I thought about it. "If this is going to get better on its own anyway, I'd rather not use anything."

He nodded. "Then it looks like you're just going to have to tough it out."

"I can do that," I assured him. "As long as it's okay for the baby."

"The baby will be fine. Just make sure you're eating and drinking well."

I moved to pick up my purse from the chair. "What about work? Is it okay for me to go back?"

"That's up to you. You're not contagious, if that's your concern."

"It is, but I'm glad to hear everything's okay. Thanks." I left his office and flagged down a cab.

Dr. Weldon was right. My cough improved after about a week, and I was able to return to work.

My illness had sapped me of energy, however, because I couldn't climb the stairs in my apartment building without needing to stop halfway up and catch my breath. I assumed it was simply pregnancy fatigue and the added weight I was carrying. Since I hadn't been getting much exercise – not since I came down with the sore throat – I resolved to go to an aerobics class for expectant mothers as soon as I felt up to it.

Later that week, I woke in the middle of the night because I had difficulty breathing.

Was this normal? I wondered as I propped myself up on a few pillows. Maybe the baby was pushing on my lungs.

I managed to go back to sleep, but when I woke the next morning, I felt more fatigued than I had the day before. Even the simple act of getting dressed exhausted me. I had to sit down on the edge of the bed for a few minutes to recover.

When I arrived at work and reached my desk, I noticed my legs and ankles were more puffy than usual, which was typical for pregnant women, so I wasn't too concerned at the time. Ida came out to the reception area to tell me about a client who was coming in that morning to get something signed, and he was in a hurry.

"You look a little gray," she said.

"I feel worse than gray," I replied. "I can't believe how tired I am. Were you this tired when you were pregnant?"

"Oh, yes," she said. "I remember sleeping for hours in the afternoons."

Her assurance eased my mind, and I did my best to put in a hard day's work. I finished all the tasks that were handed to me, which turned out to be a good thing, because something unexpected happened that night.

I didn't know it at the time, but that was to be my last day working for the firm of Perkins and McPhee. I never set foot in that building again.

ೱ

Sometime after midnight, while propped up against a pile of pillows in bed, I dreamed of the father I hadn't seen in almost twenty years. He hugged me so tightly, I couldn't breathe. My rib cage felt like it was constricting, but he wouldn't listen when I asked him to stop squeezing and let go.

I woke up fighting to suck air into my lungs. My head spun and my heart raced with panic. I was wheezing again. *Did I have pneumonia?*

It was the middle of the night, and I couldn't call my doctor, so I called a cab instead and managed to pull on a T-shirt and a loose pair of sweatpants. Somehow I made it down the stairs on my own.

"Take me to the hospital please," I said to the cab driver as I got in.

He glanced down at my belly. "Jesus, Mary, and Joseph. You're not going to have that baby now, are you?"

"I hope not," I said. "I'm barely six months." Still working hard to take air into my lungs, I held my hands up in front of my face because my fingertips were tingling.

"Hurry," I pleaded, because I feared I might pass out.

Looking back on it, I probably should have called an ambulance, but it wasn't the first bad decision I'd ever made.

The cab driver hit the gas and sped off. He swerved wildly around corners, and I was forced to hang on to avoid being tossed across the seat.

When we pulled into the hospital parking lot, he drove me to the outpatients' entrance. "Twelve dollars," he said, turning around to face me.

Still feeling terribly short of breath and aware of the perspiration on my face, I flipped open my wallet and gave him a twenty. "Keep the change." I couldn't wait any longer.

I opened the door and stepped out of the cab, but only made it as far as the information desk before everything started to swirl. My vision blurred and the world in front of my eyes turned cloudy white.

Then my knees buckled, and down I went, straight to the floor.

I have no idea how long I was unconscious, but I recall seeing my mother walk toward me on that fluffy cloud that surrounded me in front of the information desk. It was not my birth mother I saw. The person coming toward me was my adoptive mother. She held out her hands and smiled.

Then I dreamed I was floating around the hospital waiting area, feeling sorry for all the sick and injured people who had to wait to see a doctor, while I was lifted onto a gurney and fast-tracked to the trauma room.

A team of nurses ran in.

"What do you need?" one of the nurses said to the doctor.

"Get the crash cart," he replied.

I woke to the rapid whirly sound of my baby's heartbeat on a fetal monitor. Such a lovely sound. It reminded me of a skipping rope, whipping fast through the air but never hitting the ground. Around and around it went.

I didn't understand where I was until I opened my eyes and discovered the oxygen mask over my face. An IV tube was taped to the back of my hand. Turning my head on the pillow, I looked up at a bag of clear fluid dripping into the IV tube. *I hope that's okay for the baby.*

I felt groggy, and my chest hurt, but the sound of my baby's steady heartbeat on the monitor was a great comfort. That meant she was okay. But what was I doing here?

As I felt around for a button to call a nurse, I wondered if I hadn't eaten enough when I was sick. Maybe I was dehydrated or malnourished.

I found the button and pressed it with my thumb. A nurse came running in. "You're awake." She checked the tape on the heart monitor. "You gave us quite a scare."

I spoke into the oxygen mask. It muffled my voice. "Did I?"

"Yes." Her eyes met mine. "Is there someone we can call? A family member?"

I looked around the room and struggled to make sense of this. I honestly had no idea what was going on.

"Is this the ER?" I asked. "What happened to me?"

The nurse continued to check all the monitors. "You're in the intensive care unit. I'll get the doctor. He'll be able to answer your questions."

She left me alone, and I waited for what seemed an eternity, but it was probably only about ten minutes.

Finally a doctor walked in. He was an older, heavyset man with thinning hair and rimless glasses. He picked up the chart at the foot of my bed and glanced at it briefly.

His eyes lifted. "Hello Nadia," he said. He inclined his head at me. "Welcome back."

"Was I gone somewhere?"

"Yes, you were." He moved around the bed to read the tape on the heart monitor. "But we were able to bring you back."

Confused and feeling a little woozy, I stared at him. "I don't understand."

"You were in cardiac arrest when you came in," he said, "and we're trying to figure out why, so I'd like to ask you some questions."

My eyes widened, and the heart monitor next to the bed began to beep faster. I tried to sit up.

"You need to stay calm," he told me, pushing my shoulders back so I lay against the pillow. "You're not helping yourself, or your baby, by getting all worked up."

"Is my baby okay?" I asked.

"Your baby's fine," he replied. "We had you back in less than a minute, and obstetrics is involved. They're keeping a close eye on your case." He picked up the chart again. "Now let's see what we can figure out." He lowered his head and peered at me over the tops of his glasses. "Do you have a history of heart trouble?"

"No." Then I stammered as I remembered. "Wait, I was born with a hole in my heart," I told him, "but it closed up when I was three or four. It's never been a problem since. I've had it checked."

He wrote that down. "Do you smoke?"

"I used to. I quit last year."

"How many years were you a smoker?"

"Since I was fifteen," I replied, "so that would make it… twelve years."

"Any family history of heart disease?"

"I don't know. I was adopted, so I never knew my real family." I paused. "Except for a twin sister. She lives in Maine. But she never mentioned heart troubles."

He nodded. "What about drugs. Cocaine, meth…?"

"God, no!" I shouted at him. "I'm pregnant! I've been taking folic acid pills, but that's it."

He held up a hand and gave me an intimidating stare over the tops of his glasses. "What did I tell you about getting worked up?"

I clenched my jaw to keep from losing my temper, because he was suddenly rubbing me the wrong way.

"How has your health been lately?" he asked.

"Not great," I told him. "I was sick for the past few weeks."

"Tell me about your symptoms."

I described my sore throat, plugged sinuses, and the severe bronchitis. "I thought I had pneumonia," I told him. "I went to see my doctor and he said it would go away on its own. Then I was short of breath and constantly tired. I could barely climb a flight of stairs."

"Any trouble breathing at night?"

"Yes. That's why I came to the ER."

He wrote briskly in my chart while I spoke. Always in the background was the constant whirly sound of my baby's heart-beat on the fetal monitor.

"Did you notice any swelling in your legs or hands?" he asked.

"Yes, in my legs, but I'm pregnant, so I didn't think much of it." I suddenly realized I didn't know the man's name. "Who are you?"

He looked up. "I'm Dr. Vaughn. I'm a cardiologist."

"It's nice to meet you," I replied.

"Likewise." He wrote down a few more things, then closed the chart.

I was still in shock, and part of me was certain this had to be some sort of mistake. "What does it all mean?"

"I'm not certain yet," he said, "but I can tell you what we know so far. After we cleared the fluid out of your lungs to help you breathe, we did an Echocardiogram, which is an ultrasound of your heart. It told us that your heart function is down to about twenty-five percent."

"Oh, my God."

"Normal is around sixty percent," he said. "And based on what you've just told me, it's likely that you have a condition called myocarditis."

I frowned. "What's that?"

"It's an infection that causes damage to the heart muscle. The most common cause is from a flu-like virus that usually goes away for most people, but sometimes it can affect the heart."

"Are my arteries clogged?" I asked.

"No, that's not the problem. It's not because you ate too many potato chips, or didn't exercise enough. You've just had some bad luck, I'm afraid."

It made me feel sick to hear him say that, and I trembled with shock. "Will I get better?"

He paused. "I'm very sorry, but damage – as severe as you have endured – is usually permanent."

He sounded so casual about it all.

I swallowed hard as a wave of terror swept through me. "What about my baby? Will she be okay? Will I be able to give birth?"

"That's not my area of expertise," he explained, "but someone from obstetrics will be down to see you soon."

"But you must know something," I insisted. "Surely you've talked to them, or you've dealt with this before."

"Obstetrics will be down soon to answer your questions," he said.

I clenched my jaw in frustration. "You still haven't told me what's going to happen," I said. "Am I going to die? Or is this treatable?"

He removed his glasses. "We can treat it to some extent. We can keep clearing the fluid off your lungs enough so that you can function and feel better. As long as the condition doesn't worsen, we may be able to discharge you in a week or two. The goal will be to keep you healthy so that your baby can continue to grow and mature."

"And then what?" I asked. "Will I give birth?"

"I can't speak to that," he said. "The most I can tell you is that – at the level your heart is functioning now – you will likely need a heart transplant."

A heart transplant? This was too much for me to take in! I couldn't absorb it all. It didn't seem real.

Rather than suffering a complete nervous breakdown in the next five minutes, I tried to stay focused on the facts. "When would that happen?"

"Hard to say. First we need to get you on the transplant list. Then it will depend on how far down the list you are, and how soon a suitable donor can be found."

"How long can I live without a new heart?" I asked. "And will my baby survive the transplant?"

He put his glasses back on and stared at me over the tops of the lenses. "First of all, it may take a while to find a donor, and even if we had one tomorrow, it's impossible to predict the outcome of the surgery with a baby in the mix. But you should know that your baby is not helping you. It's robbing you of energy and circulation. They say a baby in the womb is the most efficient parasite there is."

"Are you serious?" I blurted out. "Did you just call my baby a parasite?"

He held up a hand. "I don't mean to offend you, but you need to be aware of the danger you're in. There are a lot of stresses on your heart right now."

I took a few deep breaths from the oxygen mask, because this doctor needed a few commonsense lessons in bedside manner. I was tempted to biff my pillow at him. If only I had the strength.

I set the mask aside again. "Will I live long enough to have this baby?"

A dark-haired female doctor in a white lab coat walked in at that moment.

"Ah, Dr. Mills." Dr. Vaughn turned to face her. "Follow me outside for a moment."

I watched them leave together. Faintly, I could hear them discussing my case out in the hall. They returned to my bedside after a few minutes.

"The patient is wondering about whether or not she can give birth," Dr. Vaughn said.

I turned to Dr. Mills, who was slim and attractive. I guessed she was about forty. She wore trendy black plastic rimmed glasses, and her long dark hair was pulled back in a sleek ponytail.

"The *patient's* name is Nadia," I pointed out.

Dr. Mills grinned at me and shook my hand. "It's a pleasure to meet you, Nadia. Looks like you had a rough night."

"That's putting it mildly."

She squeezed my shoulder. "Don't worry. You're in good hands. We're doing our best to take care of you and your baby."

Dr. Vaughn mentioned that he had other patients to see, and left me alone with Dr. Mills. I wasn't sorry to see him go.

Dr. Mills pulled a chair closer to my bed. "Myocarditis, eh?"

"Yeah," I replied. "Guess it's my lucky day."

She regarded me with compassion. "You want to know if you can give birth."

"Yes."

"Well…" She paused. "My professional opinion is that I wouldn't advise it. With your heart in the condition it's in, your body probably wouldn't be strong enough. What I am going to recommend is that you take really good care of yourself for the next six weeks, until the baby is mature enough to survive on her own. Then we'll do a C-section."

I pondered this news, and wasted no time in mentally tossing out my previous birth plan, which included herbal tea and no drugs.

"What if my condition gets worse?" I asked. "Can we take her out sooner?"

I appreciated that Dr. Mills didn't hold anything back or patronize me. She gave it to me straight.

"Statistically," she said, "an infant at twenty-four weeks has only a sixty percent chance of survival, and a seventy percent chance of neurodevelopmental impairment. The longer she stays in your belly, the better off she'll be. I'd like to try to reach at least thirty weeks, but if you're doing well, we could even try to make it to full term."

"What about the heart transplant?" I asked.

"That complicates things," she said. "It's more likely that the C-section will happen first."

I tried to imagine having major surgery, feeling as weak as I did. "Will I survive the C-section with only twenty-five percent heart function?"

"It'll be high risk, for sure," she told me, "but you'll be in excellent hands. Once the baby's out, you'll have more strength for the transplant."

I put the oxygen mask back over my face and listened briefly to the calming rhythm of the fetal heart monitor.

"What if we find a donor right away?" I asked. "Would the baby survive a heart transplant? Dr. Vaughn wasn't very clear about that."

I got the sense he would have preferred to abort the baby just to save the heart.

Dr. Mills leaned back in the chair. "It would be better to put off the transplant until your baby is delivered."

I felt tired all of a sudden, and needed to close my eyes. "All right," I said. "Let's plan for a C-section."

Dr. Mills stood up. "Good. Do you have someone to help you over the next few weeks? You'll need to get plenty of rest. Any family in the city?"

Family? Me?

I shook my head. "I don't have anyone here, but I have a sister on the east coast."

"Have you called her yet?"

"Not yet." I was ashamed to admit that she wasn't taking my calls because she had caught me making out with her would-be fiancé in a Las Vegas elevator last year.

After Dr. Mills left, I wondered if Diana would at least listen to a voicemail.

Fifty-two

Diana

There was nothing like a hot shower after yoga class on a Friday to help ease the stresses of the day.

Earlier in the afternoon, a client had walked into my office and wept for an hour. She came to me because she'd just lost custody of both her children in a prejudicial divorce settlement. The husband – who was physically abusive during their marriage – suggested that because she was in therapy (to help her cope with the breakdown of her marriage), she was emotionally unstable, therefore incapable of taking care of their children. Her lawyer had been so unprepared, he didn't even know that half of the information presented by her husband's more aggressive lawyer had been lies.

According to the woman, her husband didn't even *want* the kids. All he cared about was finding a way to avoid paying child support, and to continue receiving government checks and tax breaks for dependents.

I took her on as a client and immediately began looking into ways to appeal the judge's decision.

After shutting off the water in the yoga studio shower, I wrapped myself in a towel and returned to my locker. I pulled out my gym bag and decided to check my phone before getting dressed.

I sat down on the wooden bench and swiped my finger across the screen. There were a few emails from work – nothing urgent – and a text from my mother to let me know she and Dad would be arriving at my place in about an hour. They were on their way home to our house in Bar Harbor for a weeklong vacation, and were passing through Boston.

I texted her back and asked if she still had the extra key to my place, and if so, they should help themselves to anything in the fridge.

Then I checked my voicemail, and was surprised to discover a message from a Los Angeles phone number I didn't recognize. I listened to it:

"Hi Diana. It's Nadia…"

My stomach clenched.

Quickly, I hit the skip button and slipped my phone back into my bag. I would listen to it later, I decided, after I had a chance to put some clothes on.

I left the yoga studio and drove all the way home before I could even think about listening to the rest of Nadia's message. Just the sound of her voice – so much like my own – caused all my muscles to tense. I should have opted for a second yoga class.

What she wanted, I had no idea. Maybe she simply called to tell me about her happy condition. Or maybe she'd spent all of Rick's money already, and needed to be bailed out of a financial crisis.

There was no point speculating. I promised myself I would listen to the message as soon as I got home and had something to eat.

I arrived shortly after eight. My parents' car was parked out front, and the lights were on in the front windows of my townhouse.

"Welcome," I said to Mom as I entered the foyer. I wrapped my arms around her. "I missed you."

"I missed you, too."

Dad came to greet me as well. "Hey kiddo." He gave me a quick peck on the cheek. "How's the new practice?"

"It's growing," I replied, setting my purse and keys down on the table by the stairs. "Slow but sure." I inhaled deeply through my nose. "What smells so good?"

"I've got a pot of chili on the stove," Mom told me.

I smiled at her. "I love it when you come to visit."

We moved into the kitchen, and I pushed Nadia's voicemail message from my mind.

"You're kidding me," Mom said at the dinner table, when the three of us sat down to eat. "She's pregnant?"

Dad's eyebrows lifted as he passed me the salad bowl.

"I'm not kidding," I said. "Becky saw it on Nadia's Facebook page and called to tell me."

"And you're sure it's Rick's."

"It must be, because he paid her fifty thousand dollars to stay away and leave him alone forever."

Mom scoffed with disgust, and Dad shook his head. "You got off lucky," he said to me. "You're better off without him. You should *thank* Nadia for that."

I raised a skeptical eyebrow. "That's an interesting way of looking at it." I served up some salad, and dipped my spoon into my bowl of chili.

Mom and Dad glanced at each other.

"How long has it been since you've spoken to Nadia?" Dad cautiously asked.

"It's been months," I replied, "but she left me a voicemail message today."

Mom picked through the lettuce leaves on her salad plate. "What did she say?"

"I don't know yet. I haven't listened to it. I've been speculating about all sorts of things, though."

Mom laid down her fork. "Speculating will get you nowhere, dear, and the suspense is killing me. Don't just sit there. Go listen to it."

I met her gaze from across the table. "Don't we have an iron-clad rule about cell phones at the dinner table?"

"Oh, for Pete's sake," she said with a smile. "Go listen to it in the foyer."

I chuckled at her, and rose from my chair. After pulling my phone out of my purse, I punched in the code.

The first thing I noticed, when the message began, was that Nadia sounded exhausted, and I wondered if she'd been ill. Then, as she continued to explain why she was calling, I felt the color drain from my face.

Turning to look at my parents, who were seated at the table watching me, I couldn't speak. All I could do was stand there, numb and speechless, as I listened to my sister's message.

P lacing my phone on the polished mahogany table, I pressed the speaker button and increased the volume so we could all listen. As soon as Nadia began to speak, I sank into a chair and rubbed my forehead with my hand.

"Hi Diana," she said. "It's Nadia. I know it's been awhile since we talked, but something happened to me and I have no one else to call." She paused. "I got sick a few weeks ago – just the regular flu, I thought – but it turned out to be some kind of weird virus that attacks the heart. It's called myocarditis if you want to look it up. I'm in the hospital now, and they tell me I have only twenty-five percent of my heart function. They had to use paddles to shock me back to life yesterday. So I'm not in great shape. The doctor says I'm going to need a heart transplant, but that could take awhile and…"

The message timed out, and Mom and Dad exclaimed. "Good God! A heart transplant! Was she cut off just now? Can you get her back?"

I nodded and accessed the second voicemail message she had left.

"I got cut off," Nadia said. "I can't remember what I was saying. I think I was telling you about the transplant, but it's a bit more complicated than that. I'm not sure if you heard, but I'm pregnant. I'm six months along, and I'm…I'm afraid about what's going to happen to the baby. She's too little to come out of my tummy now, so we have to wait until it's safe to do a C-section. That's why I'm calling."

Her voice began to tremble, and I knew she was holding back tears. I locked eyes with my mother, who was white as a sheet.

"I don't know if I can make it through all of this," Nadia said, "and I'm worried about what will happen to my baby. Diana, will you please call? Will you take her if anything happens to me?"

She was cut off again, so I keyed in the code to listen to the third and final message.

This time, Nadia was weeping.

"Will you please call me? I'm all alone here, and I'm really scared. I don't like my doctor, and I can't call Rick. He doesn't want the baby. I don't want her to be left all alone in the world like I was. Please, Diana. Please call me."

It ended there.

"Oh, my God. Did she leave a number?" Mom frantically asked.

I picked up my phone. "It's listed on the call display."

My hands shook uncontrollably as I dialed what I assumed was the Los Angeles hospital where Nadia was being treated.

"Nadia, is this you?" I paced back and forth beside the dining room table. "It's Diana."

"Oh, thank God," she said on a sigh. "I can't believe you called."

"Of course I called," I said. "How are you? Are they taking good care of you?"

Her voice was weak, as if she'd just woken from a nap. "I'm in intensive care, and the nurses are really nice. They seem to know what they're doing, and the baby's okay. They have her hooked up to a fetal monitor, so I can hear her heart beating all the time. Can you hear it?"

I strained to listen, and made out the faint rhythm of the monitor in the background. "Yes, I think I can."

"I'm sorry about what happened between us," Nadia said. "I wish I could take it all back. I never wanted to hurt you. It was the stupidest thing I ever did."

"But if that hadn't happened," I said, needing to remind her of the only thing that mattered in that moment, "you wouldn't be carrying that precious baby."

She mumbled in agreement. "I'm still sorry."

"I know you are."

Did this mean I forgave her? I wondered as I paced back and forth in the dining room.

No, it couldn't be that simple. I wished I could forget my suspicions from a year ago, how I confronted her about her relationship with Rick, and how she'd lied to my face.

I wished I could forget the angst that went on for weeks, and the explosive pain I felt when I caught her and Rick kissing in the elevator.

But that was not relevant now. There were other things far more pressing.

"Did you listen to all my messages?" Nadia asked. "Did you hear what I said about the baby, in case I don't survive the surgeries?"

"You're going to be fine," I insisted, but my voice quivered on the last word. I honestly had no idea what her chances were. Twenty-five percent heart function didn't sound good.

"I need you to do a few things for me, okay?" I said, aware of my parents watching me. "I need you to tell me the name of your doctor – the one you said you didn't like."

"His name is Dr. Jeffrey Vaughn. He's a cardiologist here."

"Okay. Good. Now I need you to give him permission to talk to me. Tell him I'm your twin sister and that I'm going to call him and find out everything that's going on. Then I'm going to get on the first plane out of here. I'm in Boston right now, but I'll be in LA as soon as possible. What you need to do is relax and not worry about anything. Can you do that?"

"Thank you so much." She quietly cried.

I closed my eyes and felt her fear, as if it were my own. "I need to hang up now," I said, "so that I can book the flight. I'll call you when I know what time I'll be arriving."

"Okay."

Lowering the phone to my side, I turned to face my parents. My throat closed up and a hot tear rolled down my cheek. "She's my sister," I said, "and I have to go to her."

My mother nodded and rose from her chair. "Yes. I'll come with you."

The first thing I did was book the flights to LA, but we couldn't leave for a few hours, so I had time to call the hospital and speak with Dr. Vaughn.

I wasn't sure exactly why Nadia didn't like him, but at this point, I merely wanted to gather as much information as I could about her condition. He took the time to explain why a heart transplant was necessary, and he described the potential complications that could arise from her pregnancy.

After we hung up, I went online to do some research of my own, and wasn't thrilled to discover that Dr. Vaughn had been successfully sued in the past. I understood that cardiac surgery was a high-risk profession, and it was not uncommon for surgeons to face lawsuits, but what I didn't care for was the arrogance I had sensed on the phone.

I resolved to learn more when I met him face to face.

Ten hours later, our flight touched down at LAX. Mom and I got off the plane and took a cab straight to the hospital.

As we sped along the familiar Los Angeles freeway and cut through city streets I had once considered home, I felt no regret that I'd moved back to the east coast. In fact, I was surprised by my lack of nostalgia for LA. I was not sentimental about the years I'd spent here – I suppose my memory of the city had been fouled by the unpleasant circumstances of my departure.

When we arrived at the hospital entrance, I paid the cab driver, and Mom and I got out. The driver fetched our suitcases from the trunk, and we pulled them on their little rubber wheels through the doors and across the reception area to the elevators.

The sliding doors opened and we had to squeeze in. All the while, I tried to imagine how I was going to feel when I saw my twin again, after almost a full year.

In the end, I was not prepared for the emotions I would experience when I saw Nadia in the ICU.

Fifty-six

∾⟡∾

I was still angry with her, though I had to remind myself of that fact as I stood outside her room, looking in at her – so sick and weak – through the glass. She was six months pregnant, yet her face was gaunt. The sallow, pasty color of her skin disturbed me. It was like looking at myself in death's doorway.

But she was not me, and I was not her.

Mom waited outside while I entered the room on my own. Nadia was asleep, so I stood over her bed for a few minutes and stared at her freely.

Despite what had occurred between us, I was still fascinated by our resemblance. I could stare at her all day. Meanwhile, my emotions oscillated back and forth. I was still angry, yet I felt a distant love inside me that somehow managed to wriggle out from under the shell of my resentment.

Perhaps she sensed my presence over her bed, because her eyes fluttered open and she turned her head on the pillow to look at me.

"Oh…" She reached for my hand. "You're here."

"Yes, I'm here." I leaned down and kissed her on the cheek. "How are you feeling?"

"Better. I can breathe all right, and the baby's doing well."

"That's good news."

"How was your flight?"

"It was fine."

There was a noticeable awkwardness between us while we chatted about superficial things.

Working to stay focused on the here and now, and what needed to be done for her, I invited my mother in. She kissed Nadia on the cheek as well.

"You poor darling," Mom said. "Don't you worry. We're here now, and everything's going to be fine."

Nadia's eyes welled up. "Thank you, Mrs. Moore."

"It's Sandra."

For the next little while, we caught up on each other's news. I told Nadia about the law practice I'd joined in Boston, and she talked to us about what it was like to be pregnant. She was proud to announce that she was recently promoted at work. We congratulated her, of course, but she wasn't sure she would be able to return.

Later, Mom left to get a cup of coffee. As soon as Nadia and I were alone, she hit me with the question that had been weighing heavily on each of our minds.

"Have you thought about what I asked you on the phone?" she said.

I shifted in my chair. The fact is, I hadn't thought about it much at all – I certainly hadn't made any decisions – because I'd been too occupied with researching Nadia's heart condition, looking into the results of heart transplant surgeries, and searching for the best doctors in the country. Planning for Nadia's death hadn't entered my mind, despite the fact that I was a lawyer and I knew how important it was to plan for these things.

"Obviously, we need to talk about it," I said. "I don't mean to sound pessimistic, but do you have a will? Everyone should have one," I added, so as not to sound too morbid.

"No," she replied. "Can you help me with that?"

"Of course. We can do it today. I'll just take a few notes on my laptop."

She nodded. "That will be good, but you still haven't answered my question. Will you be my baby's mother if something happens to me?"

God, the way she phrased the question made me feel as if I'd been hit across the back with a baseball bat. The lawyer in me would have used the word "legal guardian," but a guardian was not what Nadia wanted.

"Nothing's going to happen to you," I said. "You'll make it through this, and *you're* going to be the baby's mother."

"Please, Diana," she replied. "I know you don't owe me any favors, and I certainly don't deserve sympathy from you, but you have to say yes. I don't know what I'll do if you don't."

"You'll survive," I told her. "That's what you'll do."

She shook her head and frowned in anger. "Don't try to use that to motivate me to fight for my life. Believe me, I'm plenty motivated. I want to live so that I can raise this child. I want it more than anything. But I also know – perhaps better than anyone – that sometimes things don't turn out the way you want them to. Life's not like that." She paused. "My baby can't end up without a family. Please, just say yes."

I swallowed over a painful lump in my throat and realized I couldn't imagine my twin sister's child ending up without a family either.

"Of course I'll take her," I replied. "If anything happens to you, I promise I'll scale mountains to make sure she is never left alone. She'll have all the love I have to give, and I'll raise her as if she were my own."

Strange, how there was almost no thinking involved. I realized in that moment that some decisions – even those that are enormous and far reaching – are simply made by the heart.

Fifty-seven

A week later, Nadia was discharged from the hospital. By then I considered myself a bit of an expert on C-sections, myocarditis, and all things relating to heart transplants – including the system that matched donors with patients, the complications that could arise during and after the surgery, and the prognosis and life expectancy for those who made it that far.

Two things I knew for sure – I didn't want Nadia to go through this alone, nor did I want her to be treated by Dr. Vaughn. So, with her permission, I made arrangements to have her files sent to Massachusetts General Hospital, so that she could come home with me and live in Boston.

I found an excellent obstetrician, experienced in dealing with pregnancy complications due to heart conditions. Her name was Dr. Aline Jones, and I spoke to her on the phone. She sounded perfect for Nadia.

I also found a hotshot cardiac surgeon who appeared to walk on water. His name was Dr. Jacob Peterson, and he was one of the top transplant surgeons in the country. He had even dealt with a pregnant myocarditis patient in the recent past. That case was similar to Nadia's, and the woman went on to have a successful heart transplant three months after delivering her healthy baby by C-section. This gave me hope.

I spent the week getting Nadia out of her apartment lease and arranging for movers to put all her furniture into storage, and ship her personal belongings to my home in Beacon Hill.

Since no commercial airline would permit Nadia to fly in her condition, we hired a private medevac plane to take the three of us home to Boston. Nadia did well during the flight, and my father picked us up at the airport.

When we arrived home, I settled Nadia comfortably in the spare bedroom. We went to sleep early, because we had an appointment first thing in the morning to meet her new doctor.

It will baffle me forever that when Dr. Peterson walked into his office, and I turned in my chair to watch him close the door, I felt no great spark of attraction or fascination. Upon first glance, I didn't even find him terrible handsome. My only response was a thoughtful appreciation of his expert skills as a heart surgeon, and gratitude that he had taken Nadia on as a patient.

Nevertheless, I remember every single detail about his appearance that day: the white lab coat over a blue denim shirt, the loose-fitting jeans, and the well-worn running shoes on his feet. His hair was red, his complexion freckled, and he appeared to be about forty.

As he entered the room, he didn't speak or make eye contact. His attention was focused on Nadia's chart, which we had arranged to be sent from the hospital in LA.

He moved around his desk, sat down, and took another moment to finish reading the file before his green eyes finally lifted. He smiled at us, and the little laugh lines at the corners of his eyes made me wonder if he might be older than forty. Forty-five perhaps?

"You must be Nadia," he cheerfully said, glancing at her belly.

"Yes," she replied. "This is my sister, Diana."

He inclined his head slightly as he looked at me, and to my surprise, I fell completely into the openness of his stare. Ordinarily, I was not a shy person, but I felt rather tongue-tied. Not because I was bowled over by any sort of romantic attraction; this was something else entirely. I was overwhelmed by the intelligence and confidence that radiated from his expression. Most importantly, I sensed in him a genuine kindness, a warmth and caring that convinced me I had made the right decision to bring Nadia all this way across the country. I felt very proud.

"You're twins," he said.

"Yes," Nadia replied, and his gaze returned to her.

"I hear you flew back from LA only yesterday," he said. "That was quite a brave feat in your condition. How was the flight, Nadia? Good service? Did they bring you lots of those little packets of peanuts?"

He was joking of course, because he knew I had hired a private medevac plane. I had discussed it with him on the phone days ago.

Nadia and I both chuckled, but I knew her nervousness about discussing her transplant matched mine.

"Well, it's very nice to meet both of you," he said, "and I want you to know that I'll be working closely with Dr. Jones over the coming weeks. The priority right now is to take care of your baby, then we'll start the screening process for the transplant."

"What will that involve?" Nadia asked.

"Quite a lot of things, actually. First we'll do a medical evaluation, some diagnostic tests to make sure you're a good candidate. And you'll see a social worker—"

I sat forward and interrupted him. "Why a social worker?"

His eyes turned to me, and again I felt knocked over.

"I'd like you both to become familiar with the resources available to you while you wait for the transplant. There are group sessions where you can meet other transplant candidates and recipients and learn from their experiences. There are support groups for family members as well." He paused. "Coping with everything surrounding a transplant can be stressful. Most people find the sessions to be educational and helpful."

Satisfied with his answer, I leaned back in my chair again.

"You'll also see a psychiatrist," he said to Nadia, "and a physical therapist who will work with you to make sure an appropriate level of exercise remains part of your life before and after the transplant. We have a transplant coordinator here, and she'll be available to answer any questions you might have – about anything. Mostly, I want you to consider this evaluation period an opportunity for you to learn all about heart transplantation and get familiar with the process. That way, you'll have appropriate information and time to consider all your options and decide whether or not you even want to move forward with it."

"Is *not* having it even an option?" Nadia asked. "How long can I live with only twenty-five percent heart function?"

"It's impossible to predict. Some people can live for years, while others..." He didn't finish his sentence.

"How long will the wait be," she asked, "if I decide to go ahead with it?"

"It depends how far up the list you are." He spoke frankly, but there was always an undercurrent of positive encouragement in his voice. He was nothing like Dr. Vaughn. "Your position on the list can change depending on your health," he continued, "and the health of others who are on the list with you. There are a lot of factors that go into determining a patient's placement, and you'll learn about those as we move along."

I turned to Nadia. "I read that in our country, three thousand people are on the wait list for a heart transplant at any given time, and only two thousand donor hearts are available each year."

"That's about right," Dr. Peterson said. "You've been doing your homework."

I looked back at him and nodded, and we stared at each other for several seconds. My gaze roamed over his face, and I decided his was one of the most interesting faces I'd ever seen. The shape of his lips and teeth, the length of his nose, and the strong line of his jaw…As I said before, he was not classically handsome, but he was attractively different. Even the soft velvety tone of his voice had a strange effect on me.

"If you don't have any more questions," he said to both of us, "I'd like to get started with some bloodwork this morning, and perform a few other tests just to see where we are. Then I'll set you up with the coordinator to book appointments with the rest of the team."

"Thank you," Nadia replied, "but I do have one more question. If a person is on the list, but they're not home when a heart becomes available and you can't reach them, what happens? Does the heart go to the next person in line?"

"The hospital will issue a pager," he said, "so you'll keep that with you at all times. We wouldn't want you to miss out," he said with a smile, as if it were a party invitation.

We all stood up. I held out my hand to shake his over the desk between us. His grip was warm and strong, his gaze friendly, direct, and open.

In that moment, I knew we were in excellent hands, and I was very grateful. So grateful, in fact, that when he escorted us out of the room and I shook his hand at the door, I felt an internal jolt. It became clear to me, then, that he was going to be someone very important in our lives.

Autumn Leaves

September

A few weeks after meeting Dr. Peterson at the hospital, I was standing in line at Starbucks near my house when the person behind me tapped me on the shoulder.

I turned around, and there he was – my twin sister's cardiovascular surgeon. This morning he wore loose-fitting jeans, a black turtleneck, and a brown leather jacket. His hair was windblown, and the sight of him forced me to take back my foolish first impression – that he was not particularly handsome. *What had I been thinking?*

"I thought it was you," he said with a smile.

"Oh, hi," I jauntily replied over a sudden whooshing sensation in my belly. His unexpected appearance in my neck of the woods had caught me off guard. "What are you doing here?"

Stupid question. Obviously he's getting a coffee.

"I live near here," he replied.

"No kidding." *Not so stupid after all.* "So do I. What street?"

He pointed toward the door to gesture in the direction of his house. "I'm over on Chestnut."

"That's crazy," I said. "I'm on Charles Street."

His eyebrows lifted. "We're neighbors then."

"Yes, we are."

I couldn't believe it. Nor could I stop staring at him. I felt a little frazzled.

Dr. Peterson glanced over my head. "It's your turn."

I swung around to discover a wide space between me and the counter. The clerk was staring at me impatiently. "Can I help you?"

Jostled out of my trance – which was the only word to describe my reaction to seeing Dr. Peterson in my local Starbucks – I hastened forward and ordered a tall non-fat latte.

Dr. Peterson placed his order next. Then we found ourselves waiting together at the end of the counter for our coffees.

"On your way to work?" I asked.

"Always," he said. "You?"

I nodded.

"What do you do?" he asked.

"I'm a divorce attorney," I told him. "I joined a small practice downtown a few months ago."

"A divorce attorney," he replied. "That must be a challenge."

I adjusted the strap of my purse on my shoulder. "It can be. Sometimes it's hard not to feel completely smothered by heartbreak. I just hope it doesn't make me jaded about marriage."

"You're not married?" he casually asked.

"No. I was in a relationship recently, but it didn't work out."

"I'm sorry to hear that."

I waved a dismissive hand. "Don't be. I'm much better off. It's just taken some time to put all the little pieces of my heart back together, that's all."

Oh, God, did I really just say that?

The clerk called my name. I raised my hand in response and stepped forward while he set my latte on the counter. Slipping my cup into a cardboard sleeve, I glanced up when a female clerk placed a coffee on the counter and inquired, "Jacob?"

It was odd to hear Dr. Peterson addressed by his first name. He moved to collect his coffee, and I handed him a sleeve. "Want one of these?"

"Sure. Thanks."

I waited for him so we could walk out together.

"How's Nadia?" he asked as we pushed through the door and emerged onto the sunny street.

"She's doing well, although she's a bit bored. She misses her job."

He nodded with understanding. "That's pretty standard for someone who's been through what she has. There'll be a lot of adjustments. Just make sure she gets out every day, even for a short walk around the block. When's her next appointment at the hospital?"

"She sees her obstetrician tomorrow."

"Will you be taking her?"

I inclined my head. "Unfortunately, no. I have to be in court in the morning. She'll take a cab."

I wasn't sure why I said 'unfortunately.' Was I disappointed I wouldn't bump into Dr. Peterson again?

"Why don't I give you my home number, in case you ever have questions or need anything," he said out of the blue. "I don't usually give it out to patients, but since we're neighbors…."

My head drew back in surprise. "That would be wonderful, thank you." I dug into my purse for my phone so I could add him to my list of contacts.

He gave me two numbers – one for his home landline, and another for his cell.

When I finished adding him, I said, "Do you want mine?"

"Yeah, that would be great."

He reached into his back pocket for his phone, and I wondered if he was just being polite. Why would he need my number? In case he had an emergency divorce situation?

I found myself watching his hands as he keyed in my information. He was not wearing a wedding ring, and I wished I had asked about his marital status when he'd asked about mine.

The fact that I was curious seemed rather significant, because until that moment, when it came to men, since what happened with Rick, I had been living in some sort of vegetative state.

He slipped his phone back into his jeans pocket. "Thanks for that. Now I should get going."

Thanks for what, exactly? I wondered. *What just happened here?*

"I have to get going, too," I replied. "It was nice bumping into you."

"You, too. Have a great day."

We turned and walked in opposite directions, and I had to fight a powerful urge to turn around for one more look at him.

"How did your appointment go?" I asked Nadia when I arrived home from work the following day.

She stood at the stove stirring a pot of something that smelled like chicken soup.

"It went well." She leaned over the pot to take a whiff. "The baby is still growing, and Dr. Jones said my heart sounded okay."

"Did you see Dr. Peterson at all?" I asked nonchalantly, as I shrugged out of my blazer and hung it on the newel post at the bottom of the stairs. I entered the kitchen and watched her carefully, waiting for her response.

"No. Today was just about the baby."

For some reason I was relieved to hear that, because if she'd told me she'd spent time in Dr. Peterson's office, I would have wondered what happened, what they talked about. I might have even felt a little jealous, which made no sense because he was her doctor, not mine.

I hadn't told her that I ran into him at Starbucks the day before, nor did I reveal that he lived in our neighborhood. I'm not sure why. Maybe I didn't want her to suspect that I might, possibly, have a teensy tiny crush on him.

This secret of mine felt childish – like something out of junior high school when you know you can't trust your new best friend not to go after the boy you like.

It made me realize that I still didn't trust her.

But I was glad the appointment had gone well.

A few days later, it happened again. With a tall latte in my hand, I walked out of Starbucks and nearly collided with Dr. Peterson, who was on his way in.

"We meet again," he said, and my insides performed a little flip, for I had thought about him often over the past few days. Yesterday after lunch, I tipped my head back in my chair and closed my eyes so I could replay our conversations in my head. Then – because it was my personal and private daydream – I said all sorts of interesting and witty things to him while we waited for our coffees, and he asked me out on a date.

But here we stood, in the real world, not my fantasy. He paused on the sidewalk, and I switched my coffee from one hand to the other. "How are you?" I asked.

"Good," he replied. "How did your sister's appointment go the other day?"

A customer hurried out of the coffee shop, and because we were blocking the door, we had to step apart to let her through.

"She said it went well," I told him. "The baby's growing."

I felt suddenly self-conscious, as if he could magically read me and know that I had been daydreaming about our previous encounter.

"And how are *you* coping with all of this?" he asked, stepping a little closer.

"I'm doing fine," I replied, too abruptly. Then I glanced away at the cars parked along the curb on the other side of the street.

Dr. Peterson stood in front of me, watching me intently while he waited for me to elaborate.

"It's been tough," I admitted, meeting his gaze again.

"No doubt. She's your twin sister."

I looked down at my feet, because I knew what he thought. He assumed Nadia and I were normal twins who had grown up together, wore similar outfits, and were as closely bonded as two women could be. He had no idea that until last year, neither of us knew the other existed. We had been separated at birth, and separated again recently, by circumstances just as cruel, after only a few months of friendship.

We were far from normal.

"Would you like to have dinner with me?" he asked out of the blue, and I was so startled, I nearly dropped my coffee.

"When?" I posed the question as if the time and date would dictate whether or not I would say yes, which was funny, because it didn't matter when. The answer was going to be yes, regardless.

His eyes smiled at me. "What about tonight? If you're free."

"Tonight would be great." I tried not to have a happy manic episode right there on the street. "What time?"

"Why don't you come over around 7:00?"

"To *your* place?" I was having some trouble believing this was happening, because it's exactly how it had played out in my daydream.

"Yeah, I'll cook."

I smiled. "All right. Can I bring anything?"

"Just yourself."

He told me the number of his house on Chestnut Street, then pulled open the door to the coffee shop. "I'll see you tonight."

"I'll look forward to it."

As I walked away, I did a little dance in my head. Then I wondered what I was going to say to Nadia. He was *her* doctor, and tonight I would leave her home alone to have dinner with him, in his home.

I toyed with the idea of not telling her. I could say I had some sort of work function.

But why didn't I want her to know?

There were a few different reasons, I suppose.

W ell, I did it. I lied to my pregnant sister with the heart condition. I told her I was having dinner with a client. Then I left the house, got into my car, and drove around the corner to Dr. Peterson's. It would have been much quicker to walk, because I had trouble finding a parking space and had to hoof it even farther from the opposite direction. I suppose I had that coming.

When I finally reached Dr. Peterson's townhouse, I paused a moment to look up at it. It was red brick with black shutters and a glossy black front door, almost identical to mine. Though I had colorful marigolds in my window boxes, his were full of overgrown weeds. At least they were green.

Taking a deep breath, I walked up the steps and tapped the brass knocker. Dr. Peterson opened the door, and I decided to stop thinking of him as Dr. Peterson.

"Hi Jacob," I said.

He stepped aside. "Hi, come on in. Is that for us?" He gestured toward the bottle of wine I carried, and when I held it out, he took it off my hands so I could remove my leather jacket.

Beneath it I wore jeans and a silky black blouse, with a pair of high wedge black sandals.

Jacob also wore jeans, and a loose-fitting, navy cotton shirt that made his shoulders look broad.

I followed him into the kitchen. "You're not allergic to shell-fish, are you?" he asked.

"No, I love shellfish."

"Great." He went to the stove and emptied a bag of live mussels into a pot of steaming broth.

"Everything smells delicious," I said.

He turned to me. "Wine?"

"Yes, please."

"Red or white?"

I glanced at his glass of white wine and the open bottle on the counter. "I'll have white."

He poured it and handed it to me, then leaned against the counter. "How was work today?" he asked.

I regarded him with a smile. "The polite response would be for me say 'good,' but it doesn't seem to be the right word, because I'm working on a difficult appeal right now."

"Can you tell me about it?" he asked. "If it wouldn't be breaking any rules of confidentiality…"

I reached for a slice of cheddar cheese on the plate of crackers he had set out, and told him about the woman who lost custody of her children because she'd gone to see a therapist during her separation, and how her abusive husband used it against her to imply she was unable to care for the children.

"I'll bet that sort of thing happens more often than people realize," Jacob said.

"You have no idea."

We stood in his kitchen talking about the legal system while the mussels steamed. When the shells opened up, he served them into a large stainless steel bowl, which he set on the granite-topped island. We stood over it, dipping the mussels in melted butter and devouring them while we talked, mostly about my work.

"Do you enjoy it?" he asked.

I set my mussel fork down and picked up my wine. "Yes, I do. Despite some of the frustrating things I see, I enjoy helping people turn a corner. When they come to me, they're in the process of breaking apart, and they're usually stressed and unhappy and afraid of what the future will hold. There's a fear of the unknown. But by the time we get through it all, they feel relieved, as if they can breathe again. I get lots of hugs from clients, once they reach that stage. Those are the good days." I inclined my head at him. "But you must experience the same thing in your profession."

"I do hug a lot of patients," he told me. "Sometimes they're relieved, like you said. They're overjoyed with the news I give them, but not always. I also see a lot of grief and sorrow, too. And fear."

"That's not surprising," I gently replied. "When people come to you, they're forced to face their mortality." I paused. "I suppose we all have to face that, even when we're healthy, but I think there must be some natural defense mechanism that keeps us from dwelling on it – otherwise we'd all be living in a constant state of fear and regret for all the things we didn't accomplish."

"That's probably true," he agreed, "but that mechanism must break down as we grow older. Look at how teenagers can live so fearlessly and take stupid risks, as if they're invincible. Then we hit middle age and we start worrying about our cholesterol, and every time we get on a plane…" He picked up another mussel shell and scooped out the flesh. "It really makes you think."

"I know what you mean," I said. "I never used to mind flying, but now I get a little queasy during takeoff and landing. I'm always relieved when we reach a certain altitude in the air and level off. Then, after the long descent, when the wheels finally touch down on the ground, I can't stop gripping the seat handles, even when we're taxying. Actually, the part I hate the most is when we're speeding on the ground, in those final seconds, just before lift off. I'm always afraid we're going to hit a pothole and spin out of control. Think about it. If you were driving your car that fast…"

"A Boeing 747 has to reach a speed of about 180 miles per hour before takeoff," he told me. "You wouldn't have liked the Concorde. It hit 225 on the ground. I think the airports take care of potholes though," he said with a grin.

I chuckled and sipped my wine. "Thank you, that's very reassuring." I was oddly turned on by his knowledge of jet speeds.

Later, when we sat down at the table to enjoy two perfect steaks he'd barbequed – along with roasted potatoes and fresh green beans – he opened the bottle of red wine I brought and poured two glasses.

Jacob sat down. "Thanks for joining me." He raised his glass to clink lightly against mine.

"Thank you for the invitation," I replied, and we each cut into our steaks. "It's delicious," I said, and then wondered where our conversation would go next.

"So tell me what it was like growing up as a twin," Jacob said as we cleared the table together.

I carried our plates to the sink to rinse them off. "Actually, Nadia and I didn't grow up together," I told him. "I only met her for the first time last year."

"You're kidding me." He was bending to open the dishwasher, but straightened upright to look at me.

"No, I'm not." I handed him my plate and began to rinse the others.

"What happened?" he asked. "If you don't mind the question."

I didn't mind it at all. In fact, for some reason I couldn't comprehend, I wanted to confess everything to this man about my relationship with Nadia, but I limited myself to the facts surrounding our adoptions. Because I was embarrassed by the rest of it; it was rather sordid.

"Our birth mother died when we were born," I explained, "and our biological father was married to another woman, so he didn't want to have anything to do with us. We were put up for adoption, but the agency felt it best to separate us, so that's what they did."

His brow furrowed with dismay. "Why would they think it would be better to separate you?"

"Because of Nadia's heart defect," I explained. "I was born healthy, so they figured it was better to get me placed in a home right away, rather than hold both of us back."

He closed the dishwasher door and stared at me with a look of concern, as if he were contemplating all the lifelong effects of such a decision, which we had no control over.

"I was adopted fairly quickly into an amazing family," I assured him. "My parents were wonderful, and I have a brother and a sister – also adopted. We're all very close."

"What about Nadia?" he asked. "Did she find a good home as well?"

I reached for the dishcloth and slowly wiped the counter. "She wasn't adopted until the issue with her heart was resolved, and that took a few years. But she wasn't as lucky as me. Her parents split up when she was nine, and she hasn't talked to her father since. He had a drinking problem. Her mom passed away a few years ago, so she has no family now."

"Except for you," he said.

Folding the dishcloth over the side of the sink, I found myself staring blankly at the faucet for a long time. Then I felt Jacob's hand on my arm.

"I didn't even know she existed until last year," I told him, "but somehow, we both ended up working in LA, a few blocks away from each other. How's that for a coincidence?"

Jacob's hand clasped mine. His touch was warm and soothing.

"People started making weird comments," I said, "asking how I could be working in two places at once. It was kind of freaky. I mean…what are the odds?"

"It must have been a shock to meet her for the first time," Jacob said.

"Yes."

I had trouble speaking after that. I felt emotionally spent.

"Do you want to go sit down?" he asked, nodding his head in the direction of the living room. "I could light a fire."

"That would be nice." I picked up my wine glass. He brought what was left of the bottle to the other room, and set it on the coffee table.

While I removed my sandals and curled up on the comfortable white sofa, he struck a match and lit the kindling, which had already been laid out on the grate. He remained seated on an ottoman, keeping an eye on the fire, nudging it with the poker and adding bunches of crumpled newspaper to help it along.

My body relaxed into the sofa cushions as I watched the flames snap and sizzle into a roaring blaze.

"I love the smell of a wood fire this time of year," I said.

Jacob stood. "Can I get you anything?"

"No, this is lovely."

He took a seat beside me, facing me with his arm along the back of the sofa.

I sipped my wine. For a long while I watched the flames dance in the grate and thought about our conversation in the kitchen.

"I know it's not my fault," I said, referring to what happened to Nadia and me when we became orphans, "but whenever I think about the life she had, compared to mine––"

"You feel guilty," he finished for me, and I looked deep into those absorbing green eyes.

"Yes. When I met her for the first time, it was a shock to my system, to see my exact likeness in another person, but I soon realized we had very little in common, because our life experiences had shaped us into different people."

"How so?"

"My parents had money, so they were able to send me to good schools, give me the best of everything, but it was more than that. I always felt loved. I never worried that they would abandon me, or that I would be left alone. I didn't live with that fear. Nadia didn't have any of that stability. At one point, she and her mother were so poor, they were evicted from their apartment and had to live in their car."

Jacob took hold of my hand again, and I wondered why I was the one having dinner with this amazing man; why I was the one being comforted and listened to, while Nadia was at home. Alone again.

"Now she has another heart condition because of some random virus," I said.

"But she also has *you*," he said. "The fact that you found each other is a gift and a miracle. It's something to be grateful for."

That should have been my cue to tell Jacob the truth… that Nadia and I were still strangers to each other – *worse* than strangers – because of what happened with Rick. Any emotional bond that might have existed between us had been broken. I felt no love in my heart, only a sense of duty to care for her in her time of need. There was no intimacy, no true personal connection. Our conversations were superficial, and I didn't feel that I could trust her, or be my honest self around her. My guard was always up.

I hadn't even told her I was coming here tonight because I believed that if she knew, she would begin flirting with Jacob – because I thought, on some unconscious level she wanted to be me. She wanted to possess what was mine, and if I let my guard down again, she would steal all the bounty from my life.

It was crazy, I knew. It sounded like something out of an old gothic novel.

I wasn't proud of my lack of love for Nadia, my twin sister, especially in her condition, and I couldn't bring myself to reveal that to Jacob. I didn't want him to think me callous or selfish.

And I didn't want to *be* either of those things. I hoped I would eventually find a way to work through it.

"What about you?" I asked, desperate to change the subject. "Any brothers or sisters?"

He leaned forward to pour himself more wine. "I have a younger sister who lives in Minnesota. She's a reporter. She's married to a civil engineer."

"But *you're* not married..."

He shook his head. "Not anymore. I was once, though."

"What happened?"

Looking down at our clasped hands, he entwined his fingers through mine. "She died in the twin towers."

A small breath escaped my lungs. "Oh, my God...I'm so sorry."

He nodded to acknowledge my sympathies. "So I know all about guilt, Diana," he said, lifting his gaze, "because I was the one who brought her to New York. She was happy where we were before and didn't want to move to a big city, but she was supportive of my career, and she made that sacrifice for me." He turned to look at the fire. "She was a financial analyst. Worked on one of the top floors. She couldn't get out."

Though I was curious, I didn't want to pry into the details of her death and force him to revisit that time. If he wanted to tell me more about it, he would.

"It took a long time to get over that," he said. "I was angry."

"You don't seem angry now."

He tilted his head to the side. "No, I'm not."

"What changed for you?"

He was quiet a moment, staring at the fire while I admired the way the light reflected in his eyes.

"It's been more than ten years," he said, "so I had plenty of time to wallow in my grief. Actually, I was shackled to it. My only escape was the hospital, which forced me to focus on something outside myself. I had to stay focused, or people could die." He paused and looked at me. "Sometimes, people *did* die, not from anything I did wrong, but because it's a fact of life. And I wasn't the only one in the world who lost someone that day."

"No...It was a terrible day."

He looked down at our hands again. "I know it's a cliché," he said, "but life is short and death comes to us all. So what's the point of living, if we're not going to experience real joy? At least some of the time," he added. "I'm not saying we shouldn't grieve or ever be unhappy – that's part of living, too. But we can't forget the other side of it when times are bleak."

"What other side?" I asked.

"The beautiful side."

A log shifted in the grate, and sparks flew up the chimney. I became aware of Jacob's hand on my shoulder, toying with a lock of my hair. I felt a rush of desire. I wanted to be closer to him.

"I'm sure you're right," I softly said. "I *know* you are, but sometimes we get so caught up in everything that's wrong in our lives, that we can't see what's good. I suppose we shut down to it. And it's all about feelings, isn't it? It's about letting yourself feel euphoric about something...*anything*. It's just so hard to feel joyful when your whole world is collapsing around you."

As we sat quietly in the glow of the fire, I wondered what Nadia was doing in that moment. It was getting rather late.

"You should come fishing with me," Jacob said. His hand was still moving through my hair. His touch caused a tingling sensation along the side of my neck. I shrugged my shoulder to gently trap his hand beneath my cheek, and closed my eyes. He cupped the side of my face, and I kissed his palm.

"Will you come?" he asked, his voice husky and low.

My eyes fluttered open, and I became aware of a deep emotional longing inside of me – though it was sensual, too, because I felt it in my nerve endings, like an electric current, and in the pit of my belly, like a thrilling wave of anticipation. I was still trying to make sense of it, because it was both sexual and soulful. I wanted to *know* Jacob, to know everything about him.

"Will I have to put a worm on a hook?" I asked, my eyes trained on his.

He grinned at me. "Not if you don't want to."

I was overwhelmingly aware of the rapid beat of my pulse and the rush of blood through my body.

"Then I would love to go fishing with you," I said.

He smiled again. "How about Saturday? If you don't mind getting up before dawn."

"*Before* dawn?" I replied with a note of teasing in my voice. "Sounds like you take fishing very seriously."

He nodded. "I take everything seriously."

His gaze dipped to my mouth, and I thought perhaps he might kiss me. My heart began to race at the prospect of it, but then he sat back and withdrew his hand from the crook of my neck.

"I should get going," I said. "I don't like leaving Nadia alone for too long these days."

It wasn't a lie. I felt a constant need to check in with her and make sure she was all right.

We stood up and moved to the foyer. Jacob pulled my leather jacket from the closet and held it up for me. I slid my arms into the sleeves. Then he reached for his own jacket.

"Are you going somewhere?" I asked.

"I'm walking you home," he replied, as if it was obvious.

I wasn't about to admit that I had driven my car around the corner to his place, and besides that, I'd had too much wine to get behind the wheel. So I accepted his offer, and we held hands as we walked leisurely from his house to mine. We were at my front door in less than five minutes.

We said goodnight, and he kissed me on the cheek – which left me quite hungry for something more.

Perhaps Jacob was hungry, too, because he texted me the following morning and asked me what time I'd be at Starbucks. I texted back.

In twenty minutes.

We arranged to meet at the same time each morning for the next two weeks. Instead of getting our coffees to go, we arrived early enough so that we had time to sit at a table and chat.

On the second day, he asked me about the relationship I'd mentioned the first time we met there.

"How long were you together?" he asked.

"For a few years," I replied, "while I was living in LA. His name was Rick and he was a sports agent."

Jacob raised his eyebrows. "That sounds interesting. You said it didn't work out. Can I ask what happened?"

I fiddled with the cardboard sleeve around my coffee cup. "I caught him cheating on me. We were at a casino resort in Las Vegas and he went missing for a while, then I found him on an elevator kissing another woman."

I don't know why I kept the rest of the story from Jacob – the part Nadia had played in the end of my relationship. Part of me wanted to believe that I was protecting her, because I didn't want Jacob to think badly of her. I wanted him to save her life. But perhaps I felt that anything Nadia did reflected poorly on me as well, because I was her twin. I certainly didn't want Jacob to think I was the cheating type.

"That must have been rough," he said.

"It was, but it was for the best," I said. "We were having troubles before that anyway."

"What kind of troubles?"

When I hesitated, he held up a hand. "Sorry. I'm asking too many questions."

"No. It's fine," I replied. But it took me a moment to figure out how to explain it. "We wanted different things out of life," I finally said. "I wanted marriage, eventually, and children. But Rick wasn't keen on a lifelong commitment. Don't get me wrong. He was wonderful for the first few years, and very devoted. But as soon as I wanted to talk about marriage…that was too much for him. He'll probably always be a serial monogamist. He enjoys falling in love. He just doesn't enjoy *staying* in love. And children?" I shook my head. "Not for him."

Jacob reached across the table, raised my hand to his lips, and kissed it. "I'm sorry that happened."

"I'm not."

"You're not?"

"No, because if it hadn't happened, I wouldn't be sitting here right now."

He kissed my hand again.

On another morning, Jacob asked about my parents.

"They've been married for almost forty years," I told him. Then I squinted through the bright, sunny window. "Sometimes

I wonder if they're an anomaly, because they're still so happy and in love. They go for walks and hold hands, and my dad still kisses my mom every morning when he leaves for work, and every night when he comes home."

Jacob and I were again holding hands across the table.

"Thank God for them," I said, "because in my line of work, I need to know there's still hope that *some* marriages will last forever."

His eyes were full of warmth. "Sounds like you learned from the best."

I looked down at the table. "I'm not sure how much I learned, because it didn't keep me from walking out on a two-year relationship that I thought was going to last forever."

"He wasn't the right one for you," Jacob said matter-of-factly. "And you weren't married to him."

I nodded, and the subject changed to our upcoming fishing trip on Saturday. Jacob told me about his cabin on the lake. He described the mist rising off the glassy water at dawn and the peaceful silence of the woods. I couldn't wait to be there with him.

As our Friday morning date at Starbucks came to an end, the idea of not seeing Jacob until the following morning seemed like an eternity to wait. I realized, as we walked out of the coffee shop together, that my 'teensy tiny crush' on my sister's doctor had mushroomed into something much bigger.

We paused to say good-bye on the street as we always did. He gave me a kiss on the cheek. As soon as we turned our backs on each other, however, he said, "Diana, wait."

I stopped and swung around.

"Would you like to see a movie tonight?"

Could it be that he was just as enamored as I was?

"I'd love to," I replied with a smile. "Anything special you want to see?"

"Not really. I'm game for anything. Why don't you check the listings and choose something for us. Surprise me."

I wanted to bounce up and down on my toes. "All right."

He hesitated. "I'd suggest that you invite Nadia, but––"

"You're her doctor," I finished for him.

He nodded.

"I understand," I replied.

A short while later, as I got into my car, I was thankful for the clear line that was drawn in the sand between Jacob and Nadia. He was her doctor, and it would be a breach of ethics for him to form any sort of intimate relationship with her.

Not that I feared – for a single second – that Jacob would do that. I knew in my heart that he was nothing like Rick.

It was Nadia I was unsure of. I didn't know how she would maneuver through this if she knew.

"I need to talk to you about something," Jacob said that night, taking hold of my hand as we walked out of the movie theater together.

I glanced up at him uncertainly.

"I think it would be best if I turned Nadia's case over to a colleague," he said.

I stopped in my tracks. "Why?"

The rest of the crowd moved past us in the theater lobby. Someone bumped my elbow and knocked me slightly off balance.

"Because of what's happening here," Jacob quietly replied. He stepped a little closer. "I don't want to be presumptuous, but I like you, Diana. I want to see where this goes, and if we're going to do that, it would be best if I wasn't your sister's cardiologist."

I looked down at my feet. "You're not being presumptuous. I like you, too. A lot."

I wanted to continue seeing Jacob – I wanted it more than anything – and I didn't want to cause him any problems with the professional ethics committee.

At the same time, I didn't want it to be my fault that Nadia received less than the very best medical care.

"You're the best heart surgeon at Mass General," I said to him.

We began walking again, slowly falling behind the pace of the crowd.

"I appreciate the compliment," he replied, "but some people might disagree."

"You're being modest."

He squeezed my hand. "We're a team at Mass General, Diana. Everyone is top notch. I'd like to hand Nadia's case over to Dr. John Reynolds, if that's okay with the two of you. He's an excellent surgeon and a good friend."

"But she's so comfortable with you," I argued. "That first day when we met in your office, I believed you were the right doctor for her, and I still believe it."

"I'll always be nearby," he assured me, "available to consult about anything. Like I said, Dr. Reynolds and I work as a team."

We pushed through the theater doors, and when I still didn't agree to Jacob's suggestion that we move Nadia to another doctor, he stopped and took hold of my arm.

"Diana, the main reason I want to take myself off her case is because I don't want to hold anything back when I'm with *you*. She's your twin, and there's a gray area there, in terms of ethics. Do you understand? Also – and this isn't easy for me to say – if anything happens to her, I'm afraid that every time you look at me, you'll be reminded of how I couldn't save her, and how I failed you."

I swallowed uneasily, then nodded to indicate that yes, I understood. He was choosing the possibility of a future with me over Nadia's medical case. I was pleased, of course, that he wanted to explore what might be possible between us, but at the same time, I was hesitant to take him away from my sister. After everything she'd been through, could I really do that?

It was nearly midnight when Jacob pulled up in front of my house. A jazz tune was playing on the radio, but he turned the volume down so we could say goodnight.

"You'll be ready to go at 5:00 tomorrow?" he asked.

"I'll set three alarm clocks," I replied, "just to make sure I don't sleep in."

He smiled. "Good. And I promise it'll be worth it. You know what they say – every hour spent fishing——"

"Adds an hour to your life." I chuckled. "Are there any statistics to prove that?"

"I don't know, but I like the sound of it."

"Me, too."

He reached for my hand, raised it to his lips, and kissed the back of it. The soft pressure of his mouth on my skin sent a current of desire rushing through me.

Jacob's eyes met mine, then he leaned in for a kiss. The moment our lips touched, I was overcome by a jolt of pleasure that erupted in every part of my body, all at once. I slid my hands across his shoulders and up the sides of his neck to the strong line of his jaw. The quickened pace of his breathing matched mine, but for me, it was so much more than physical. I felt as if the bond forming between us was not new. It had always been there beneath the surface of my existence, waiting quietly and patiently to be discovered. All that had been required was for us to meet.

As we drew apart, I fought to catch my breath and gain control over my desires, because I had to go inside soon.

"Your cheeks are flushed," Jacob whispered with a smile. He rested his forehead on mine.

"That's because I'm happy," I replied.

"So am I. I haven't felt like this in a very long time."

I swallowed over my disbelief. Was this really happening? "I don't think I've *ever* felt like this."

He nodded in agreement.

"I should go inside before I attack you," I said.

My words caused him to press his mouth to mine again, but this time his passion was fierce. His kiss filled me with desperation and a mad need to go home with him that night – because the thought of a single hour away from him felt like torture.

It took every shred of discipline I possessed to lay my hands on his chest and put a stop to this. "If I don't go inside right now," I breathlessly said, "things are going to get out of hand."

He nodded. "You'd better go. I'll see you in the morning."

My hands trembled as I reached for the door handle and got out.

"Good night," Jacob said, leaning across the passenger seat to smile up at me.

As I stood on the curb, I felt completely dazed and beguiled. I closed the car door and turned to walk up my front steps.

I inserted the key into the lock and entered the foyer with a smile on my face, but turned to discover Nadia, standing in the center of the living room in her fleecy blue bathrobe. She stared at me with a frown.

"You didn't tell me you were going out on a *date*," she said accusingly. "Were you lying about that?"

I set my purse and keys down on the table by the stairs and inhaled deeply. *Here we go.*

"Who was he?" Nadia asked, before I had a chance to explain anything. She crossed to the window and pulled the curtain aside to look out. Thankfully, Jacob was gone by then, but I wondered how long she'd been watching us.

I moved into the living room. "I'm sorry I didn't tell you. I was going to, but with everything you've been through lately, I didn't want to cause you any stress."

"Why would it cause me stress?" she asked.

"Because of who I'm dating," I answered honestly.

She tilted her head. "And who is that?"

Clearly, she already knew the answer to the question. She just wanted to hear me admit it.

"I was with Jacob Peterson tonight."

She pointed her thumb into her breastbone. "*My* doctor."

"Yes."

Her shoulders rose and fell as she exhaled. "How long have you been seeing him?"

"Not long. A couple of weeks."

"Why him?" she asked. "Of all the men in Boston."

"I didn't plan on it," I explained. "We bumped into each other at Starbucks, that's all. It was a coincidence. Turns out he lives in our neighborhood."

"But your date with him tonight wasn't a coincidence," she said, and I saw the wheels turning in her head. "When you went out for dinner with clients last week…Were you lying about that, too?"

My mouth became dry. I wet my lips. "Yes."

Nadia's nostrils flared. The next thing I knew, she was storming past me toward the kitchen.

I followed her, but remained in the kitchen doorway.

"I'm sorry," I said, "but I really like him."

She opened the cupboard door over the microwave and pulled out a small box of herbal tea, and slammed it down on the countertop. "Are you just doing this to get back at me for what happened with Rick?"

"Of course not. This has nothing to do with that."

"Are you *sure*?" she answered reproachfully. "I know you haven't forgiven me for it. You didn't answer my texts or emails for almost a year. I was on my *deathbed* before you would return a phone call, and now that I'm here, you never talk to me. I think the only reason I'm in your home is because you feel it's your moral duty to be a good person – always the perfect Diana – but you don't really want me here. You'd be much happier if I was still in LA and out of your life."

My thoughts began racing dangerously, and all of a sudden I was back in that ritzy Vegas penthouse, while Nadia looked past me and focused all her attention on my future fiancé.

"Fine," I said, "if you want to go there." I strode forward to where she was rifling through the box of herbal teas. "Yes, I'm still angry about what happened between you and Rick. He was the man I wanted to marry. What do you expect? You're standing in front of me with his kid in your belly."

Her eyes grew wide with shock. "I told you I was sorry about that. And you said yourself that you're better off without him. I did you a favor."

"Hah!" I shouted. "I didn't realize a knife in the back was considered a favor. And why did you do it anyway? Did you want to hurt me, or did you just want to have what I had? Did you feel it was owed to you, that you had a right to it, because we were twins and you should have everything I had? Was it jealousy? Resentment?"

She wagged a finger at me. "Stop talking about it as if it was all my doing, as if I orchestrated everything, and stole your boyfriend from you. Rick was as much to blame as I was, if not more. The way he treated me..." She stopped. "He was so charming, and I wasn't used to that. I just..." She paused. "I fell."

"You fell." I should my head in disbelief. "What does that even *mean*?"

"It means I fell head over heels in love with him," she said, "and I couldn't stay away. There. Is that what you wanted to hear?"

"Not really," I scoffed.

She glared at me, then left the kitchen without boiling any water for her tea.

"Where are you going?" I asked.

"To bed."

I followed her up the stairs. "Wait. We're not done here. I still need to talk to you."

"About what?"

"About the situation with Dr. Peterson."

Nadia reached the top of the stairs and disappeared into her room. She was shrugging out of her bathrobe when I arrived in her doorway.

"I don't want you to see him anymore," she said to me.

I walked all the way in. "I'm seeing him tomorrow. He's picking me up at dawn and taking me fishing. I'm not going to cancel that."

"But he's *my* doctor."

I worked hard to wrestle my anger to the ground and speak in a calm voice. "That's what I need to talk to you about. Tonight he told me that he would prefer to hand your file over to another surgeon. His name is Dr. Reynolds, and he's supposed to be very good."

She stared at me in horror. "I don't want another doctor. I want Dr. Peterson. Was it *you* who suggested that?"

I took another deep breath and counted to ten. "Dr. Reynolds is just as good, and they'll work together as a team."

"Didn't you hear me? I said *no.*"

My head drew back at the firm note of command in her voice. She was a guest in my home. I was doing everything humanly possible to help her, despite the fact that she had betrayed me and broken up my last relationship. Now she had the nerve to tell me I wasn't permitted to see a man I was falling in love with?

"Are you forgetting that I'm the one who found Dr. Peterson in the first place?" I asked. "I made all the calls and all the arrangements. I paid for your travel to come here to Boston. I could just as easily have chosen Dr. Reynolds for you, and you would have been perfectly fine with that. You're only digging your heels in now because you don't want me to have any more advantages. Any more happiness. You think I've had more than my share, and that anything good from now on should go to *you.*"

"What if I said *yes,* it should be my turn now," she replied.

I honestly didn't know what to say to that.

She shook her head at me. "You have everything, Diana, and I've had nothing – or whatever I did have was taken away. I lost my dad, my mom, Rick, and I even lost you. The only truly good thing that's happened to me is this baby, so I'm not going to apologize for getting pregnant. I don't care if you were hurt by it. I want this child. She's all I've got, and if I'm going to survive long enough to raise her, I need a damn good doctor."

For a long moment, I stood there in shock, staring at her. Then I slowly began to back out of her room. "You'll have one," I said, gripping the doorknob to gently close the door behind me. "And his name is Dr. Reynolds."

My alarm went off at 4:30, well before sunrise. At least I thought it was my alarm when my eyes fluttered open and I sat up groggily in bed.

In actuality it was only 3:00 a.m. I must have been dreaming.

I pushed my hair away from my face and listened through the silence. Then I heard it again – *the sound of Nadia's voice, calling my name.*

Tossing the covers aside, I leaped out of bed and ran barefoot to her room. "What is it?"

Her lamp was on, and she was sitting up against a pile of pillows. "It's happening again," she said. "I woke up because I couldn't breathe."

I was still half asleep, and it took me a second to comprehend what she was saying.

"Can you call Dr. Peterson? she asked. "I think it's my heart again. You said he lives in our neighborhood."

"Maybe I should call 911," I replied, thinking we were going to need an ambulance.

"No, please call Dr. Peterson. He can get here faster, right?"

Warning bells went off in my brain. She knew I was supposed to go fishing with Jacob at dawn. Was this an act? Was she just trying to prevent me from going? Or was I crazy to think so?

She was pasty white and perspiring, so I ran back to my room to grab my phone. With trembling fingers, I found Jacob's home number and called it. He answered after two rings.

"Jacob? It's Diana."

"Hey. Is something wrong?"

"Yes, it's Nadia. She can't breathe very well and she thinks she might be in heart failure."

"Hang up and call 911 right away," he said. "Then unlock your front door. I'll be there in three minutes."

True to his word, Jacob made it to our house in three minutes flat and came bounding up the stairs. "Where are you?"

"In here!" I called out to him. I was sitting on the edge of Nadia's bed, holding her hand when he appeared in the doorway wearing black pyjama bottoms and a gray sweatshirt. He carried a black canvas backpack.

I quickly got out of his way so he could take my place at Nadia's side.

"How are you doing?" he asked in a friendly, relaxed manner – as if everything was completely under control. I could have hugged him.

Nadia put her hand over her chest. "Not good. I can't breathe. It feels just like last time."

He looked up at me. "Did you call 911?"

"Yes, they're on their way."

He reached into his medical bag and withdrew a stethoscope and a blood pressure cuff, which he wrapped around Nadia's upper arm. "Everything's going to be fine," he said as he placed the ear buds in his ears. "Just try to relax."

He squeezed the rubber ball a number of times in quick succession to inflate the cuff. Nadia and I were very quiet while he listened to the pulse in the crook of her arm and watched the dial.

The Velcro on the cuff ripped noisily when he removed it.

"My baby," Nadia said. "Is she all right? I haven't felt her move or kick since this started."

Jacob placed the stethoscope on top of her belly. Closing his eyes to listen, he moved it from one spot to another. The tension was thick in the room while we waited forever for him to say something.

At last his eyes opened. "Everything's fine. She must be sleeping. It's the middle of the night, you know," he said to Nadia with a hint of humor, which helped her to relax.

"Do you mind if I check your legs?" He rose to his feet and pulled the covers aside.

I was surprised to see how swollen Nadia's legs were. I didn't think that was normal, not even for a pregnant woman. Jacob made no comment. He simply covered Nadia back up and sat down beside her. "The ambulance will be here any minute."

Just then, I saw the glow of flashing lights through the window. I ran downstairs to open the front door.

Naturally, I blamed myself for Nadia's heart troubles that night. It was the stress of our argument that caused it, I believed. I wished I could take it back, but all I could do was sit in the hospital waiting area, whispering quiet prayers that everything would be okay.

It had been almost two hours since the paramedics wheeled Nadia out of my house on a stretcher. I followed the ambulance in my car, while Jacob rode in the back with her. When we arrived at the hospital, he promised to keep me updated about her condition, but he hadn't come out to see me yet, and I was growing anxious.

Slouching down in the chair, I tipped my head back against the wall and closed my eyes.

Maybe I dozed off. I'm not sure.

"Diana…"

I jumped, startled by a hand on my shoulder, shaking me. I opened my eyes to discover Jacob, dressed in a pair of OR greens, standing over me.

Instantly alert, I sat up. "How is she?"

"Not well, I'm afraid." He took a seat. "She's in intensive care right now because she went into cardiac failure again. There's a lot of extra fluid in her lungs and we're trying to get rid of that. We're doing everything we can to stabilize her."

"What about the baby?"

"I've been talking to the obstetrician," he explained, "and the baby's heart has deep decelerations, which means it's slowing down for long periods of time, and we're worried about that. Bottom line is the baby has to come out. Nadia needs a section as soon as possible, but she also needs to be stable. It's a balancing act."

I buried my face in my hands. "Oh, God. This my all fault. We had an argument tonight."

"It's not your fault," he assured me, squeezing my shoulder. "Her heart's in bad shape. Anything could have brought this on. The good news is, the baby's at thirty-two weeks now, so she has a good chance."

"But what about Nadia?" I asked. "How can she survive the surgery if her heart is that weak?"

A nurse came through a set of double doors and hurried toward us. She looked panicked.

"Dr. Peterson, we need you."

He stood up to go, but stopped and turned back briefly to say, "If there are any friends or family you feel should be here, you should call them now."

I stared at him in shock. Then he started running, and disappeared through the double doors to the ICU.

First I said a prayer. I ran to the hospital chapel, got down on my knees, and pleaded with God to help Nadia through this. I made promises and bargains.

Then I called my parents in Washington and asked them to call Becky and Adam. Finally, I scrolled through my list of contacts and found Rick's number. I wasn't sure if Nadia would want me to call him, but he was the baby's father, and I felt he deserved to know what was going on.

"Hello?" he answered, sounding half asleep.

"Hi Rick. It's Diana." When he didn't say anything for a few seconds, I added, "Diana *Moore*."

God, was this really necessary?

"Yeah…yeah," he mumbled. "I know. I'm sorry, it's the middle of the night here. What's going on?"

I stood up and paced slowly around the waiting room. "I wasn't sure if I should call you or not," I said, "but Nadia's not doing well. Did you know she's been having heart troubles?"

"No," he replied. "What kind of troubles?"

Feeling exhausted suddenly, I covered my forehead with a hand and pushed my hair away from my face. "She caught a virus which caused damage to her heart. The condition is called myocarditis, and things are pretty serious right now. I'm calling from

Mass General, and they're about to do a C-section to get the baby out, but Nadia's in bad shape."

"Will she be all right?" he asked.

I hesitated. "I don't know. It's not looking good, but I don't want to lose hope."

He was quiet for a long time. "Should I come out there?"

I thought about it. Carefully.

"No," I replied. "That's not necessary. Unless you want to. I just thought you should know what was happening."

If he had insisted on coming, I certainly wouldn't have stopped him, but he merely said, "Okay. I appreciate the call. I hope she'll be all right. Will you let me know?"

"Yes."

I was about to end the call, but he wouldn't let me go.

"*Wait*, Diana…" There was a note of desperation in his voice. "What about the baby? I mean, if anything happens to Nadia…"

I knew in that moment that he was not concerned for Nadia's welfare, or the baby's. He was worried about his own personal freedom and what responsibilities might fall to him if Nadia didn't make it through the C-section.

"Relax," I said. "I've already agreed to become the child's legal guardian in the event of Nadia's death. She signed a new will a number of weeks ago."

I could just picture him letting out a huge breath of relief.

"I suppose you took care of that for her," he mentioned.

"Yes."

I had nothing more to say to him.

"That was good of you. You're a good sister." He paused. "Look, I'm sorry about everything."

I wondered if there was a new woman in the bed beside him, listening to the conversation, and was comforted by the fact that I genuinely didn't care.

"I know," I replied, "but that's all in the past now. I really need to go."

"Okay. Take care, Diana."

"You too."

I ended the call and sat in silence for a long while, staring at the wall.

About a half an hour later, Jacob emerged from a different set of double doors and walked toward me. He looked exhausted and shaken, and there was blood splattered on his OR greens. I stood up and immediately burst into tears.

❦

Jacob put his arms around me. He held me tight, and stroked my hair while I wept on his shoulder.

When I finally pulled myself together, he took me by the hand and led me to a chair away from the other people in the waiting area. "We did the section," he said, "and the baby's doing fine. I can take you to see her in a little bit."

I wiped my nose with the back of my hand. "Thank God. What about Nadia?"

"She's back in the ICU," he said, "so she's hanging on, but it was rough. When they came to get me earlier, she was arresting, and the baby was in distress, so we had to do an emergency section, even though Nadia wasn't stable. A few minutes after we got the baby out, we lost her, and it took a while to get her back. I had to shock her a number of times. She's a fighter, that one."

Thank you, God.

"Has she woken up yet?"

"No, and she's not out of the woods yet. But I promise you, we're doing everything we can."

"Will she recover?"

He hesitated. "I won't lie to you, Diana. Her heart function is very poor. That virus hit her hard, and the pregnancy didn't help. If she can make it through the next twenty-four hours there's a chance, but she's definitely going to need a new heart. I've got my team working to get her on the transplant list right now."

"How long will it take to get her a new heart?" I asked.

"It's impossible to predict." Then he touched my knee. "I'd like to take you to see the baby now, if that's all right with you."

I nodded, and he offered his hand to help me rise.

"She's a few weeks premature," Jacob said, "so she'll have to remain in an incubator for the time being." He opened the door to the neonatal intensive care unit. "But everything's looking good."

He escorted me inside, where a number of newborns were lying in glass cribs.

"She's over here," Jacob said.

As we approached the fully enclosed glass case, I looked in at my niece and felt a giant swell of joy and love in my heart. I couldn't believe what I was looking at – the little person who had been growing inside my sister's belly for the past eight months.

This was the beginning of a new life. This child would be part of my world forever. She would grow into a curious toddler, perhaps a rebellious teenager, and eventually a woman. This baby was family, and the protective, loving bond I felt for her was both powerful and instantaneous.

"She's so beautiful," I softly said. "She looks like Nadia."

"She looks like you, too," Jacob replied, meeting my gaze over the top of the incubator. "If you'd like to open one of the portholes, you can reach in and touch her."

"It's okay for me to do that?" I asked, glancing over my shoulder at the nurses.

"Yes. It's important for her to get to know your voice and your touch."

I opened the little round door and reached in to caress the baby's tiny head. "Her hair is so soft," I whispered.

Overcome with fascination, I touched her hand and she gripped my finger. A tear spilled across my cheek. I laughed.

When I removed my hand and closed the door, I met Jacob's gaze uncertainly over the top of the glass case. "There's so much I need to tell you," I said, "about Nadia and me, and the argument we had last night."

I wasn't sure how to explain that this baby's father was the man I almost married – the man I'd caught kissing another woman in an elevator in Las Vegas. And that woman was my sister.

"There's plenty of time for that," Jacob said.

I looked down at my niece again. "I'm sorry we didn't get to go fishing this morning."

"There's plenty of time for that, too," he replied.

But I wasn't so sure, because while I was on my knees in the dimly lit hospital chapel – and Jacob was shocking Nadia back to life on the operating table – I had made a desperate promise.

If all my prayers were answered, I was going to have to keep that promise.

For the next eight hours, I sat at Nadia's bedside and continued to pray. I wasn't sure if she could hear me, but I talked to her anyway and described the beautiful baby who was waiting to meet her.

"You have to wake up so you can give her a name," I whispered in Nadia's ear.

But she wouldn't wake up.

She simply couldn't.

My parents arrived that evening to help keep vigil at Nadia's bedside. We held hands and prayed together and talked to her constantly, urging her to keep fighting and come back to us.

I also took my parents to see the baby, one at a time so that someone was always at Nadia's side, willing her to come back.

Jacob, too, was a constant presence. He came by often to check on Nadia and answer any questions we had. I introduced him to my parents and explained that he was our neighbor and friend, but I made no mention of the fact that I was had been falling in love with him over the past few weeks, and had selfishly argued with Nadia the night before about moving her case to another doctor. I still blamed myself for her heart failure that night, and I was ashamed of the fight we'd had. I should have been able to let go of my anger. And she was right; I should have talked to her more, instead of shutting her out.

These things I grappled with. I wondered 'what if' I had handled things differently. What if I'd been able to forgive her earlier on? Maybe we could have gone back to the way things were. Maybe she would have moved out to Boston sooner and might never have caught that virus.

_⌒_

When the hour grew late, we were told to go home and get some rest. The head ICU nurse promised to call if there was any change.

My parents came home with me, and after sharing a pot of chamomile tea at the kitchen table, we all went to bed. I fell asleep as soon as my head hit the pillow. When I woke up, the sun was beaming through my window, casting a long ray of diagonal light across the room. I checked my clock. It was almost eight. There had been no phone calls from the hospital during the night, so I could only presume there was no change in Nadia's condition.

My presumptions proved correct. When we arrived at the hospital later that morning, she was still in ICU and looked the same as the day before.

I decided to go and see the baby. This time I was permitted to hold her in my arms. I sat in a rocking chair and sang her a lullaby, and in those moments, all the stresses of the world simply faded away. I felt nothing but love and gratitude that she had made it this far. At least some of my prayers had been answered.

When I returned to the ICU, my parents were there. I pulled a chair closer to the bed and clasped Nadia's hand.

"I hope you wake up soon," I said, "because your sweet baby wants to meet you. I got to hold her just now, and she's perfect. She's the most beautiful little person in the whole wide world."

To my surprise, Nadia squeezed my hand. Then her eyes opened and she turned her head on the pillow and frowned at me.

L ater, I wondered if Nadia willed herself to wake up because she was agitated that I had held her baby before she did. If that was true, I decided not to dwell on it. The only thing that mattered was that she'd opened her eyes – and that meant there was hope.

I turned to my mother. "Can you get a nurse? She's awake."

Mom hurried from the room, while I stroked Nadia's hair away from her forehead. "How are you feeling?"

She nodded, and the first words out of her mouth were, "My baby...?"

"She's fine," I said. "She's doing really well. They're taking good care of her in the nursery." I paused. "Do you remember what happened?"

Nadia shook her head, while a nurse came in and checked her vitals.

"They had to do a C-section yesterday morning," I explained, "but it went fine. Your baby's adorable, Nadia. She's the most beautiful thing in the world. Now you just need to recover and get your strength back."

I looked up when Jacob walked in. "Nadia," he said, approaching her side. "How are you feeling?" He withdrew a penlight from the pocket of his lab coat and shone it in her eyes.

She turned her head on the pillow and stared at me with questioning eyes. "Where's Dr. Reynolds?" she whispered.

I shook my head. "Dr. Peterson is your doctor. He was there for everything yesterday, including the C-section. He saved your life, and he's going to continue to be your doctor."

She looked up at him. "Thank you."

His eyes met mine, and all I could do was stare at him with an agonizing mixture of love and sorrow. "Thank you for bringing her back," I said.

He merely nodded, and I knew he understood what was in my heart.

Sometimes there are lessons we need to learn, different ways we need to grow, but we don't know what direction to grow *toward* until we meet someone who is everything we aspire to be. Some people call them role models. Heroes. Mentors.

Jacob Peterson was all of those things to me. He may have saved my sister's life on the operating table, but on that day, he also saved mine, because through him I discovered what I was capable of, and it went beyond a robotic moral duty to do the right thing. There was something in my soul, something that came alive in me because of what I felt for this man. And for my sister.

A few hours after Nadia woke up, I left the ICU and went searching for Jacob on the cardiology floor. His office door was closed, so I asked the receptionist if it would be possible for me to speak with him. "I don't have an appointment," I explained. "I'm a neighbor of his."

"What's your name?" she asked.

"Diana Moore."

She picked up the phone and called him. "Diana Moore is here and she's wondering if you have a minute?" She hung up. "He said to go right in."

Nervous knots invaded my belly. I felt as if I were walking up the steep steps to the gallows. "Thank you."

When I entered his brightly lit office, Jacob was already rising from his chair and moving around his desk to greet me. I closed the door and remained there, leaning against it.

He stopped in the center of the room, gazing at me with understanding. Or was it dread? Either way, I sensed he already knew what I came to say.

"It's been difficult," he said.

I merely nodded, because I wasn't sure I could form proper words. All I could do was move slowly toward him, wrap my arms around his waist, and lay my cheek on his shoulder. Closing my eyes, I melted into the warmth of his arms as they enveloped me in a caring embrace.

His hand stroked the back of my head, and I was immensely grateful that he did not rush me to say what I'd come here to say.

"I don't want to let you go," I whispered after a moment, and he kissed the top of my head.

Finally I summoned the will to take a step backward. His hand skimmed down the length of my arm until only our fingers were entwined.

"I want to be with you," I said, "but Nadia needs you more."

It wasn't easy to stand there in his presence when all I wanted to do was dash back into his arms and kiss him passionately until I collapsed with rapture. My thoughts drifted to an image of the two of us sitting on the dock at his lakeside cabin at dawn, fishing off the end of it. I imagined lying back on the weathered boards, gazing up at the sky, while he moved over me and pressed his body to mine. Suddenly, I wanted him with an intensity that made me dizzy.

I had to stay focused, however. I needed to explain. "Remember when we were in the nursery yesterday, and I said there were things I wanted to tell you?"

"Yes," he replied.

I sighed deeply and searched for the right way to begin. "My relationship with Nadia is complicated," I said. "We've been apart more than we've been together and…"

I stopped a moment, then somehow found the strength to continue. "The baby you helped deliver yesterday…The father is the man I was seeing in LA. When I told you I caught him cheating with another woman, I didn't tell you that the other woman was Nadia."

Jacob's eyebrows pulled together in a frown. His thumb rubbed over the back of my hand.

"I couldn't even *think* about forgiving her," I confessed, "which is why I left the west coast and came here. I probably never would have spoken to her again if she hadn't gotten sick. So we've been struggling to get along since then, and she thinks I'm only helping her because of a need to be perfect, not because I care for her, or trust her, or love her."

"Do you?" he asked. "Do you love her?"

"Yes," I replied, without hesitation. "How could I not? She's my twin sister, and that bond is somehow…unbreakable. I just couldn't feel it before because I was so angry with her. But now, after seeing her come so close to death, I realize that the love in me is stronger than the anger. I don't want to lose her, Jacob, and if she's more comfortable with you as her doctor, then I don't want to get in the way of that. She's had so little that's *good* in her life, while I've had so much."

His clear, observant eyes held me captive.

"You can't change the past," he said.

I lowered my gaze. "I know. But I can change the future, my own future, at least. I want Nadia to be the one who gets everything right now." I looked up. "And *you're* everything. So I'm begging you to stay on as her doctor. If you care about me, please don't leave her."

The phone on his desk began to ring, and I let out a breath, feeling deflated, because I wanted an answer from him. I needed to be sure that he understood how difficult this was for me to let him go. To not be with him when I wanted him so desperately.

He turned to answer the phone. I waited until he finished the call and hung up. Then he faced me again.

"Diana," he said. "I don't want to lose you either."

There was no other way to say it. "But I couldn't live with myself if you chose me over her. I wouldn't be the person you deserve."

I turned to go, but as I opened the door, he followed and pushed it closed. Standing behind me, he brushed his lips lightly over my ear, and I feared I might dissolve because of the electric current that raced through me.

"Please know," he whispered, "that I'm going to do everything in my power for your sister. I give you my word."

"I know."

With only that, I walked out.

Until that day in Jacob's office, my rivalry with Nadia had weighed down upon me like an oversized suitcase on my back. I'd kept everyone at a distance, even my family, until Jacob came along and reminded me that I was still capable of affection and intimacy. And sexual attraction. He made me see that the walls I'd built around me weren't as thick as I'd tried to make them, and I began to believe they also might not be permanent.

As Nadia grew stronger day by day, I felt as if my prayers were being answered. I also felt more whole – more worthy and confident – having surrendered to the idea of forgiveness. When I watched her sit in the rocking chair in the hospital nursery and hold her baby for the first time, I felt weightless, as if I were floating upwards toward the clouds. Nadia wept softly, and somehow I knew this was the first time she had ever experienced such a deep and profound joy.

Our eyes met, and a warm glow moved through me.

"Diana," she whispered, "how can I ever thank you?"

"For what?" I asked.

"For taking such good care of me, even after everything…"

I shook my head. "That's in the past now. Besides, you were right. You *did* do me a favor. A huge one. I just didn't realize it at the time."

She continued to rock gently in the chair and look down at her baby.

"Now I'm glad it happened," I firmly said, "because if it hadn't, you wouldn't be holding that precious little bundle in your arms. And we're going to love her like there's no tomorrow. You and me, together."

"Even if there was no tomorrow," Nadia said, "I would go to bed happy tonight, knowing I was able to hold her – just this once – and knowing that she'll have *you*."

I frowned. "Don't talk like that. You're getting stronger every day."

She glanced up at me briefly and nodded, but I couldn't escape the feeling that she knew something I didn't – something even the doctors couldn't know.

"I think I'll name her Ellen," she said. "Do you like that name?"

"Yes. It's lovely."

Ten days later, Nadia and Ellen were discharged from the hospital, and I hired a full-time nurse to take care of them at home while I was at work. Because I wanted Nadia to get plenty of rest, I took over the night feedings and diaper changes. Though I was exhausted in the mornings, I loved every precious minute I spent with little Ellen, singing lullabies and bouncing at the knees while I walked with her around the house in the middle of the night.

Though I needed coffee more than ever in the mornings, I stopped going to my regular Starbucks because I was afraid I might bump into Jacob. I suppose I didn't trust myself to truly let him go.

Weeks passed. I missed him terribly, and I had no idea what he was feeling. We hadn't spoken or texted each other since Nadia left the hospital, though she had been to see him a few times for checkups. I chose not to accompany her. Maybe he was hurt by that…

Maybe he assumed I didn't care, or that I wasn't thinking of him.

Then, four weeks after Nadia's discharge from the hospital, something happened on a Saturday afternoon.

We were sitting at home eating lunch together, when her hospital-issued pager went off.

It took me less than an hour to get Nadia to the hospital, and she was immediately taken in for blood work and other preparations. Because it was a Saturday, our home care nurse was off duty, so I took Ellen with me in the stroller. I brought a large diaper bag with extra bottles and everything I would need if we had to remain in the hospital for an extended period of time.

I was permitted to stay with Nadia while she waited, and when a nurse came in to check her IV, I couldn't help but ask, "Will Dr. Peterson be performing the surgery?"

"Yes," she said. "He should be out of the OR soon. He's removing the donor heart now."

"The donor is here in the hospital?" I asked, having expected the heart to be flown in from somewhere else.

"Yes," the nurse replied. "It's not often that happens."

The idea that Nadia's new heart had been beating in another living person, right here in this building, filled me with intense emotions. I couldn't help but think of the family members who were, at this very moment, losing a loved one.

And Jacob...He was not far.

I had dreamed of him just last night. I dreamed that he was running up a hill, drenched in sweat. I didn't know what that meant.

"Diana," Nadia said.

I realized I was staring off into space, pushing the stroller back and forth to help Ellen fall asleep. "Yes?"

"I need to say something to you."

Focusing all my attention on my sister, I moved closer to the bed.

"Thank you for letting Jacob be my doctor," she said. "I know it hasn't been easy for you, these past few weeks."

"It's been fine," I assured her. "I wouldn't have it any other way."

"No, it hasn't been fine. You've been very gracious, not saying anything about him, but I know how you feel. I see it in your eyes sometimes, and I can't blame you. He's a wonderful man."

I swallowed uneasily. "And an excellent surgeon, which is why I want him to stay focused on *you*."

"I appreciate that," she said. "And I want you to know that everything you've done for me has made me believe in something I never believed in before."

"What's that?"

"The forever kind of love. I never really felt like I was truly part of someone else's life before, but now I understand what it means, and what it means to be family. I understand because of how I feel about Ellen, and also because of how I feel about you. You've given up a lot for me, and I'm grateful for the time we've had."

I laid my hand on her arm. "We're going to have plenty more of that," I said.

Her attention was diverted when someone entered the room. I turned to look, and my heart nearly beat out of my chest when I found myself staring at the man I had dreamed about last night, running up that hill.

When our eyes met, I recognized something in his expression
I didn't want to see.

Disappointment.

~⑥~

"I'm sorry," Jacob said, "but the donor heart wasn't a good match.
We won't be doing the surgery today."

Nadia sat forward and covered her face with her hands, while
I couldn't seem to move from my spot on the floor.

We had known this was a possibility – that we would be
called into the transplant center, but the organ wouldn't be right
for Nadia. It would go to someone else. I had no idea, however,
that the news would be so devastating.

We'd gotten our hopes up. Now they were crushed.

"I wish I had better news for you," Jacob said. I couldn't tear
my gaze away from his. "I really wanted it to be a match."

Nadia nodded and sat back.

"Thank you," was all I could say to him.

He nodded, then turned around and walked out.

~⑥~

While Nadia spoke to a social worker about what had occurred
that day and made arrangements to see the psychologist, I waited
alone in a long corridor, pushing Ellen's stroller up and down, up
and down.

She slept soundly, and I wondered why all of this had to be so
difficult. Why couldn't Nadia have some good luck for a change,
for once in her life? Hadn't she been through enough?

Feeling emotionally drained, I stopped walking, closed my eyes, and leaned my head back against the wall.

After a few seconds, all the hairs on my neck stood on end, and I felt a tingling sensation everywhere.

I opened my eyes to find Jacob standing in front of me. He wore a clean pair of OR greens.

A sudden commotion erupted inside me. We stared at each other for a long moment without saying a word, then Jacob wrapped his hands around the handle of Ellen's stroller and gestured for me to follow him. He pushed Ellen down the length of the corridor, and took us into a supply closet.

The next thing I knew he was pulling me into his arms, where he held me close for a shuddering moment. I wrapped my arms around his neck and clung to him like a lifeline. Then he pulled back and smothered my mouth in a fierce kiss that knocked the wind right out of me. Straining against him, I ran my hands through his wavy hair. The pleasure was intoxicating, and my body trembled. I felt like a starving person who had just been led to a swimming pool filled with delicious ripe fruit, and I had leapt into it.

My head was spinning; my knees turned to pudding. When Jacob broke the kiss, he held me close and whispered in my ear, "I had to see you."

My answer came on a breathless sigh. "I've been in agony for weeks, missing you."

He kissed me again and cupped my face in his hands. "I wanted to fix everything for you today," he said. "I wanted to give Nadia a new heart. I'm so sorry it didn't happen."

"It's not your fault," I replied. "And we won't give up hope. There will be other hearts."

Jacob nodded. He started kissing me again, but his pager went off. He checked it and said, "I have to go."

I backed away.

He squeezed my hand, kissed the back of it, and quickly walked out.

While driving home, Nadia rode the entire way in silence with her head resting against the window, staring out at the passing streets.

"Are you okay?" I asked. I glanced briefly at her, then over my shoulder to check on Ellen, who was buckled into the rear-facing car seat behind Nadia.

"I don't know how much longer I can hang on," she told me.

It wasn't the first time I'd felt some concern that she might sink into a depression. She knew her limitations, and she couldn't do all the things she wanted to do. She couldn't take Ellen for long walks in the park, she couldn't travel; she couldn't apply for a job. The future couldn't really exist for her until the waiting came to an end, which made it difficult for her to remain hopeful.

"Let's consider this a dress rehearsal," I said. "And you know what they say about a dress rehearsal that goes badly."

I expected her to finish the thought for me, but she continued to stare vacantly out the window.

I laid my hand on her knee and drove into our neighborhood. "It'll go better next time," I assured her, though I didn't have the power to keep that promise. No one did.

I helped Nadia inside first, then removed the car seat from my vehicle and carried Ellen in. Ellen began to cry, so I set the carrier on the kitchen floor and went to prepare a bottle.

"I'd like to take a bath," Nadia said, while standing at the bottom of the staircase. "But I don't think I can make it up there. I don't have the strength."

My own heart throbbed with despair. "I'll carry you."

"Are you sure?"

"Yes," I replied, "and tomorrow, I'll see about having one of those elevator chairs installed."

It wasn't easy, but somehow I managed to carry my sister in my arms, all the way to the top.

"Thank you for taking care of Ellen," Nadia said, her arms gripped tightly around my neck.

"You don't need to thank me. I love doing it." I carried Nadia to the washroom, set her down, and started the water running. Then I went back downstairs to change and feed Ellen.

Ellen finished her bottle and fell asleep in my arms, so I took her upstairs to her crib and laid her down. Quietly, I tiptoed out of her room.

Pausing in the hallway, I pressed my ear to the bathroom door to listen for water sloshing about in the tub, but it was quiet in there. Too quiet. After the day we'd had, I was concerned that Nadia might not be able to handle the stress.

I knocked on the door. "Nadia?"

She gave no answer, and my pulse began to race.

"Is everything okay in there?" I asked.

Then I heard the sound of movement in the tub, and I waited for her to answer.

"The door's open," she said. "You can come in if you want."

I accepted her invitation and entered to find her up to her earlobes in frothy white bubbles.

"That looks great," I said. "What's the fragrance? Is it mango?"

"Passion fruit," she replied, and swiped a hand over the suds, tossing a few bubbles into the air. "Sit down for a second," she said. "I need to talk to you."

I closed the lid on the toilet, took a seat, and leaned forward, resting my elbows on my knees.

"I've been thinking," she said. "I'm grateful for everything you've done for me. Really, I am. But things didn't go so well today, and I think it's time I tried a new doctor."

"What do you mean?"

"I met Dr. Reynolds today," she said, "and I liked him a lot."

Laying her head back on the rim of the tub, she stared at me intently.

"What happened today wasn't Jacob's fault," I said. "I'm sure he made the right call with that heart. It's important that we get the right one for you, so that your body doesn't reject it."

"I don't blame Jacob," she said. "Today wasn't the right day, that's all. But I really liked Dr. Reynolds. He was nice."

I twirled my pearl ring around on my finger. "You don't have to do this," I said. "Jacob is the best, and we've come so far."

"We certainly have," she agreed. "I feel very blessed. But I saw how you looked at him today, and how he looked at you. Like I said in the car, I'm not sure how much longer I can keep holding on, and when I think about Ellen growing up without me, I need to know that she's going to have the thing that I missed out on – a real family that stays together. Parents who love each other and treat each other with kindness and respect. I'm doing you a terrible disservice by keeping Jacob for myself, when clearly he's meant to be with you. So I've already made up my mind. I called the hospital a little while ago and asked for my file to be moved to Dr. Reynolds."

I closed my eyes and looked down at the floor. "I only want what's best for you," I said.

"And I want what's best for *you*," she argued. "So maybe we're going to have to duke it out and see who wins. But since I have a heart condition, I think it's only fair that you allow me a handicap."

I smiled at her.

"I know you want to be with him," Nadia said. "Don't even try to deny it. You can't hide that from me. I'm your twin, for pity's sake. I know everything."

She scooped up a pile of soapsuds in the cradle of her hand and threw them at me. "Go call him, you idiot."

The thought of contacting Jacob made me want to weep uncontrollably with happiness. "Maybe I'll just send him a text," I said.

"That'll do."

I stood and felt all the barriers between us falling away. Our lives apart had thrust us to very different places in the world, yet here we were, back to where we belonged, together as sisters, willing to sacrifice anything, and everything, for each other. "Thank you."

"It's no sweat,"

With a chuckle, I went downstairs to dig through my purse for my phone. A soon as I found it, I scrolled through my list of favorites and typed in a message.

Hey you. Nadia just told me she met Dr. Reynolds today and she liked him. I'm making a pot of tea right now. Are you home? Would you like some?

I set my phone down on the kitchen counter, stared at it, waiting impatiently for it to vibrate. It sat there like a dead fish.

Five minutes later, as soon as the kettle began to boil, there was a knock at the front door. I eagerly went to answer it.

One month later

What a delight to discover that everything Jacob had told me about fishing was true. After spending an hour with him at sunrise, standing on the edge of the dock at his lakeside cabin, while watching the mist rise up off the gleaming water, I was quite certain I had indeed added an extra hour to my life. Perhaps even two. I hoped the same would be true for Nadia.

Four weeks had passed since the false alarm that summoned her to the hospital to receive a new heart, which turned out to be the wrong one for her. Unfortunately, her condition had worsened since then. She rarely left the house and had to keep an oxygen tank nearby, but we remained ever hopeful that a new heart would be found in time to save her life.

Since the night I texted Jacob, he and I had met in Starbucks every morning, and eaten dinner with Nadia and Ellen on the nights he was home at a decent hour. If not, he came over later to spend time with us. Sometimes we watched television, or took Ellen for short drives around the neighborhood to help her fall asleep. Occasionally he and I went out alone together, to a movie or a late supper.

On this particular Saturday morning, the four of us – me, Jacob, Nadia and Ellen – had risen early after spending the night in his cabin, and ventured outside to marvel at the sunrise. Nadia was very weak, but she wanted this experience with a desperation and determination that moved me.

Jacob carried her down to the rocky beach, where he set her gently in a chair so she could hold Ellen in her arms and watch us fish off the dock.

A short while later, Jacob slipped a worm on a hook and cast a line. The reel made a whizzing sound, and the hook and bait went *plop* in the still water, creating a circular ripple effect that eventually reached the shore.

Ellen was fussy, however. Nadia sang to her.

"She's scaring the fish away," Jacob said with laughter. "We may have to eat steak tonight."

"That wouldn't be such a bad thing," I mentioned as I laid my hand on his shoulder. "You do make an excellent steak. But it will have to be a lean one."

He gave me a sexy smile and jiggled the rod, dragging the hook through the water. The rod quivered and bowed, and he tugged it back. "There's a nibble."

The line tightened and he reeled it in until a giant trout came flying out of the water.

"You've got one!" I cried.

Ellen screamed even louder.

"Looks like we'll be dining on fish after all." Jacob reeled in the trout. It landed on the dock and flopped around.

I squatted down to watch Jacob remove the hook and toss the fish into the bucket.

"Well done, surgeon," I said.

He looked at me with those flirtatious green eyes that never failed to take my breath away.

"*Diana!*"

The panic in Nadia's voice sent my insides into a frenzy. Jacob and I both rose to our feet, and I ran the length of the dock to reach her.

"What is it?" I asked.

She was scrambling awkwardly to reach for something in her pocket, while shifting Ellen from one arm to the other.

"It's my pager," she said. "It just went off."

Our eyes locked on each other's while she checked to make sure she hadn't imagined it. I turned to Jacob.

"Her pager just went off," I told him.

He immediately pulled out his phone and called Dr. Reynolds at the hospital. "Hey," he said. "What's going on?"

He listened for a moment, and checked his watch. Then his eyes lifted and he nodded at both of us. "We'll be there in under two hours." He ended the call. "Looks like today could be your big day," he said to Nadia. "Are you up for it?"

She smiled at him and her eyes filled with moisture. "Yes, I am."

I took Ellen from her arms. Then Jacob offered his hand and helped Nadia rise to her feet.

Epilogue

Nadia

When the four of us drove from Jacob's cabin to the hospital for my surgery, I spent a great deal of time watching Ellen in her car seat. I also gazed out the window at the colorful autumn leaves in the forest, and felt a surprising sense of calm.

I told Diana and Jacob that no matter what happened, I had never been happier, and on that crisp October morning – while sitting on the quiet beach at dawn with my daughter in my arms – I felt somehow closer to heaven. I truly believed that if I died on that day, I would leave this world knowing I had lived a full and complete life – for I had achieved something not everyone can achieve.

By some miracle, I had broken through the walls of my childhood isolation and learned how to trust and love. Despite the years apart from my sister, and our differences, and the appalling mistakes I had made, she loved me regardless, and forgave me for my mistakes.

Then I was blessed with the knowledge of motherhood – though none of it was ever handed to me on a silver platter. I had fought tooth and nail to survive long enough to hold my baby in my arms. The love I felt for her was a love I never imagined could exist, and it gave me great strength.

As we drove to the hospital, I wondered if my birth mother had known this kind of love before she passed on. Was she able to hold Diana and me in her arms, even just for a moment? Maybe one day I would meet her again, and she would tell me everything.

But on that particular day, I had something important to do. My fight wasn't over yet. I had to see if someone else's heart might be right for me, and if it was the right one, I would accept it and be grateful for my donor's generous gift.

But this is a terrible thing I am doing here – keeping you in suspense like this.

Dr. Reynolds was brilliant during the surgery, and I am in his debt.

It's been three weeks since my transplant, and I am home again with Ellen and Diana, though the transplant team is still monitoring me closely. I take medicines to prevent my body from rejecting the new heart, and so far, there have been no complications, but it will be a long, hard road to a full recovery.

Meanwhile I wonder about the person who signed the donor card that saved my life. What were the circumstances of his or her death? I have been given limited information due to issues of confidentiality, but I can't help but think of the family, and how difficult it must have been for them. I hope they know how grateful I am.

So I will cherish my time here, because every moment – every heartbeat – is a gift, and I have learned that no gifts should be squandered.

Please do not forget that, even when life seems hopeless. Especially then. Because you never know when it might take a sudden turn for the better, and you'll find yourself in a situation you never could have predicted.

Maybe there is someone in your future who will change everything. Maybe there will be gifts that will surprise you.

Live for it. Dream of it. Or if you already have it, treasure it.

Questions for Discussion

1. In what ways are Nadia and Diana mirror images of each other?

2. In Chapter Forty-seven, after Diana returns to Bar Harbor, she says: "In the beginning – when I was fresh out of law school – I'd wanted to help people through a difficult time as quickly and smoothly as possible, be their advocate, and share with them my hope and optimism about the future. Unfortunately, the longer I practiced, the more jaded I became. Conflict and bitterness surrounded me on a daily basis, and after what happened to me in LA, I suddenly understood that a messy divorce could happen to anyone, even me." How does this compare to what is happening to Nadia at the same time? What are the similarities and differences in their life trajectories?

3. When Diana and Nadia argue in Chapter Sixty-six, who did you sympathize with more? Did you feel Diana was wrong to date Dr. Peterson? Was Nadia unreasonable to ask Diana not to continue seeing him? Explain your reasoning.

4. In chapter Sixty-seven, when Nadia calls for Diana in the middle of the night because she's having heart troubles,

and asks her to call Dr. Peterson, did you wonder – as Diana did – if she might be faking it? Or did you think Diana was irrational or paranoid to suspect such a thing?

5. At any point, did you feel Nadia was Diana's 'evil twin'? Or did you ever feel that Diana filled that role? If so, when? And how does personal point of view create that label for each one of them?

6. In what ways are Diana and Jacob mirror images of each other?

7. What did you think of Rick in the early part of the novel? How does this compare to how you felt about him at the end? How would you describe him as a person? Is he true to life?

8. Do you believe Diana and Jacob were truly meant for each other? Will their relationship last?

9. How many acts of sacrifice can you identify in the novel?

For more information about this book and others in the Color of Heaven series, please visit the author's website at www.juliannemaclean.com. While you're there, be sure to sign up for Julianne's newsletter to be notified about when a new book in this series is released.

Read on for an excerpt from *The Color of a Dream*, book four in the Color of Heaven series.

Prologue

Jesse Vincent Fraser

Sometimes it's difficult to believe that coincidences are simply that: *coincidences.*

How could it be that easy when the most unlikely events occur and we find ourselves connecting with others in ways that can only be described as magical?

Until recently, I didn't believe in that sort of thing—that fate, destiny, or magic played any part in the outcome of a man's life. I always believed that what happened to me later, when I became a husband and father, resulted from the decisions and choices I made along the way, with a little luck—good or bad—tossed into the pot for good measure.

Things are different for me now. How can I not believe in something more, when what happened to me still feels like a dream?

It's not difficult to pinpoint the exact moment when my world began to shift and all the puzzle pieces began to slide into place. It was a month before Christmas almost twenty years ago. A heavy, wet snow had just begun to fall.

I was fourteen years old, and it was the day I began to hate my older brother.

One

Some people said we lived in the middle of nowhere because the road wasn't paved and ours was the only house for many miles.

I didn't think it was nowhere. I liked where we lived on the distant outskirts of a quaint little town where our father was the only dentist.

I suppose it was a bit remote. Once you drove past our house, which stood at the top of a grassy hill with pine trees behind it, you reached a bend in the road and were suddenly surrounded by thick forest on either side. It was extremely dark at night.

That didn't stop people from speeding, however, because it was the only alternate route between our town and the next and there were plenty of country folk who preferred to avoid the interstate. Partly because our road provided a more direct route into town, but mainly because it was where the bootleggers lived. If you wanted liquor after hours—or if you were underage—a fifteen-mile drive down a deserted gravel road was only a minor inconvenience.

More than a few times, we were awakened in the night by drunks who drove into the ditch where the road took a sharp turn not far from our home. We always left our outdoor lights on all night, so we were the first house they staggered to. Luckily, the ones who came to our door were always polite and happy drunks. There hadn't been any fatalities and my father never refused to let them use the phone to call a tow truck.

The event that changed my relationship with my brother, however, occurred in the bright cold light of day during the month of November, and we weren't coming from the bootleg-ger's shack. We were on our way home from a high school football game where we'd just slaughtered the rival team—thanks to my brother Rick, who was captain and star quarterback.

Earlier in the day, Rick had been coerced by our mother to let me tag along to the game. Now he was dropping me off at home so that he and his buddies could go celebrate.

As we turned left onto the gravel road, the tires skidded and dust rose up in a thick cloud behind us. Rick was doing the driving and I was sandwiched into the back seat between two keyed up linebackers.

"Did you see the look on the other coach's face when you scored that first touchdown?" one of them said. "We were only five minutes into the game. I think that's when he knew it was going to get ugly."

"Ugly for them, but not for us," Greg said from the front seat. He high-fived Rick, who lay on the horn five or six times.

The car fishtailed on the loose gravel as he picked up speed, eager to get rid of me no doubt.

"Hey," Greg said, turning to speak over his shoulder to Jeff, the linebacker to my right. "What are you going to do if Penny's there?"

I may have been only fourteen years old, but I'd heard all the gossip surrounding the senior players on the team. They were like celebrities in our town and if the school could have published a tabloid, these guys would have been on the front cover every week.

"She better not be there," Jeff replied, referring to the house party they were going to as soon as they dropped me off. "She knows we're done."

"She won't take no for an answer, that one," Rick said.

"He speaks from experience," Greg added, facing forward again.

Everyone knew the story. Penny dated my brother for three months the year before, but when she got too lovey-dovey he broke it off with her. She wouldn't stop calling him though. Then she had a minor mental breakdown and lost a lot of weight before her parents finally admitted her to the hospital. She was out of school for a month.

This year, she'd set her sights on Jeff and they'd had a brief fling a few weeks ago. Now he was avoiding her and everyone said he had a thing for some girl in the eleventh grade who just broke up with her longtime boyfriend. I heard he went off to college in September, joined a fraternity and decided he didn't want to be tied down anymore. She was heartbroken and Jeff wanted to step in and lift her spirits.

We all knew what that meant.

I felt sorry for her. I also felt sorry for Penny, who kept getting her heart stomped on and would probably end up in the hospital again. From where I stood at the sidelines, it seemed obvious that she should steer clear of the football team and maybe join the science club instead, but girls just didn't seem to go for guys like me who were good at math. They liked big muscles and stardom. Even if it was only small town stardom.

We drove past the Johnson's hayfield and I wondered what the cows thought of the dust cloud we were creating as we sped up the gravel road.

When at last our large white house came into view at the top of the hill, Rick didn't slow down and I wondered how he was going to make the turn onto our tree-lined driveway.

That was the moment I spotted Francis—our eleven-year-old golden lab—charging down the hill to greet us.

I grabbed hold of the seat in front of me and pulled myself out of my sandwiched position between Jeff and Rob.

"Slow down," I said to Rick. "Francis got loose."

What was he doing out of the house? I wondered. Our parents weren't home. They'd left early that morning to visit my grandmother. Rick was the last one to leave the house and before that I was sure I'd seen Francis asleep on his bed in the family room as I walked out.

"I'm not slowing down," Rick said. "We're already late for the party, thanks to you."

It all seemed to happen in slow motion after that…as I watched Francis gallop down the hill, his ears flopping. The sound of our tires speeding over the packed dirt and gravel was thunderous in my ears.

"I think you better slow down!" I shouted, hitting Rick on the shoulder.

"Shut up," he said. "He's not stupid. He'll stop when he gets closer."

My heart rose up in my throat as our two paths converged. I prayed that Rick was right about Francis knowing enough to stop when he reached the road.

Then *whack*!—the horrendous sound of the vehicle colliding with my dog.

Only then did Rick slam on the brakes. "Shit!"

"Did you just hit your dog?" Jeff asked as the car skidded sideways to a halt and we were all tossed forward in our seats.

"Lemme out!" I cried as I scrambled over Jeff's lap.

Rick was quicker to open his door and leap out to see what had happened.

My whole body burned with terror at the sight of Francis, more than ten yards back, lying still at the edge of the road.

I ran to Francis as fast as my legs would carry me and dropped to my knees. I laid my hands on his belly, rubbed them over the contours of his ribs and shoulder blades.

"Francis!" I cried, but he didn't move.

Rick shoved me aside. "Move Jesse! Let me check him!"

I was practically hyperventilating as I stood up, only vaguely aware of the other three guys coming to take a look.

"Is he okay?" I asked, while Rick pressed his ear to Francis's chest to listen for a heartbeat. Then he put his fingers to Francis's nose. "Shit!" he shouted. "He's dead."

What? No! He can't be! I dropped to my knees again and laid my head on Francis's side. There were no signs of life. I stared at his belly, willing it to rise and fall. I needed to see him breathing, to know it wasn't true.

"Maybe we should take him to the vet!" I pleaded, unable to accept what I knew to be true. "Maybe they can save him!"

"It's too late," Rick said. "He's gone."

The words, spoken so straightforwardly, made my eyes fill up with tears while blood rushed to my head. My temples began to throb.

"Why didn't you slow down?" I demanded to know. "He was running straight for us."

"I didn't think he'd hit us," Rick explained.

"What a stupid dog," Greg said.

"He's not stupid!" I sobbed. Then I stood up and slammed my open palms into Greg's chest to shove him away. He was built like a tank, however, and barely took a step back.

"Settle down," Rick said, hitting me in the shoulder and shoving me.

"This is all your fault!" I cried. "And what was he doing outside? Didn't you shut the door when you left?"

He stared at me for a long moment, then shoved me again. "This isn't my fault. It's *your* fault, jerk, because we wouldn't even be here if Mom didn't force me to drag you along. We wouldn't be late for the party. We'd be there right now, and Francis wouldn't be…"

Thank God he stopped himself, because I don't know what I would have done if he'd finished that sentence. Actually said the word.

Still, to this day, I fantasize about tackling Rick in that moment and punching him in the head.

But my anger was tempered by grief. I felt as if I were dissolving into a thousand pieces. I swung around and sank to my knees again, gathered my beloved dog—we'd had him since I was three years old—into my arms and wept uncontrollably.

"Jesus," Jeff said. "What are we gonna do? We can't just leave him here."

"No," Rick agreed. "We'll have to take him up to the house."

I felt his hand on my shoulder and this time he spoke more gently.

"Come on Jesse. We have to get him off the road. Help me lift him. We'll put him in the car."

I glanced back at my father's blue sedan. "How?" I asked, wiping at my tears with the back of my hand.

"We'll put him in the trunk."

"The trunk?" I replied. "No. He can't be in there alone."

"It's the only way," Rick replied. "We'll cover him with the blanket. Now get up and help me. Guys? You gotta help too. He's gonna be heavy."

Each breath I took was a hellish, shuddering ordeal as I slid my hands under Francis's torso and raised him up. He was limp and it took four of us to carry him to the car. In hindsight, we should have backed the car up closer, but we were all pretty shaken. Well, at least I was shaken, and I can only assume Rick was as well, though he certainly didn't show it. Maybe it was because his friends were there. He seemed more irritated than anything else.

Awkwardly we placed Francis in the trunk and Rick covered him with the green plaid blanket my father always kept on hand in case we got stranded in a snow storm.

"Stop crying," Rick said as he shut the trunk. "It's over now and we can't do anything to change it."

I felt the other guys staring at me as if I was a wimp, but I didn't care. I opened the car door and got into the front seat, forcing the other three to pile into the back together. I'm sure they weren't happy about it, but they had the sense not to object.

Before Rick got in, he went around to the front of the car to check for damage.

"How's it looking?" Jeff asked when Rick got in.

"The fender's dented."

"At least it's just the fender," Greg replied. "You won't even need to tell the insurance company. You can just hammer that out."

Rick started up the engine. This time, he drove slowly as he turned up our driveway and began the long journey up the hill.

I could barely think. I felt like I was floating in cold water, bobbing up and down while waves splashed in my face. I had to suck in great gulps of air whenever I could.

At last we reached the house and everyone got out of the car. I have no memory of the next few minutes. All I recall is sinking down onto the cool grass in our front yard next to Francis while Rick stood over us.

"We have to go," he said. "When Dad gets home, make sure you tell him it was an accident and that Francis came out of nowhere."

"But he didn't," I replied.

"Jesus, he was running like a bat out of hell."

He was just excited to see us, I thought, as I ran my hand over Francis's smooth coat.

"You *better* tell him it was an accident," Rick warned me as he returned to the car, "because you were there, too, and this wouldn't have happened if you weren't."

"I told you to slow down," I insisted.

"No, you didn't."

"Yes, I did."

"It's your word against mine," Rick said, pausing before he got into the car, "and I have witnesses. On top of that, I'm pretty sure you were the last one to leave the house, remember? Mom's always telling you to shut the back door."

It wasn't true. I hadn't left the door open. I was waiting in the car when Rick came out with his gear slung over his shoulder, running late as usual.

I couldn't wait to tell my father the whole story when he got home. And I was going to tell the truth, whether Rick liked it or not.

Four

❦

I'd always suspected that Rick was my father's favorite. He was his firstborn child after all, my father's namesake—though my father went by Richard.

When you compared Rick and me, I realized it must have been difficult for my mother to pretend I was as special as him because he excelled at everything he did. He was good looking and popular, he played a number of sports equally well, and he possessed a fierce charisma that seemed to put most people in some sort of hypnotic state. Every other person in a room seemed to disappear when Rick walked into it. All eyes turned to him and everyone was mesmerized. He knew all the right things to say, especially to grownups, and everyone who met him was suitably impressed.

'You sure hit a home run with that boy, Richard,' friends of my father would say when they came over to the house—or 'He's going to be a heartbreaker,' women said to my mother at the supermarket.

I suppose I was invisible in the glare of such perfection, but to be honest, I didn't mind because I was a bit of an introvert, which was why I didn't go seeking a spotlight by trying out for sports teams or running for student council. I was quite content to sit quietly in the corner of a room while Rick carried on conversations or told stories that made everyone laugh.

Naturally he was voted most likely to succeed during his senior year of high school—which turned out to be a good prediction because he ended up working in LA as a sports agent, earning millions from celebrity clients.

But that came much later. I shouldn't be skipping ahead when you probably want to know what happened when my parents came home and found me huddled in the front yard with Francis in my arms.

It was dark by the time they drove up the tree-lined drive. I should have at least gone into the house to get a warmer jacket at some point, because it was late November in Connecticut and near the freezing point on that particular day after the sun went down. But I didn't want to leave Francis, so I sat there shivering in my light windbreaker until the car headlights nearly blinded me.

My mother was first to get out of the car. "Oh my God, what happened?" She strode toward me and crouched down, laid her hand on Francis's shoulder.

"Rick hit him with the car," I explained as my father approached. He'd left the headlights on.

My rage had been boiling up inside me for nearly two hours and I'm not sure what I sounded like. I think I might have achieved more if I'd remained calm and rational, but I was fourteen years old and didn't possess Rick's clever way with people.

"He murdered him!" I shouted.

"Who murdered who?" my father asked with growing concern.

"Rick killed Francis. He drove right into him, even when I told him not to."

"That can't be true," Mom said, looking up at my father who glared down at me with derision. "Rick loves Francis. He would never do something like that. Certainly not intentionally."

"You're not making any sense, Jesse," my father said in his deep, booming voice. "You're upset, which is understandable, but accidents happen."

He knelt down and stroked Francis's head. "Poor boy. How long ago did it happen?"

"A couple of hours," I replied.

"And you've been out here with him all this time?" my mother asked, laying a sympathetic hand on my cheek.

I nodded, grateful for her gentle warmth in light of my father's severity.

She looked down at Francis and rubbed his side. I could see her eyes tearing up.

"Did he suffer at all?" she asked.

"I don't think so," I replied. "It happened really fast. As soon as we got out of the car, Rick said he was dead."

My father's eyes lifted and he regarded me from beneath those bushy dark brows. "How did he get loose? Did you leave the door open again?"

"No! I swear I didn't! It was Rick! It had to have been."

My parents exchanged a look and I knew they didn't believe me.

"Well," my mother said gently, "whatever happened, we can't change it now and we can't bring Francis back. This was a terrible accident, Jesse, but you mustn't punish yourself. It's no one's fault."

Why did everyone seem to think it was *me*? That *I* was the one who had something to answer for?

"Yes, it *is* someone's fault," I argued. "It's Rick's, because he was driving."

"Now, see here," my father scolded. "I won't hear talk like that. If Francis got out of the house, it could have happened to any of us. It was an accident and if I hear you say otherwise to your brother, you'll have to answer to me. He must feel guilty enough as it is. Do you understand?"

"But it *was* his fault," I pleaded. "He was driving too fast and I told him to slow down but he wouldn't."

My father's eyes darkened. "Did you not hear what I just said to you?"

I'd been raised to respect and obey my father—and to fear him. We all did, even Mom. So I nodded to indicate that yes, I'd heard what he said.

That didn't mean I had to believe he was right.

Rick didn't come home that night. He slept at Greg's so it was left to me to help Dad bury Francis at the edge of the yard under the big oak tree. My mother suggested the spot because it was visible from the top floor windows of the house, and I agreed it was the right place.

It was ten o'clock by the time we finished. I was so exhausted afterwards, I went straight to bed, but I hardly slept a wink all night. What happened that day had been a terrible ordeal and I couldn't stop replaying all the vivid images in my mind: Francis bounding down the hill to greet us; the sound of our car striking him; then finally the eerie sight of my father shoveling dirt on top of him while I held the flashlight.

I imagined we must have hit Francis in the head with the car, which was why he died so quickly. At least, if that was the case, he probably felt no pain.

That thought provided me with some comfort, though I couldn't overcome the white-hot rage I felt every time I remembered how Rick stood over me in the yard blaming me for what happened.

That perhaps was the real reason I couldn't sleep. My body was on fire with adrenaline, and I wanted to hit something.

Seven

I woke late the next morning, having finally drifted off into a deep slumber sometime before dawn. Sleepily, I rose from bed, used the washroom, and padded downstairs to the kitchen in my pajamas. "Mom?"

My voice never echoed back to me in the kitchen before and the implications of that fact caused a lump to form in my throat.

"Mom? Dad? Is anyone here?"

When no answer came, I went to the front hall and looked out the window. Both cars were parked in the driveway, which meant Rick had come home.

"Rick?" I climbed the stairs to check his room, but it was empty and the bed was made.

Suddenly it occurred to me where everyone must be and a feeling of panic swept over me. I hurried to the window in Rick's room, which looked out over the back field and apple orchard, and sure enough, there they were, my mother, father and Rick, all standing over Francis's grave.

I had no idea what was going on out there, but I felt very left out. Without bothering to get dressed, I hurried downstairs, pulled on a pair of rain boots and a jacket, and ran out the back door.

It was not one of my finer moments. I will admit that. When I reached my family, I shouted at all of them accusingly.

"What are you doing out here? Why didn't you wake me?"

My mother turned and looked at me with concern. "You seemed so tired last night, Jesse. I thought you could use some extra sleep."

"If this is Francis's funeral," I said, "I should be here."

"It's not his funeral," my father informed me, impatiently. "Rick just got home and he wanted to see where we buried Francis."

"He was my dog, too," Rick said with a frown, as if I was being selfish.

Maybe I was, but I was only fourteen and I was grief-stricken and angry.

"Come here," Rick said, holding out his hand to wave me closer.

I slowly approached.

"I was thinking," Rick said, "that we should get some sort of monument. Maybe a small headstone. I have enough in my savings account to pay for it."

"That would be a fine gesture, Rick," my father said, "but please let me cover the cost."

Rick laid a hand on my shoulder. "What do you think we should have engraved on it?" he asked. "His name of course, but maybe we should come up with some sort of epitaph."

I thought about it for a moment. "What about: Here lies Francis, beloved dog and best friend?"

My voice shook and I didn't think I could speak again without breaking down.

"That sounds perfect," Rick said. He looked down at me meaningfully. "I'm really sorry, Jesse. I don't think I'll ever be able to forgive myself."

He closed his eyes and pinched the bridge of his nose, as if he, too, could not speak about it anymore.

My father squeezed his shoulder and patted him on the back.

Eight

Five years later

"Hey, Bentley. Where's your leash?"

Bentley's head lifted, his ears perked up and he jumped off the sofa in the family room. I rose from my chair at the kitchen table and headed for the laundry room. With tail wagging, Bentley followed me in.

Dad waited only a month after we lost Francis before coming home one afternoon with a brand new puppy—an adorable black lab I fell in love with at first sight.

From that moment on, Bentley and I were best pals. He formed a closer bond with me than anyone else because both my parents worked and I was the first one home every afternoon to take him for a walk. I made sure his food and water bowls were always full in the mornings, and he slept on the floor in my room on a large green pillow. I loved him dearly.

After attaching the leash to Bentley's collar, I led him out the front door. While I stood there locking the door behind me, I heard a car speed by on the road at the bottom of the hill. A few years earlier, a crew had come in and paved the road all the way to the next town, so we now had a steadier stream of traffic moving at a faster clip in front of our house. In addition to that, a number of new homes had gone up since the paving project was announced. We were no longer the only house between the main road and the bootlegger's shack—which as far as I knew was still there.

There had been other changes to our lives as well. Rick graduated from high school with honors and received a scholarship to UCLA. He was still there, living out west, working on an MBA.

As for me, I was still living at home, working at the airport as an operations assistant until I figured out what to do with my life. My father wanted me to enroll in a science program and go to dental or medical school. I certainly had the grades for either of those options, but I just wasn't that keen on following in my father's footsteps. We were different, he and I, and I wanted to choose my own path. Maybe it would have something to do with aviation. I'd always had an interest in that. I just wasn't sure yet.

That's when I met Angela. She, too, had decided to take a year off after high school and she was working as a waitress in one of the airport restaurants. Just like seeing Bentley for the first time, it was love at first sight when she approached me in the staff parking lot, needing help because she'd locked herself out of her car. I called AAA for her and waited for them to arrive, but when she finally got into her car, the engine wouldn't start. So after arranging to have her vehicle towed to a repair shop, I gave her a lift home.

Three weeks later, we were seeing each other every day and I was head over heels in love. I hadn't had much experience with girls and I never imagined it could be like that, but everything about Angela suited me. She was a bit of a math geek, like me, and she hadn't had much experience in the dating scene either. I couldn't understand why, because I thought she was the most beautiful creature to ever walk the earth. Her hair was jet black, cut in a shoulder-length bob with bangs, and she had giant brown eyes and a soft, smooth ivory complexion. She was very petite at five-foot-three and went to yoga class three times a week. Every time I saw her, I felt like I'd been run over by a truck. She was fun and sweet and incredibly kindhearted. Bentley loved her, too.

Before long I started thinking about moving out of my parents' house and getting a place of my own. My parents didn't approve, of course, because they still wanted me to go to university and make something of myself.

When I brought it up at the dinner table one night, my father's bushy eyebrows pulled together and two large vertical creases formed between them. He set down his fork and knife and leaned back in his chair.

"How will you ever go to a good school if you're tied down to some waitress here in town, struggling to pay your rent every month?" he asked.

"Maybe I don't want to go to a good school," I defiantly replied. "Maybe I just want to keep working at the airport." My mother fidgeted uncomfortably and her eyes pleaded for me to walk away from this one.

He scoffed at me, as if I were a fool. "Believe me, when the shine wears off of this exciting new relationship and you're stuck in a dead end job, arguing with that girl about how you're going to pay the phone bill, you'll feel differently, and you'll wish you had listened to me."

"Maybe so," I replied, "but it's my life and I'm not a kid anymore. I'm nineteen and you have to let me make my own decisions."

He and Mom exchanged a look, as if they were carrying on a mental conversation I wasn't privileged to be a part of.

Then Mom leaned across the table and clasped my hand. "Jesse, it's not that we don't like Angela. She's probably a very nice girl. But you've had so little experience in that area. How can I say this…?" She paused, then continued. "It's important to try on some different styles and sizes before you make a commitment you can't get yourself out of."

She was so much gentler than my father. Nevertheless, I frowned at her. "It's not like we're moving in together." Though the idea wasn't far from my mind. Angela and I had only been seeing each other for a month, but I figured—and hoped—moving in would be the next step. For now, I just wanted a place where I could have my privacy to be with her.

My father still hadn't picked up his fork. "Your mother's right," he said in that deep, reverberating voice that made everyone quiver. "You should be dating lots of girls before you settle for just one."

"Like Rick does?" I tersely asked. I set my fork down and leaned back in my chair. "He dates all kinds of girls and manages to have a whale of a time. Do you want me to be more like him and break lots of hearts?"

"That's not fair," Mom said. "Rick has always worked very hard at school and sports. He's incredibly busy and doesn't have time for a serious relationship, that's all."

"And look where he is now," my father added. "In the MBA program at Anderson Business School. He'll have his pick of high-paying jobs the minute he steps off that campus."

I took a deep breath and let it out because I knew this conversation was pointless. My parents wanted me to be a great "success" like Rick, but when it came right down to it, my definition of success differed from theirs. I didn't need to make a million dollars. I didn't want to have a series of superficial relationships with girls I had nothing in common with. I'd already found the girl who was right for me and I just wanted to be with her. It didn't mean I was going to give up any thought of doing something more with my life. I just wanted her at my side, no matter what I chose to do.

"It's my decision to make," I said, pulling my napkin from my lap and tossing it onto the table. "Excuse me, Mom. I'm finished now."

My father stared up at me with displeasure as I carried my plate to the kitchen. "Fine," he said, "but don't expect any help from me when you can't pay your rent."

"I'll remember that." On my way upstairs, I picked up the newspaper from the front hall so I could check out the classifieds.

CHAPTER

Nine

A week later, I signed the lease on my first apartment, which came cheap because it was a mile from the airport and the roar of the planes flying overhead turned off most prospective renters. It was convenient for me, however, because I could reach work in ten minutes by bicycle, and Angela could come and stay over anytime she liked.

My dad was true to his word. He didn't help me with anything. He didn't let me take any of the furniture from my room—not a single item—so I had to purchase a bed and a table at yard sales. My mother couldn't stand with me on this, but I remember the lump in my throat when she quietly slipped fifty dollars into my hand on the day I moved out.

It was Angela who helped me shop for plates and kitchen utensils, bedding and a small television set, all of which we found at second hand stores. Her parents gave me a sofa they wanted to get rid of anyway.

Ironically, the one thing my father let me take from the house was the only thing I really wanted.

He let me have Bentley.

I didn't call my parents or speak to them for over two months. I wasn't trying to punish them. I just had no interest in being lectured about why I was making the worst mistake of my life. So I waited it out and thought maybe, eventually, they would accept my decision and let me choose my own path.

The way I saw it, even if I *was* making a mistake, it was *my* mistake to make, and I was ready and willing to learn from it— and all the others I would likely make in the coming years.

Wasn't that part of life? To follow your heart? Explore the unknown and engage in a little trial and error?

Angela, for the most part, agreed with me, though she worried about me losing touch with my family. She certainly didn't want to feel responsible for that, so when a third month passed and there was still no communication, she suggested I pick up the phone.

"Call when you know your father won't be there," she suggested one evening while we were out walking Bentley. "How much you want to bet your mom will be thrilled to hear your voice and she won't even tell him you called if you don't want her to."

I considered that. "If she wants to hear my voice, she could call me any time," I said. "I'm in the book."

"No, you're not. You won't be in the book until the next one comes out."

"When will that be?" I asked.

"I have no idea," she replied with a chuckle.

Bentley paused briefly to lift a leg and pee on a telephone pole, then continued on.

"I'm sure Mom knows the number for directory assistance," I mentioned.

Playfully, Angela shoved me into the chain-link fence that ran along the sidewalk. "You're impossible," she said.

I bounced off the fence and returned to her side. "Yep, and that's why you love me."

"Is it?" she replied with mischief in her eyes. "I thought it was for another reason entirely."

I smiled and wrapped my arm around her. We walked on, our steps in perfect unison while a giant Boeing 767 passed over our heads—taking off for some exotic location, no doubt.

The thought of what unexplored territories were over my own horizon filled me with hope and excitement. I felt like one those jetliners, finally lifting off the runway. Everything in my world seemed new and full of promise.

It's a shame that feeling didn't last longer. Two weeks later I was forced to come down from the clouds when my mother called with some news.

Suddenly, I was back on the ground, living among the pressures of my old world.

The C O L O R *of* H E A V E N

A deeply emotional tale about Sophie Duncan, a successful columnist whose world falls apart after her daughter's unexpected illness and her husband's shocking affair. When it seems nothing else could possibly go wrong, her car skids off an icy road and plunges into a frozen lake. There, in the cold dark depths of the water, a profound and extraordinary experience unlocks the surprising secrets from Sophie's past, and teaches her what it means to truly live…and love.

Full of surprising twists and turns and a near-death experience that will leave you breathless, this story is not to be missed.

"A gripping, emotional tale you'll want to read in one sitting."
　　　　　　　–New York Times bestselling author, Julia London

"Brilliantly poignant mainstream tale."
　　　　　　　　　–4 ½ starred review, *Romantic Times*

The COLOR of DESTINY

Eighteen years ago a teenage pregnancy changed Kate Worthington's life forever. Faced with many difficult decisions, she chose to follow her heart and embrace an uncertain future with the father of her baby – her devoted first love.

At the same time, in another part of the world, sixteen-year-old Ryan Hamilton makes his own share of mistakes, but learns important lessons along the way. Twenty years later, Kate's and Ryan's paths cross in a way they could never expect, which makes them question the possibility of destiny. Even when all seems hopeless, could it be that everything happens for a reason, and we end up exactly where we are meant to be?

The COLOR *of* HOPE

Diana Moore has led a charmed life. She is the daughter of a wealthy senator and lives a glamorous city life, confident that her handsome live-in boyfriend Rick is about to propose. But everything is turned upside down when she learns of a mysterious woman who works nearby – a woman who is her identical mirror image.

Diana is compelled to discover the truth about this woman's identity, but the truth leads her down a path of secrets, betrayals, and shocking discoveries about her past. These discoveries follow her like a shadow.

Then she meets Dr. Jacob Peterson—a brilliant cardiac surgeon with an uncanny ability to heal those who are broken. With his help, Diana embarks upon a journey to restore her belief in the human spirit, and recover a sense of hope - that happiness, and love, may still be within reach for those willing to believe in second chances.

The COLOR *of* A DREAM

Nadia Carmichael has had a lifelong run of bad luck. It begins on the day she is born, when she is separated from her identical twin sister and put up for adoption. Twenty-seven years later, not long after she is finally reunited with her twin and is expecting her first child, Nadia falls victim to a mysterious virus and requires a heart transplant.

Now recovering from the surgery with a new heart, Nadia is haunted by a recurring dream that sets her on a path to discover the identity of her donor. Her efforts are thwarted, however, when the father of her baby returns to sue for custody of their child. It's not until Nadia learns of his estranged brother Jesse that she begins to explore the true nature of her dreams, and discover what her new heart truly needs and desires…

The COLOR *of* A MEMORY

Audrey Fitzgerald believed she was married to the perfect man - a heroic firefighter who saved lives, even beyond his own death. But a year later she meets a mysterious woman who has some unexplained connection to her husband....

Soon Audrey discovers that her husband was keeping secrets and she is compelled to dig into his past. Little does she know... this journey of self-discovery will lead her down a path to a new and different future - a future she never could have imagined.

The COLOR *of* LOVE

Carla Matthews is a single mother struggling to make ends meet and give her daughter Kaleigh a decent upbringing. When Kaleigh's absent father Seth—a famous alpine climber who never wanted to be tied down—begs for a second chance at fatherhood, Carla is hesitant because she doesn't want to pin her hopes on a man who is always seeking another mountain to scale. A man who was never willing to stay put in one place and raise a family.

But when Seth's plane goes missing after a crash landing in the harsh Canadian wilderness, Carla must wait for news… Is he dead or alive? Will the wreckage ever be found?

One year later, after having given up all hope, Carla receives a phone call that shocks her to her core. A man has been found, half-dead, floating on an iceberg in the North Atlantic, uttering her name. Is this Seth? And is it possible that he will come home to her and Kaleigh at last, and be the man she always dreamed he would be?

The COLOR *of* THE SEASON

Boston cop, Josh Wallace, is having the worst day of his life. First, he's dumped by the woman he was about to propose to, then everything goes downhill from there when he is shot in the line of duty. While recovering in the hospital, he can't seem to forget the woman he wanted to marry, nor can he make sense of the vivid images that flashed before his eyes when he was wounded on the job. Soon, everything he once believed about his life begins to shift when he meets Leah James, an enigmatic resident doctor who somehow holds the key to both his past and his future...

Praise for Julianne MacLean's Historical Romances

"MacLean's compelling writing turns this simple, classic love story into a richly emotional romance, and by combining engaging characters with a unique, vividly detailed setting, she has created an exceptional tale for readers who hunger for something a bit different in their historical romances."

—BOOKLIST

"You can always count on Julianne MacLean to deliver ravishing romance that will keep you turning pages until the wee hours of the morning."

—Teresa Medeiros

"Julianne MacLean's writing is smart, thrilling, and sizzles with sensuality."

—Elizabeth Hoyt

"Scottish romance at its finest, with characters to cheer for, a lush love story, and rousing adventure. I was captivated from the very first page. When it comes to exciting Highland romance, Julianne MacLean delivers."

—Laura Lee Guhrke

"She is just an all-around wonderful writer, and I look forward to reading everything she writes."

—*Romance Junkies*

About the Author

Julianne MacLean is a *USA Today* bestselling author of many historical romances, including The Highlander Series with St. Martin's Press and her popular American Heiress Series with Avon/Harper Collins. She also writes contemporary mainstream fiction, and The Color of Heaven was a *USA Today* bestseller. She is a three-time RITA finalist, and has won numerous awards, including the Booksellers' Best Award, the Book Buyer's Best Award, and a Reviewers' Choice Award from *Romantic Times* for Best Regency Historical of 2005. She lives in Nova Scotia with her husband and daughter, and is a dedicated member of Romance Writers of Atlantic Canada. Please visit Julianne's website for more information and to subscribe to her mailing list to stay informed about upcoming releases.

www.juliannemaclean.com

OTHER BOOKS BY JULIANNE MACLEAN

The American Heiress Series:

To Marry the Duke
An Affair Most Wicked
My Own Private Hero
Love According to Lily
Portrait of a Lover
Surrender to a Scoundrel

The Pembroke Palace Series:

In My Wildest Fantasies
The Mistress Diaries
When a Stranger Loves Me
Married By Midnight
A Kiss Before the Wedding - A Pembroke Palace Short Story
Seduced at Sunset

The Highlander Series:

Captured by the Highlander
Claimed by the Highlander
Seduced by the Highlander
The Rebel – A Highland Short Story

The Royal Trilogy:
Be My Prince
Princess in Love
The Prince's Bride

Harlequin Historical Romances:
Prairie Bride
The Marshal and Mrs. O'Malley
Adam's Promise

Time Travel Romance
Taken by the Cowboy

Contemporary Fiction:
The Color of Heaven
The Color of Destiny
The Color of Hope
The Color of a Dream
The Color of a Memory
The Color of Love
The Color of the Season

Printed in Great Britain
by Amazon